SHE's DIVINE

By Lenny Williams

A Romantic/Spirit Novel

I0587177

Published by Melanin Origins LLC

PO Box 122123; Arlington, TX 76012

Copyright 2018

First Edition

Copyright © 2018 Lenny Williams

Library of Congress Control Number:2018953125

ISBN: 978-1-62676-740-9 hardback
ISBN: 978-1-62676-747-8 paperback
ISBN: 978-1-62676-746-1 ebook

DEDICATION

This book is dedicated to anyone who's ever lost a loved one, family member, or friend. Although it's hard to live without them, and you yearn for them every day, I want you to know that in due time you will see them again. It may happen in your dreams, it may happen in your memories, but it will certainly happen in the afterlife. I hope you understand that they are waiting for your return. The moment you see them again, all the pain and heartache you feel right now will vanish. For my healing, I look up to the sky and the stars, and above those beautiful creations I find the heavens. The heavens of the universe are where all our positive energies and angelic spirits assemble.

Much love and peace to you all!

lennysimagination.com

~ ~ ~

melaninorigins.com

ACKNOWLEDGMENTS

I truly have to thank the universal God for using me to bring this story to life.

I want to thank all of my family, friends, and supporters for encouraging my first novel and my previous children's books. As always, I hope that you enjoy reading this work as much as I enjoyed writing it.

I have to be honest, producing this story took a lot out of me. I thought that the project would be derided and considered distasteful. However, I was constantly told to create it anyway and share it with the world.

Last October, finding out that my cousin passed away sucked the life right out of me. After receiving that devastating phone call, I dropped to my knees and wept like a baby. The horrible feeling hit too close to home. I hadn't felt that way since my uncle passed ten years prior.

During that month and the next, I didn't feel like doing anything at all; I felt as though the news and social media reported nothing but death. I experienced the pain and agony known only to those who have lost precious people. Throughout the following months, my soul was empty, I wished for a lot. I wished that everyone's dead loved ones could somehow be brought back to life. I wished that everyone could at least be blessed with the power to see our departed loved ones whenever we wanted.

I knew that these desires weren't possible and could not be granted. However, even in my depressed state, I continued to wish.

In the midst of my sadness, I started to randomly have consecutive dreams. All I will say about these dreams is that someone kept telling me to create this story because it would not only resurrect my love for writing but it would also give many people hope and faith about seeing their loved ones again. I was told to appreciate the beauty of life and cherish every moment while I can.

I took that dream person's advice. Which I believe ultimately saved my life, and healed me from my depressive state of mind. Within three months, I had a rough draft completed. When I finished, I was astonished. I had to save the memory forever:

Today is January 29, 2018, and I've just completed the rough draft of my very first novel. At the tender age of 23, I'm still trying to figure out why the universal God chose me to create this particular story and why I was blessed to have my dreams. Regardless, I'm grateful for it all.

Rest In Paradise to all of our loved ones

Until We Meet Again

SHE's DIVINE

1

CONGRATULATIONS

It was a bright and sunny afternoon in the city of Silverside. Children were playing at the park, people were jogging and walking their dogs, and everyone was outside enjoying the weather—everyone besides Noah King, that is. Noah was in the Silverside University library getting a jump start on his psychology project.

A woman spotted Noah alone in the computer lab section. He was typing extremely fast, as if he were running late for something. Surprised, she approached him. "Mr. King? What are you doing here? It's the first day of spring break. I'd figured you'd be at the beach with your friends by now."

Noah took a quick break from his work to see who was talking to him. "Oh, hello Professor Wright. I'm just getting an early start on the *How The Brain Works* project you assigned. That's all."

Professor Wright smiled, then sighed. "Noah, the project isn't due until the end of the semester. That's two months away. And remember, you can call me Mrs. Wright or Ms. Angela. I'm one of the cool professors here."

Noah giggled. "I know, Professor—um, Mrs. Wright. I just love keeping busy."

Mrs. Wright pulled up a chair and sat down. "Okay. Well, since you're here now, I have some great news for you."

Noah's eyes lit up. "What is it?"

"I got a call from the Paradise Home Care Center yesterday. You've been selected for their new internship program. You are now officially a psychotherapist in training. Oh, and it pays $300 a week, too!" Mrs. Wright joyfully announced.

"Hold on!" Noah gasped and then gave her a tight hug. "Mrs. Wright are you serious? Wow! I can't wait to tell my parents that I'm finally getting started with my career. I've been waiting three long years for this."

His professor smirked. "That makes me extremely pleased to hear. I know the wait was worth it. So when would you like to start? Right after finals, or sometime after graduation?"

"How about tomorrow?" Noah replied excitedly.

Out of the blue Mrs. Wright's eyebrows rose. "Tomorrow's Saturday. Are you sure? I wouldn't want it to interfere with your social life, or your school work for that matter. You don't think this will affect any of that, do you?"

"Oh no, not at all Mrs. Wright, I'll be fine," Noah responded, still grinning hugely.

While cheerfully beaming Mrs. Wright stood up, and twisted her dreadlocks into a ponytail. "Of course, you'll be fine. You're a 4.0 student! All right, I'll let the administration staff know that you'll be there tomorrow morning at ten a.m. If you need anything, have any questions, or want to tell me about how it went, just give me a call."

"Will do! Thank you so much!" Noah replied as his professor walked away.

Later that evening, Noah rushed home to tell his parents and baby brother the good news. When he burst through the door, he found all three of them sitting on the living room couch.

"Mom, Dad, I finally got the internship! You're looking at Paradise Home Care Center's newest therapist—in training, that is."

"That's incredible, son!" Mr. King said, embracing him. "You truly deserve it! All that hard work paid off."

"Oh, that's wonderful! I'm so proud of you Noah!" Mrs. King added. She kissed him on the cheek while holding his baby brother, Nathan, in her arms. "When do you start?"

"Thank you! I start tomorrow." Noah told them before shifting his focus to his baby brother. "Hey what's up Nathan! How are you feeling, little guy?" Noah asked, placing his index finger on Nathan's tiny hand.

"What are you going to do to celebrate?" Mr. King asked.

"Nothing much, Dad. I'm just going to do some research on how I should prepare for my first day. You really have to be mentally ready for this kind of job."

As he took off upstairs, Mrs. King called after him,

"Okay, honey! Well, to celebrate we're going to make your favorite! SHRIMP ALFREDO!"

"Okay, cool! Thanks Mom!" Noah yelled back.

Mrs. King exhaled slowly as she sat down and started rocking the baby to sleep. "This is Noah's senior year in college, and he still doesn't go out to party with the other students. He doesn't even hang out with anyone his age. All he does is work and come home, every day. Should we be worried?"

Mr. King scratched his head. Then he sat down and put his arm around her. "Nah, I don't think so. He chose not to go to an out-of-state school, so being home a lot is normal, and Noah's just a secluded guy now. I know we always said that once he got into college he'd break out of it. But the truth is, he'll never really be the same after that whole prom situation happened his eleventh grade year. Shoot, if you ask me Noah is just supremely mature for his age," Mr. King reassured his wife.

"He sure is. Still, I just always pray that my baby isn't depressed, because a lot of young people his age are committing suicide. Almost every day I see families suffering from these tragedies at work." Mrs. King sadly disclosed. "I hope we aren't overlooking any signs."

"Natalie, I know you're worried about our boy, but trust me, he's fine. He's not depressed. He's just a remarkable genius. His goal in life is to heal people. That's a lot like what you do, and those types of people are hard to come by. Luckily, I've got two of you right at home."

"Aw Robert, you always know how to make me feel better," Mrs. King said with a huge smile.

"That's why I'm your husband," Mr. King declared with a chuckle.

2

FIRST DAY

The next morning, Noah woke up at 9:00am sharp. "Today's your first day, man! Make a good impression and be great!" he said as he hopped off the bed and started preparing for his first day as a therapist.

When Noah arrived at the Paradise Home Care Center, he was greeted by a man with pale white skin and white hair, about five inches taller than Noah's six-foot height. He shook Noah's hand firmly.

"Hello! You must be Noah King. Your professor has told me so much about you, and I'm glad you'll be joining us. My name is Richard Manning, I'm one of the directors here at the center. I work with the head administration to make sure things are running smoothly."

"Thank you for having me, Mr. Manning. So, how is this process going to work?" he asked eagerly.

"I'm glad you asked. Well, every morning you're going to clock in with this badge I'm handing you. At ten a.m., you'll have a session with Mr. Dave Wise, and at twelve you'll have a session with Mrs. Joanna Divine. Your sessions will be two hours or less. Luckily for you, Mr. Wise and Mrs. Divine are the only people who've signed up for these therapeutic sessions."

"Oh, okay . . . so I only have two clients?" Noah asked with a disappointed look. He spoke again quickly, before Mr. Manning could respond. "Never mind that. Is there anything that I need to know specifically about Mr. Wise or Mrs. Divine before I start?"

Mr. Manning beamed. "That's another great question. Well, Dave Wise is an army veteran who served two years in Korea, and a former civil rights activist. He's recently been diagnosed with PTSD and depression. Oh, and he's bipolar as well. And I mean really bipolar, you would think his first language was profanity. You'll see what I mean when you meet him. Then Joanna Divine, she's a sweet lady, and she's always loved it here. Mrs. Divine is suffering from depression too, because of a sudden death in her family last year. I can't remember which of her family members died off the top of my head. And that's basically all you need to know about these two. I'm sure they'll provide you with more information today."

Noah took a deep breath and rubbed his hands together. "Alrighty. Well, if that's everything, then I'm ready to begin when you are."

"Okay. This way. Follow me, please." As Mr. Manning escorted Noah down the aisle toward his new office, he struck up the conversation again to fill the silence. "Did you know that we're ranked among the top five old folks' homes in the country?"

Noah shook his head. "No, I didn't know that, but I've always heard great things about this place."

Mr. Manning nodded in appreciation. "Yes, we do what we can to make sure that all our members are happy here, and that they're treated with the best of care."

He opened the office doors and laid a ring of shiny bronze keys in Noah's hands. "Here are your keys. One more thing, Noah. Mr. Wise and Mrs. Divine will be giving me updates once a week about how much better or worse they feel after talking with you. I'm sure that you'll receive great reviews. And please continue to wear long-sleeved collared shirts and solid-colored ties. It makes the elderly folks here a lot more comfortable to see people dressed more old-fashioned. Just giving you a heads up." And then he left Noah to himself in the office.

3

THE 1ˢᵀ SESSION

A few minutes later, an elderly black man with a full head of grey hair and a grey beard, walked into Noah's office and sat down on the couch.

"Hello. You must be Mr. Wise," Noah said to the man.

"Yup, that's me all right," Mr. Wise replied with a huge grin.

"So how are you doing, Mr. Wise?" Noah asked.

"I'm doing good and getting better." Mr. Wise answered.

Whatever the old man had on his mind, he seemed

happy to let it all out this day. "First let me just say this. I'm 84 years old, okay. And I was born amid the decade of hard times as an innocent child. My momma was a God-fearing woman, and was really strict about my siblings and I going to church . . . and worshipping God. But even with all that godly stuff pushed into our brains, this society ruined my soul!" Mr. Wise suddenly frowned, and all the joy he had shown when he entered vanished abruptly.

"Interesting." Noah was intrigued. "Why do you think this society ruined your soul?"

Mr. Wise violently slapped the couch. "MOTHER-FUCKER! I was trying to get to the point before you cut me the fuck off! And I don't think this society ruined my soul. I KNOW IT DID! OKAY?"

Feeling nervous, Noah quickly gulped down his saliva. "Yes, sir. Uh, sorry about that."

"Shit, man, I was born during the Great Depression era, I grew up during the peak of Jim Crow and segregation, and I got drafted to go to the Korean War at twenty years old."

The elderly man was infuriated. He swiftly turned their session into an interrogation. "Do you think I wanted to be part of that shit, man?"

Noah shook his head. "No sir, not at all."

"And you young black folks think y'all got it hard!" Mr. Wise violently slapped the couch again. "Shit, man, we paved the way for you motherfuckers. If it wasn't for us and the civil rights movement, y'all wouldn't be able to do half the shit y'all doing today. Right?"

Noah nodded. "Yes, sir."

Mr. Wise abruptly grew calm again. "Okay then, man, that's all I'm saying, and young people today need to know that America is doomed."

I hope he doesn't curse me out again, Noah thought as he

worked up the courage to ask another question.

"Why is that, Mr. Wise?"

"Because of all the greed and evil going on around here." Mr. Wise sat back on the couch and leered. "The universe is about to give America a taste of her own medicine, and it's going to continue to get worse," he explained calmly.

Noah's eyebrows flared. "Well, what can we do to make this country better?"

Mr. Wise laughed hysterically at the question. "Oh, there's absolutely nothing you can do. It's all in the creator's hands now. So just sit back, relax, and watch the show," he finished through uncontrollable giggles.

Noah wanted to bring positive energy back into the session, so he asked the best question he could come up with. "Now Mr. Wise, do you have any grandchildren who fulfill your day?"

"I sure do." Mr. Wise's huge grin returned. "I have twelve grandchildren and twenty-seven great grandchildren, and they all make my day better. They're healthy, living well, and are the most kindest human beings on the planet. Ya know, most of my grand-babies didn't want me to come to the Paradise Home Care Center after my wife, Mary, died a few years back. They were like, *No, grand-dad, you can come stay with us,* including my kids, but I told them, don't worry about me, and to go live their lives to the fullest. They visit me every other day, and I'm grateful for that."

"I'm sorry to hear about your wife." Noah said.

"Ain't no need to be sorry! Shit, I'm going to see her again, man." Mr. Wise chuckled. "Hopefully this year. Every day I hope to check out of this world to be with my wife again." Mr. Wise leaned in toward Noah as if he were about to reveal a secret. "Listen, young buck. Ain't nothing wrong with me. I don't have PTSD or depression, but I might be bipolar, *HA HA*. These sons of bitches are just crazy and want me on medication. I'll make a deal with you. If you let these people know that I'm getting better, then I'll let them know that you're doing a great job."

Noah snickered and shook the old man's hand. "Okay, Mr. Wise, you have a deal."

4

THE 2ND SESSION

When his two-hour session with Mr. Wise ended, Noah took a deep breath to prepare himself for whatever emotional distress the next client was going to bring in. It was noon, and an elderly, fair-skinned black woman walked into the room. Noah thought she sort of resembled Lena Horne, the actress and singer from the 1940s. He only knew of her because his father always watched classic African-American films.

"Oh, hi! I'm assuming you're Noah King," the woman said to him.

Noah stood up and gently shook her hand. "Yes, I am! And you must be Mrs. Joanna Divine. Hey, has anyone ever told you that you look like—"

"—Lena Horne," she interjected. "Yes, I've heard it a million times." She added while giggling with flattery as she sat down on the couch opposite Noah. "You know, I used to act and sing myself."

"Wow, that's amazing. I'm sure that was a great experience," Noah replied.

"Yes, it really was. I performed on Broadway in New York City, and I modeled here and there too. In those days, so many people would say I looked like Lena Horne. It started to get a little annoying, though, so I eventually put acting and singing off to one side and pursued my modeling career full-time."

Noah nodded, making an effort to retain everything Mrs. Divine had said. "Was it hard for you to put aside the acting and singing?"

"No, not at all! See, in the 1940s and 1950s, the movie studios only allowed three or four beautiful black women to act in major motion pictures, and most of the time they'd have to give something up sexually to land those roles. And I knew I wouldn't be able to do that. Besides, I adored watching Lena Horne, Eartha Kitt, Dorothy Dandridge, and Ruby Dee excel in the arts. It was like watching my family make it to the big leagues."

Noah enjoyed listening to Mrs. Divine speak about her life as if she was his own grandmother. "So what was your modeling career like? Was it good for you financially?"

Mrs. Divine grinned from to ear to ear. "Oh yes, my it was amazing. I traveled all over the world. I went to Paris, London, Italy, Japan, Brazil, Ghana, and Egypt. My most memorable year was in 1958. That's when I met—him." Mrs. Divine's grin grew even wider.

"And who's that?" Noah questioned.

"Barry, the love of my life. My husband. I met him in Los Angeles around the time my modeling career was taking off. He was a well-known photographer. Though if you ask me, he should of been in front of the camera too."

Mrs. Divine sighed as if she were falling in love all over again. "Barry had a resemblance to Sam Cooke. He couldn't sing like him, but he darn sure looked like him."

"Wow!" Noah became even more curious. "How did you two meet exactly?"

"Well, in the spring of 1958 I was hired to model bathing suits for *Ebony* magazine and *Sunny* magazine."

Noah interjected. "Oh, okay, let me guess. Barry was the photographer who took your pictures."

"Yes, he was!" Mrs. Divine snickered like a high school girl thinking about her crush. "He was very quiet during the photoshoot though. The only thing he would say was, 'You're doing a great job.' He would say that every ten minutes, and I could tell he was really shy."

"When did you really start to talk?"

"We had our first conversation two minutes after the photoshoot was over. I was outside the studio waiting for one of my girlfriends to pick me up. Barry tracked me down, tapped on my shoulder, and said, 'Hello, Miss. I just wanted to tell you that you did a great job today.'

"I looked Barry directly in his ravishing brown eyes and said, 'I know, silly. You told me that a million times during the shoot.'

"After that, Barry asked what my name was. I only gave him my first name, but then I asked for his. He shook my hand gently and twinkled at me with his glistening white teeth and said, 'Barry Divine.' At that exact moment I fell in love with him.

"The next year, we got married in San Francisco. We

were both twenty-four years old with the whole world ahead of us. Barry was such a romantic. We did everything together! We went on dates to the park, the movies, and vacationed outside the country.

"By 1970, we were thirty-five years old and had everything we wanted from our careers, so we decided it was time to have a baby. That November, we had our first and only child, Barry Vincent Divine Jr. That boy looks just like his father when it comes to his facial features, but he has my green eyes. And he didn't inherit his father's glowing chocolate skin either, ha-ha. He's a shade lighter than his father was."

"Barry seems like an incredible man. Is he here at the Center too?" Noah asked.

"Oh, no. Barry died five years ago from lung cancer. All that second-hand smoke from our early years finally caught up to him. All through the forties, fifties, and sixties, every celebrity he took pictures of had a whole posse around them who smoked in the studio. Barry himself couldn't stand it!"

"I'm sorry for your loss. Did you have family members to help you cope through this tragedy?" Noah queried gently.

A glum look suddenly struck upon Mrs. Divine's face. "Yeah—my son, Barry Jr., and his wife Vivian have a daughter named Diana. When I moved here after my husband Barry died, Diana would come to visit me every day, and we'd talk for hours and hours until she had to go to class—or go home to get some sleep." Mrs. Divine gazed at Noah for a few seconds. "How old are you, dear?" she asked.

Noah was startled by her question. "Me? Oh, I'm twenty-one."

"Oh, yeah, Diana was . . ." Mrs. Divine became

slightly teary-eyed and choked up.

"It's okay, Mrs. Divine. Take your time," Noah said soothingly as he handed her a box of tissues.

She wiped her face and gathered herself together. "Diana was close to your age when she died in a car accident last May. She was twenty-two and had just finished from college. That night after her graduation, she and her girlfriends went out to celebrate, and they were struck by a drunk driver."

Mrs. Divine began to cry softly. "Diana was the only one who didn't survive. She was in the passenger seat, and that side of the car took the most damage." She murmured, "You know the saying, 'A parent should never have to bury their child'?"

"Yes, I'm familiar with it," Noah replied.

Mrs. Divine nodded. "Well a grandparent should never have to bury their grandchild, because the feeling is even worse."

Noah felt sympathy for her. "I'm really sorry to hear about that. Tragedies are a difficult thing to overcome. What are some of the coping mechanisms you used? Or would like me to try to help you heal?"

"Well, it's been ten months since Diana's death. I used to write in my journal a lot, but what really helps me now is when I sleep. Sleeping helps me because Diana appears in my dreams," Mrs. Divine divulged.

Noah started jotting ideas in his notebook to figure out how he could help her. "Ah . . . so what happens in these dreams?"

"Well, for starters, it's always in the same place, on the front porch of my and Barry's old house. It's always peaceful and quiet, and the sun is always setting, giving the sky a beautiful orange glow, but with perfect weather. I'll be sitting on my old wooden rocking chair, and she'll be sitting on her Pop-Pop Barry's old rocking chair, and we'll have a beautiful view of Silverside Lake."

"Oh, wonderful. Do you two ever talk about anything in these dreams?" Noah asked as he continued to write.

"Yes, we talk about a lot actually. And you know, I'm really starting to think they aren't dreams. Well they're dreams, but they're like real dreams at the same time."

"Oh, my." Noah's eyebrows lifted. "What do you mean, and why do you think that?"

"Because everything we do and talk about is based on the present and what's happening to us now. I remember the night after her funeral; she came to me in my dream and ran up to hug me. That's something Diana would do whenever she saw me when she was alive. When her body disappeared and went through mine, she was so upset because she couldn't feel me anymore. But we could both sit down on the chairs and walk around on the porch with no problem. She was grateful to at least hear me and see me again.

"I also remember asking her if she'd seen her Pop-Pop yet, but she told me he wasn't around. She believes her Pop-Pop Barry is on the third floor of some spirit dimension she always talks about. Apparently, the third floor is the highest. We also know it as Heaven. She told me that some big mysterious guy who is probably an angel explained to her that on the third floor, you meet all your dead family members, loved ones, and friends. And it's so massive that it takes millions of years to explore." Mrs. Divine giggled. "But hey, the people there have all eternity, so millions of years is nothing to them."

Noah smiled at the joke. "That's interesting. Have you ever asked Diana why she hasn't entered the third floor yet?"

"No. I do know she's free to enter it whenever she

pleases, but I think the poor child is waiting for me to come with her. Every time I see her in my dreams, she gets extremely excited and says she's been waiting for me all day." Mrs. Divine added.

"I see—do you have this dream every night?" Noah questioned.

"Yes, these so-called dreams have been happening every night since her funeral." Mrs. Divine paused. "Noah, I want to thank you because you've really helped me today. I've been really wanting to get all this—whatever it is—off my chest so bad lately. I didn't want to bother my son and his wife about what I'm going through. It's already been a bad enough year with them losing Diana too. The last thing I need to be is a burden to them. When I signed up for your therapy sessions, I told my son that these were just happy, therapeutic talking sessions that I would be joining for fun so that I wouldn't get bored here."

"I see. So does your son Barry vis—"

"Barry Jr," Mrs. Divine interjected pleasantly.

"Oh yes, sorry. Do Barry Jr. and his wife Vivian visit you often?"

"Yes they do, every single weekend actually. They'll take me to church, we'll have something to eat, or we'll visit Diana's gravesite. We do our best to make our weekends memorable and beautiful."

Mrs. Divine continued to gaze at Noah thoughtfully. Finally she spoke. "You know Diana would've really liked you. I can tell you're just a great young man. No kids, I assume?"

"Oh, no! No kids at all!" Noah responded with a giggle.

Okay, yeah, I see. So no kids, you're in school, handsome, well mannered. I can tell you have no criminal record. You're just perfect!" Mrs. Divine said as if she were about to set him up with someone.

Noah was flattered. "Thank you, Mrs. Divine I appreciate everything you said. And it looks like our time here is almost up. I just have one more question to ask you. How has this session helped you heal, and what do you look forward to talking about next?"

Mrs. Divine sat back and exhaled deeply. "This session has helped me heal by allowing me to release my emotions, and it made me realize that the more I talk about Diana the better I feel. When Diana visited we always talked about her Pop-Pop Barry, and that helped me appreciate my memories of him. So in our next session, all I have to do is talk about Diana more, and about my dreams, and then I should be fine. I'll even bring in a picture of Diana so that you can see what my beautiful grandbaby looked like."

"Okay, that'll be great Mrs. Divine. I'm glad this session has helped you heal a little," Noah said as he helped her out of the office.

When Noah got home that evening, his mother greeted him with curiosity. "Noah! How was your first day on the internship?"

"Hey, Mom. It was a cool experience overall. I only have two clients so far, Mr. Wise and Mrs. Divine, but I definitely learned a lot about them. And I have to say, elderly people sure can talk." Noah joked. "But I don't mind. It was great hearing their stories."

Mr. King had a proud look on his face. "That's great, son. You're on your way to becoming the most requested therapist in Silverside. And you're absolutely right, though, elderly people can sure talk your head off," he laughed.

5

THE PICTURE

The following week, Noah called Mrs. Wright before preparing for his clients' follow-up sessions. "I just wanted to thank you again," he told her, "and let you know that I'm really enjoying my internship. It's been a great experience so far."

"Oh, Noah that's fantastic! I'm so proud of you! Mr. Manning told me he heard great things from your clients. I shouldn't have said that, so act surprised when he tells you, ok? I could ask you a billion questions, Noah, but I don't want to hold you up. So I'll see you in class next week, okay?"

"Okay, will do! See you next week! Bye-bye." Noah hung up the phone.

An hour later, entering the lobby of the Care Center, he ran into Mr. Manning.

"Oh, hey, Noah! Great news! Mr. Wise and Mrs. Divine absolutely love you, man! They said that talking with you is really helping their state of mind. So whatever you're doing, keep it up."

Noah acted surprised. "Wow!" he exclaimed, "I'm glad to hear it. Thank you, Mr. Manning!"

Noah was waiting in his office when Mr. Wise arrived a few minutes later.

"Hey, young brotha!" he offered cheerfully.

"Hey, Mr. Wise! How are you?"

Mr. Wise giggled. "Shit, man, I'm still here ain't I? Like I told you, I'm just ready to check out of here so I can see my wife Mary again. Every night I go to sleep hoping I'll wake up by her side in heaven, but other than that I'm doing good. How's your morning going?"

"Oh, it's going great. I—" Noah didn't have a chance to complete the sentence.

"Let me tell you about how beautiful and great my wife Mary was." And with that, Mr. Wise continued talking for the next two hours. Noah simply made sure not to interrupt him as he went on about his wife, the war, the government, and everything else that was on his mind.

After his session was over, Mrs. Divine entered Noah's office excitedly, carrying a stack of photo albums. "Hello, Noah!"

"Hi, Mrs. Divine. Please make yourself comfortable."

"Hey, so Barry Jr. and Vivian are here too. I told them how great a therapist you are, and how young and intelligent you are too, and they would just love to have the chance to meet you. Can they come in really quick and say hello?"

"Sure, absolutely!" Noah agreed.

"Hey, guys! Come on in," Mrs. Divine called. When they entered, Noah saw that Mrs. Divine had not been exaggerating about her son's appearance. Barry Jr. definitely had his father's genes. He looked like Sam Cooke, but just a shade lighter and with Mrs. Divine's green eyes.

Sam Cooke and Barry Sr. must have been distant relatives, he thought. *Or long lost brothers.*

"Hello there, young man. I wanted to thank you for helping my mother. She's been telling me all about you this week." Barry Jr. said delightedly. "This is my wife, Vivian," he added.

Vivian greeted Noah with a radiant smile. "Hi, darling!" Noah was stunned by how young and ravishing Vivian looked. She didn't seem to be a day over 25. She had smooth dark-skin, a slim, fit build, fine curves, and long flowing black hair. "I've been hearing about you all week, so I thought it was only right if I brought you in some lemon cake and lemonade to snack on."

Sounds good!

"Wow! Thank you—you really didn't have to do that." Noah said.

"Are you kidding? It's the least I can do. When Momma Divine just kept going on and on about how incredible you were, we just had to meet you."

Noah noticed that Vivian had an accent, but he couldn't place it.

She must be from, like India, or Ethiopia . . . or France? Brazil? I don't know. She's definitely not from America.

"So, Noah, what school do you go to?" Barry Jr. asked.

"I attend Silverside University, sir, nothing special."

"That is special! It's pretty amazing, actually! That school is on its way up there with the Ivy Leagues. I'm guessing you're pretty smart. What year are you in?"

"My senior year, but I'll be finishing a couple of months early, since I have one more project and a final exam left."

"Good work! And you're already getting a jump start on your profession. Shoot, is there anything else you do besides school and this?" he joked.

"Well, since you ask . . . every Christmas, I buy toys for children in foster care or orphanages. But that's about it," Noah replied humbly.

Barry Jr. and Vivian were blown away. "Well, I'm glad my mom chose you, young man," Barry Jr. said.

"So am I! Keep up the great work!" Vivian added.

"See? I told you this young man here is something else," Mrs. Divine put in.

Noah really couldn't think of what to say. He felt a little awkward with everyone talking about him while he was sitting right there. "Uh . . . thank you!" he finally said, rubbing his head.

"All right, well, we're going to leave you two be. It was nice meeting you, Noah," Barry Jr. opened the office door.

"It was nice meeting you both as well. Have a great day," Noah replied as they left.

"We really need to set Noah up with Amber," Vivian whispered to her husband as they walked down the hall. "He's perfect for her. Oh my, and if only Diana were here. They would have made a great couple."

"True, that would've been nice to see." Barry Jr. responded as he placed his arm around his wife.

~~~

When Mrs. Divine had finally settled in, she pulled out her photo albums. "I know I said I was only bringing in one photo, but I couldn't help myself."

"That's okay, I understand." Noah twiddled his fingers and sneered. "Did you have another one of those dreams again?" he asked as he tried to get into his therapist mode.

"Mm-hm, I sure did." Mrs. Divine responded as she looked through her photos. Suddenly she started speaking. "Oh, look, these are pictures Diana took at the Silverside Zoo. Diana wanted to take after her grandfather and me, so she got into photography and modeling at a young age. She was twelve years old when she started taking pictures." She said as she showed the photos to Noah.

Noah just nodded and smiled as he took a quick glance at each picture. "What did you and Diana talk about in your dream last night?"

Mrs. Divine was so engrossed in the pictures that she didn't hear the question. "Look! Here's Diana with her Pop-Pop Barry on her third birthday. They're so precious. He was wiping the icing off her face. They look so happy, don't they?" She snickered as she held up the picture.

Noah finally gave in and became more engaged in what Mrs. Divine was showing him.

"Oh, and here's my favorite picture of her, wearing this red sweater with her black pants. This is one of the last pictures Diana ever took." Mrs. Divine handed the picture to him.

Noah gazed in awe at the picture of Diana.

My god! This is Diana?

"Wow," he said, "she's—she was beautiful." He kept staring at the picture.

"My grandbaby sure was! In that photo she was modeling a new clothing line her friend Amber started."

Noah had never seen a woman so beautiful before.

She's so alluring. And angelic. She literally looks like an angel.

He looked at the picture more closely, paying attention to every detail. Diana was fit like her mother. She had unblemished medium-brown skin that gleamed like a star. Her lips looked naturally smooth and delicate, and her long black hair flowed like a river. She had glimmering hazel eyes that captivated the soul.

What am I doing? Noah thought as Mrs. Divine talked and showed him more pictures of Diana.

She's dead. Have some respect for yourself. And for this girl's family.

When the session wrapped up and Noah turned around to put some notes into his briefcase, Mrs. Divine slipped a wallet-sized picture of Diana into his back pocket. Luckily, he didn't notice a thing. Then she gathered her belongings and said, "It was great speaking with you again, Noah. I think I might tell Diana about you tonight, and how you're helping me. I know that might sound strange, and maybe these are just dreams, but it's still great to have some form of communication with my grandchild. You don't think I'm some crazy old lady, do you?"

Noah smiled. "Not at all, Mrs. Divine. In fact, you're perfectly normal."

6

WHAT A NIGHT

Through the afternoon and evening, Noah couldn't stop thinking about Diana. By the time midnight arrived, he had decided to find out more about her and logged in to his computer. "Okay, she attended Bay Valley High School, and then she went to Bright-Fire University. Wow! Those are expensive schools. I guess the Divines are pretty wealthy people," Noah said under his breath as he searched the internet.

Silverside News Online:

Recent Bright-Fire University graduate, Diana Divine, was killed in a car accident while heading to a party.

"Yup, I already know that," Noah muttered as he scrolled through more articles.

Today in Silverside:
Diana Divine was the granddaughter of well-known African-American photographer Barry Divine and his wife, Joanna Divine, a famous African-American model in the 1950s and 1960s.

"And I know that too," Noah said in aggravation. He sat back on his rolling chair and thought.

"Social media!" he suddenly blurted out. "She had to have a social media account while she was alive. Let's see, everyone has a *Gossip Place* account nowadays, that's how you keep up with people." Still talking to himself, he entered Diana's name in the site's explore bar. "Let's see, let's see . . . Diana Divine. There she is!" Her profile picture was a head shot of her senior class photo from high school.

He looked at her timeline.

Guess she didn't post much. There are only three pictures on here.

The first photo showed Diana and five friends posing like 80s kids in front of their lockers. The second photo showed her on stage hugging a guy very intimately. He wore a black and blue tuxedo and a crown, and she wore a blue gown and a tiara.

This must be her prom, and that's obviously her boyfriend. He was definitely an athlete. He probably played basketball or football and was like the star of the team.

The last photo showed Diana and her grandparents at

her high school graduation. Underneath were thousands of comments, mostly repeating the same things: "R.I.P. Diana miss you," "Love you Diana," "Rest in Peace," "I can't believe it ⊗," "Gone but not forgotten." A highlighted comment from Bright-Fire University read "Rest in Paradise, our Bright-Fire Alumni. You will truly be missed."

And that was that. There were no other documents of Diana Divine online. "There would probably be less information on me if I died," Noah said to himself exhaustedly as he shut the computer down. He rolled into bed still wearing his work attire.

Sometime later, Noah woke to the sound of whispering in his room. He opened his eyes slowly. The ceiling seemed to have a dark blue tint, but that didn't bother him. He figured it might have been a weird reflection coming from the moon through his window. Since he could no longer hear anything he shut his eyes again. The whispering suddenly came back, and grew louder near his right ear.

"Hey, you!" The voice said.

He turned and opened his eyes to see a glowing woman smiling and waving at him. "HOLY SHIT!" Noah shouted. He panicked and hid under his bedsheets. "I'm dreaming, I'm dreaming, I'm dreaming, I'm dreaming!" He shut his eyes tightly and tried to wake up from the nightmare.

Oh my god! He can actually see me! The woman thought.

"Hey, can you see me? I'm so sorry! I really didn't mean to scare you." She crept slowly toward Noah's bed.

"I'M DREAMING!" Noah repeated, still hiding in a fetal position and ignoring the sound of her voice.

The woman sat on the edge of his bed, and tapped his shoulder.

Wow! I can touch him too!

"Nope," she said soothingly. "Unfortunately, you aren't dreaming."

As Noah reluctantly removed his sheets, he saw that the woman talking to him was Diana Divine. His heart was beating rapidly, but the sight of her face gradually eased his anxiety. She looked just like the mesmerizing picture Mrs. Divine had shown him. There she was, sitting right on his bed, wearing the same red fitted sweater and black fitted pants he'd seen before.

Due to the brightness of her spiritual body, her medium-brown skin was glowing in the dark like a nightlight. Her long black hair flowed like a river, almost reaching the full length of her back, and her glimmering hazel eyes captivated Noah's soul. Everything else in his room now consisted of a dark blue tint. Still convinced that what he was seeing wasn't real, Noah rubbed his eyes and blinked, telling himself that Diana would suddenly disappear.

"You know what? Maybe I'm hallucinating," Noah whispered.

Diana gently tapped him on the shoulder again. "You're not hallucinating. This is really happening," she whispered back.

Noah was speechless. The beautiful woman he couldn't stop thinking about was in his room.

How the hell is this even possible? This can't be real! he thought.

He sat up to gather his thoughts. Then he said, "But you're dead!"

"Yeah, I know!" Diana replied sarcastically.

"Okay, so, um—what exactly are you doing here? I mean, like . . . why are you here . . . in my room . . . tonight?" he asked.

Diana stood up and set her hands on her hips. "Um, excuse me, I should be asking you the same thing. About an hour ago I was relaxing in my favorite world, minding my own damn business. And then out of nowhere I was sucked into a portal and dropped here in your room. I tried to get out of here by opening up my own portal back to the spirit dimension, but no matter how many times I tried I couldn't leave. Heck, I even tried climbing out of your window! I think there's like some force field keeping me here. I tried to wake you up without freaking you out and all, but I obviously failed when it came to the freaking you out part." She rambled while pacing back and forth in Noah's room.

"Did you say *world?*" Noah asked. He hopped off his bed.

"Yes. I was in a spirit world, but right now that's neither here nor there," Diana answered. After a slight pause she slowly began to approach Noah. "What I really need to know is . . . why have you been thinking about me?" she asked, piercing him with her hypnotizing eyes.

"What?" Noah played clueless, pretending he didn't know what Diana was talking about.

"Why have you been thinking about me?" She repeated with a sneer. "You've been thinking about me long and hard all freaking day! Now usually when my friends and family members are thinking about me or missing me, I can send down the memories we have together. That eases their pain, and it allows me to show them that I'm always with them. It's the only thing I can do besides entering their dreams—well, so far I can only enter my Mom-Mom's dreams. Anyway, God knows it's damn near impossible for me to enter the first floor of the spirit dimension here on Earth. I haven't been here since the day of my funeral."

Diana sat down on Noah's rolling chair as she continued to ramble. "But you . . . you're a stranger. I'm not trying to be harsh or anything, but I have no memories to send you because I have no clue who you are. I tried to pay you no mind and thought your portal would just disappear, but it somehow pulled me in."

Noah scratched his head and tried to come up with a good explanation. "Oh, sorry . . . um, I know your grandmother Joanna, and . . ." Noah was distracted by noticing his physical body still lying down in bed. He looked down at his hands and saw that they were glowing like Diana's, and he immediately freaked out again. "YO! What the hell happened to me?" he shouted frantically.

For some reason, Diana thought Noah freaking out was the most hilarious thing imaginable. She was laughing so hard she almost fell off the chair.

"This isn't funny! I think I'm dead!" Noah shouted in panic.

"Oh relax, you'll be fine. You're just going through astral projection . . . I think." Diana told him after she finished laughing. "No, wonder you can see me and feel me. You were astral projecting this whole time. I didn't notice your actual body lying there till now."

Noah was confused. "Astral projection?"

"Yes. It's a rare gift in which the living are able to have out-of-body experiences and can visit the spirit dimension as they please. So congratulations. You're one of the few human beings who can do this." Diana explained with a touch of humor.

"Oh . . . so my physical body is asleep while my spiritual body is awake," Noah muttered.

"Yup. Don't you read about these geeky type of things all the time?" she asked with a condescending smile.

Noah frowned. "No, why? What is that supposed to

mean?"

"Huh, you just seem like the type, that's all." Diana said while observing his perfect posture and formal attire. "Now, what were you saying about my Mom-Mom Joanna before you flipped out?"

"Oh, yeah, I'm your Mom-Mom's therapist at the Paradise Home Care Center."

Diana looked concerned. "A therapist? I never saw you when I visited. As a matter of fact I never even heard of the Care Center having therapist." She folded her arms across her chest.

"Yeah." Noah sighed. "They just started a new therapy program there. Your Mom-Mom signed up to help her cope with your death."

"What!" Diana hated hearing that. It saddened her to know that her grandmother needed to seek therapy because of her death, and what really sucked was that there was nothing she could do about it. "I visit Mom-Mom in her dreams all the time, and she seems fine. I wish she would have told me she was seeing a therapist."

Oh, damn, so Mrs. Divine's dreams about Diana are real, Noah thought.

He suddenly loosened his tie then directed his eyes back to Diana. "Maybe she didn't want you to worry about her in that way. That's where I come in—to help fill that void and heal patients like your grandmother."

Diana suddenly squinted at Noah and then gave him a mysterious look. "All right, so now that I know you're my Mom-Mom's therapist that answers one question, but you still didn't answer my first question."

"What question?" Noah asked, purposefully playing dumb again.

At that moment, Diana finally got fed up with Noah's stalling and dancing around her question, even though she found it kind of cute. She marched up until she was a foot away from him and asked again, "Why have you been thinking about me all day?"

After a slight pause, Noah finally gave in. "Ugh, all right, when your Mom-Mom showed me a recent picture of you, I was blown away. You were in the exact outfit you're wearing now. Honestly, and I'm not bullshitting you here, you're the most beautiful woman I've ever seen! Like, it's ridiculous! How is it possible to look that perfect? It's like you found a way to swindle the human anatomy to work in your favor."

Diana blushed and giggled a little as Noah continued.

"Anyways, after one glance at that picture I couldn't stop thinking about you. I couldn't get you out of my head. I had no clue that my thoughts would cause this to happen." He then hung his head in embarrassment after revealing his big secret. "Okay, now go ahead. I know you want to call me a creep or a weirdo."

Please let this be some type of lucid dream, because I'm humiliating myself.

Diana wore a slight smirk and was biting her lip. She started twirling her hair around her index finger and slowly swaying from side to side. She looked in every direction, suddenly too shy to look at Noah. "Oh my god, now I'm blushing and don't know what to do with myself, like some ditsy girl."

Noah suddenly had a smirk on his face too. "Yeah, you seem like the type," he teased.

"Good one!" Diana rolled her eyes and playfully stuck out her tongue. "I see you've got jokes, but okay, I had that coming."

Abruptly they heard a baby whining from across the hall.

"Nathan!" Noah opened his door and ran across the

hall into his parent's room. "Hey Diana, when you fell through the portal, nothing followed you here, right?"

"Nope, I came all by myself."

"That's a relief!"

When he entered, he saw his baby brother vaguely crying. Directly across from the crib, Mr. and Mrs. King were in such a deep sleep that they couldn't hear him.

Okay he's safe! I don't see any other ghosts in here.

"Damn, I can't pick him up. I don't want my parents waking up to a floating baby," Noah muttered as he stood over the baby. "What's wrong, Nathan? Do you need your bottle? Do you have to burp or something?"

Diana peeked her head over the crib to see the baby. "Aww, is that your son?" she asked timidly.

Noah grimaced. "No, it's my one-year-old brother Nathan."

Oh, thank God!

"Aww, he's so cute!" she said happily. In a few seconds, Nathan stopped crying and started staring at them.

"Wait, he can see us?" Noah couldn't believe it.

"I think so." Diana squinted in deep thought. "I've always heard that infants and toddlers can see spirits because of their innocence, but I've never actually witnessed it until now." She flipped her hair back behind her shoulders. "Look, he's smiling at us!"

"Hey, little man!" Noah said. He quickly noticed a pacifier at the end of Nathan's pillow. "Oh, that's why you were crying! You dropped your pacifier, huh? Here you go," he said as he retrieved the pacifier and placed it in Nathan's mouth.

Diana tried to gently rub Nathan's head, but her hand passed right through him. Noah was startled. "That doesn't make sense—how come I can touch him but you can't?"

he wondered.

"I don't know . . . maybe it's because you're still alive." Diana looked disappointed.

"Damn, it must suck being a ghost."

She scowled. "Ghost? I'd prefer it if you called me a spirit, please!"

Noah raised his palm to Diana's lips. "Shh! Keep it down!" he whispered. "He's falling back to sleep."

"Oh, sorry!" she whispered back. "But I really would rather you call me a spirit, not a ghost. *Ghost* just sounds . . . eerie."

Less than a minute later, Nathan dozed off soundly.

"Now he's knocked out just like your parents," Diana noted. "Well, I'm assuming those are your parents over there, right?"

"Yes, they are ," Noah answered.

The sight of Noah's parents reminded Diana of hers. "Your parents are some pretty hard sleepers. What do they do all day?"

Noah glanced over at the sleeping forms. "My dad is an IT technician. He works with a lot of corporations programming their computer software. And my mom here is an ER doctor."

Diana took a closer look at Noah's mother and found her face very familiar. She had a sense of where and when she might have met her, but she didn't say anything and continued to let Noah talk. "Thank God for baby Nathan bringing some life back into this house. I could tell that my mom's job has been really stressing her out for the past few years. I'm glad she's finally using some of her vacation days from work too, because she really needs it."

Noah slowly walked out of his parent's room, and Diana followed suit. "Because their shifts are so draining, I always try to comfort Nathan quickly whenever he cries at night. That's why I rushed out so fast when I heard him."

I also thought there was another ghost in his room.

"I guess I just like to take the load off them. They already do so much for us as is."

The signs of maturity Noah showed began to make a lasting impression on Diana. "That's sweet. You're an incredible big brother and son, did you know that? Shoot, there are so many guys your age that can't even take care of one responsibility." She gazed at Noah. "Speaking of age, how old are you?" she asked as they entered his room.

"Twenty-one," he said while leaving his door cracked. "I'll be twenty-two in May."

"Oh, okay. I'm about a year older than you. I'll be turning twenty-three next week, on March 31st. Well I would have been, if I were still alive." Diana pursed her lips momentarily. "Ugh, this crap sucks. I wish I had the chance to celebrate my birthday with my loved ones just one last time," She said despairingly.

"Hey, I wish you had that chance too. It would have been cool to meet you while you were alive." Noah put in with charm.

Diana laughed. "Yeah, instead of scaring you by your bedside."

Noah shook his head and giggled. "Well, you have to excuse me. I'm not used to running into ghosts every day."

Diana gave him another scowl.

"My bad—I mean *spirits*."

"Ha-ha, it's okay. You'll learn to use the right term sooner or later." She paused. "So, uh, what's your name?"

"Noah—Noah King," he responded.

"Wow! Noah King, huh? That's a lovely name."

"Not as lovely as Diana Divine," he countered.

She smirked as she sat down on his chair again. "So you and your baby brother are twenty years apart?"

"Yup, twenty years. Crazy, right?"

"No it's not crazy." Diana smiled. "It's pretty unique. Your parents look really young, though. How old are they?" she asked.

"I know, that's because they're both thirty-nine. They had me during their senior year of high school when they were eighteen. My dad proposed to my mom at their graduation," he added.

"Aww, so they're high school sweethearts still going strong. I love that!" Diana said.

"Yeah." Noah agreed. "A lot of people say they have an incredible story."

~~~

After a split second, Noah had something else on his mind. "Hey Diana, can I ask you a question?" He asked while standing a couple of feet in front of her.

She spun around once in his chair and then stopped herself to answer. "Sure. It looks like I'm going to be stuck in this house for a while, so ask away."

Noah twiddled his fingers, and sat on his bed. "I just hope it isn't too soon, or too harsh of a question."

Diana snickered, "Oh my god, Noah your question isn't going to kill me, you know! I'm already dead!"

Shit, please don't flip out on me for what I'm about to say.

At that moment he decided to go for it and ask. "Okay, here it is! What was it like the day you died? How did it feel?"

7

DIANA'S DEATH

Diana strolled over to the end of Noah's bed and sat beside him. She was so close that he could smell her flowery lavender scent and feel the warmth of her left arm brushing the right side of his body.

"I remember that day so vividly. I woke up happy as ever because I was finally graduating from college. Before leaving my room, I looked out my window and up at the sky and said, 'This is all for you, Pop-Pop!' Then I went to the mirror and tried on my Bright-Fire cap and gown."

Noah grimaced. "That school is mad expensive. I

thought about going there, but I didn't want to use my scholarship money and my parents' salaries to pay for a school that only cares about rich people."

Diana rolled her eyes. "Hey, it's not *that* bad."

Noah didn't respond. He just continued to bore into Diana's eyes until she finally gave in.

"All right, yes, unfortunately that's true. The school staff took better care of students like me—and my friends Amber and Samantha—because of how rich our families were. They knew about my mother and Amber's mother being fashion designers, and Samantha's parents are well-known filmmakers. But I can't really help what I was born into!"

"I knew it . . . Well, sorry for interrupting. Go ahead, you can finish your story," Noah said calmly.

Diana smiled. "It's okay. So I drove to school and met up with Amber and Samantha in the auditorium to prepare for the ceremony. We were so excited. We even planned on taking a girls' trip to Miami the next week to celebrate.

"During our ceremony, I remember being overwhelmed with joy as I waited in line for my name to be called. Then the magical moment happened when I heard the dean say, 'Diana Divine'. A big smile grew upon my face as I walked across the stage. When the dean handed me my diploma, I turned to the crowd and found my Mom-Mom and parents waving at me cheerfully. That's a memory I've cherished till this day. When our elegant ceremony ended, I had goosebumps all over my body. I couldn't wait to celebrate.

"Before I went home with my family, Samantha came running across the auditorium to me, super-excited. She said that some guy named Raymond she'd been crushing on from her film class had invited us to a party with his boys at the Silverside Club. I was hesitant, because I really just wanted to spend the rest of the day with my Mom-Mom and my parents, but the party was starting late, around 10:30, and Samantha wanted me to come really badly, so I agreed. I figured my parents would be tired or asleep by that time anyway, and Mom-Mom would be back at the Care Center.

"The ceremony had taken up most of the morning and afternoon. By the evening, I was home with my family. My mom cooked her favorite Ethiopian dish, Kitfo. She always made that on special occasions."

Noah interjected, "Oh, that's what she is—Ethiopian! I knew she was from outside the country when I heard her accent, I just couldn't put my finger on where." By the look on Diana's face, he could tell she had questions. "Oh, I forgot to tell you—I met your parents too, when they came to visit your Mom-Mom. But please go on."

"Wow, you're just getting yourself all acquainted with my family, and we haven't even gone out on our first date yet," Diana joked as she nudged him flirtatiously. "But yeah, along with the Kitfo my mom baked a lemon cake and made her special lemonade. My God, I miss her cooking." Diana took a deep breath, trying to keep her composure and not cry in front of Noah.

"After dinner I remember my dad walking up to me and giving me the tightest hug ever. As he held onto me he said 'My little girl is all grown up. Yesterday I could have sworn I was walking you to your first pre-k class, and now you're a college graduate. I love you so much, Diana, and I'm proud of everything you've done. Keep it up, okay? Here's a $1,000 gift card. You can spend it anywhere you'd like, so go ahead and enjoy yourself tonight, all right?'

Damn! $1,000 for one night. Noah thought as Diana continued with her story.

"I gave my father one more hug and told him I loved him, and that was the last time we spoke to each other. He was sound asleep in his room moments later.

"After I helped my mom put the food away, Mom-Mom called me out to the front porch. I knew she wanted to have one of our talks. I always loved our talks. I sat on Pop-Pop's old rocking chair as Mom-Mom Joanna sat on hers. She glanced over at me and said, 'Baby this is a true milestone for you. By walking across that stage, you completed the final stage of your childhood. Oh, I know you're twenty-two and they say that you're an adult at eighteen, but hey, what do they know. The way I see it, you're entering the first stage of adulthood now. This stage of your life is going to be more joyful and at the same time much more stressful. But there's a flipside to it. Are you ready to hear what's going to happen next?'"

Diana's smile grew wide. "I said, 'Yes, Mom-Mom I'm ready to hear it.'

"And then she continued. 'You're going to find a man who is going to win your heart and sweep you right off your feet.'"

Diana suddenly laughed, "That woman is something else. I thought she was going to tell me something much deeper than that. I told her that I'd probably never have a prince charming like she did. But she kept telling me to be patient, and that the magic of romance would happen naturally. I agreed with her words of wisdom, and I told myself that I would keep them with me forever. Right before my Mom got ready to drop my Mom-Mom off at the Care Center, Mom-Mom Joanna gave me these diamond stud earrings I'm wearing." She pulled her hair back behind her ears to show Noah the earrings. They were glistening like stars.

"They look great on you." Noah said mesmerized by her glow. "Where did she get them from?"

"Thank you! My Pop-Pop Barry had given them to her on their one-year wedding anniversary. She told me it was my graduation gift.

"Later that night, I went outside again, but this time I felt a sudden chill in the air. The moon was full and bright, lighting up the entire night sky. I gazed up at the stars and said, 'I did it, Pop-Pop! I'm finally finished with school.'

"At that moment, Samantha called to say she was twenty minutes away and would honk the horn when she was in front of my house. I went upstairs to change, since it was chilly, and I put on this sweater that Amber had made for her start-up clothing line. I looked in the mirror for about fifteen minutes, checking my makeup, my figure, my hair, and my outfit . . . patting down my sweater and my black pants . . . fitting into my black heels. I knew that the night would be great. When I checked my phone, it was already 10:50, and Raymond's party had started twenty minutes earlier. I didn't mind being fashionably late, though. Amber and Samantha loved making guys wait to see if they would show up, so that they could make a grand entrance.

"A few minutes later Samantha picked up Amber, right down the road from me. Then she pulled up at my house and honked. When I came outside, she was blasting music on the stereo and tapping the beat out on her steering wheel. Amber was in the back seat, still changing and trying to put on make-up at the same time.

"As I got into the passenger seat, I sensed this weird energy. It was the first time I'd ever felt that way. I felt like something bad was going to happen, like I had to expect the unexpected, but I didn't say anything. I really didn't know what to do. I just ignored the feeling and tried to enjoy the night.

"After five minutes of driving, we were all having a good time, blasting music and singing along. At a red light, Samantha turned the music down and said, 'Hopefully Raymond has a cute ass friend for you, Diana!'

"Amber stopped doing her make-up for a second and said, 'And for me! You need to hook me up too, girl!'

"When the light turned green Samantha laughed, turned the music back up, and shouted, 'We'll see!'

"She put her foot to the gas and then—BAM! . . ." Diana paused, and tears began rolling down her cheeks as she could no longer hide her emotions. She hid her face in her palms and started sobbing uncontrollably.

Instinctively, Noah put his arm around Diana. As he touched her shoulder, he gently drew her closer. "I'm sorry," she mumbled as she laid her head against his chest.

"No, no, don't be sorry. It's okay if you don't want to talk about it anymore. You don't have to," Noah whispered. He wanted to remove all her pain away.

Diana wiped the tears from her eyes. "No, I have to keep going. I have to get this off my chest. I never even told my Mom-Mom this story, and I talk to her every night in her dreams." Diana scooted into a more comfortable position, wrapping her arms around Noah's waist but leaving her head on his chest.

"Okay, I understand," Noah said as he stroked her shoulder.

She took a deep breath and resumed her story. "At the moment of the crash, my head collided with the side window and then the dashboard before the airbag released. And yes, I had my seatbelt on. Thank God," she kidded, "or it would've been a closed-casket funeral.

"Anyways, everything went black and I couldn't even

feel the pain I'd felt during that split second. A few minutes later I woke up, and the first thing I noticed was that my vision was different. I mean, I could still see clearly, it wasn't blurry or anything, but everything had a dark blue tint. For some reason, though, that part wasn't what freaked me out. It was when the police and firemen and paramedics arrived.

"A police officer opened the door, and shouted 'Get her out of there!' So I stepped out of the car on my own and said, 'It's okay, I got it. I'm fine.'

"The officer ignored me, though. He said, 'Come on get her out quickly.' I should've known something was off then. But a moment later the paramedics ran right through me. LIKE, right through my body! I couldn't believe it. Then I heard Amber and Samantha screaming my name, so I turned around to face them.

"As I turned I saw the paramedics taking me out of the car and rushing me into the ambulance. Everything slowed down for me. I could see my body, but somehow I wasn't in it. I looked down at my hands, and they were kind of glowing but transparent at the same time. For a moment, I hoped that it was all just a nightmare. The realization kicked in when I saw Amber and Samantha crying and giving statements to the police officers.

"From then on, I started to think and move quickly. I thought I had a great chance of getting back into my body, so I hopped into the back of the ambulance before they shut the doors.

"It was weird and petrifying to see my body lying there lifeless. While they were trying to revive me I took action myself and tried to get back into my body. But it didn't work at all. I would just go right through my old flesh, again and again. It was so frustrating! No matter how many times I tried getting my physical body back, the results were the same. I was a spirit now, and there was nothing I could do about it. It's crazy because the moment you die . . . you realize that you don't have the power to do the things you did while you were alive. You don't have the ability to communicate, and say goodbye to your family and friends for the last time. You can't touch anyone or move anything, but if you concentrate hard enough you can enter vehicles, homes, and other places—it's really weird. And time basically doesn't exist. You're just completely stuck. I felt so alone in that moment, and all I could do was put my head down and cry.

"When the paramedics arrived at Silverside Hospital, they told the doctors they couldn't revive me. But one ER doctor—the head doctor, I believe—was determined to bring me back. I could see it in her eyes. As I followed her and her team of doctors in their race to help me recover, I spotted my mom and dad, who had just arrived, crying together in the hallway and praying that I would be okay. They were waiting outside the emergency room hoping that the doctor would come back with great news. I tried to hug them and get their attention, but it obviously didn't work.

"Across the hall, I could see the ER setting up all sorts of breathing machines, and using these shock paddles on me. I just knew I had to come back, so I walked through the wall and into the operating room. But when I tried jumping back into my body, I fell right through it and the hospital bed. I heard the doctor shouting, 'Come back to us honey, I know you're still there! Come on back to your family!' as she searched for a pulse. She was operating on me for about an hour and a half. I admired her persistence, because her team had already given up and told her there was nothing they could do, but she refused to give up.

"But after my many failed attempts of getting my body

back, I had realized it was over. And after many failed attempts to bring me back to life, the ER doctor knew it too. Soon after, she emerged with a depressed look, as if she had just lost her own child. She gave my parents the terrible news that I didn't make it.

"My mom dropped to the ground and screamed, 'Diana!'

"My dad was so shocked he couldn't move. He just stood still like a statue with endless tears flowing down his cheeks. I felt pitiful, like I'd done something wrong. Then I started yelling, 'MOM, DAD, I'M RIGHT HERE! I'M RIGHT HERE!'

"Do you know how it feels to yell with all your might and still not be heard? And to have your family yearn for your presence even though you're standing right in front of them?" Noah shook his head from side to side. Diana could feel the motion of his gesture.

"Good. I hope you never have to go through that. I wouldn't wish it on my worst enemy.

"From then on, I was just a spectator to the life I once knew. When Amber and Samantha got to the hospital, my parents told them the bad news. They cried for hours.

"My father made the conscious decision not to call my Mom-Mom at the Home Care Center, since she was most likely asleep already. He thought it would be best to tell her in person anyway.

"That night was just dreadful. My parents were completely silent during the ride home, and when they arrived they just stayed in my room the whole night looking through old photos of me and smelling my clothes.

"My mom kept repeating herself. Every time she had a short outburst and would say, 'God, why is this happening?'

"All I could do was sit by her and tell her that

everything was going to be okay, and that I would always be by her side, even though I knew she couldn't hear me or see me. My dad did his best to stay strong for my mom by keeping in all of his emotions, so luckily he was there to tell her everything I was already saying.

"The next morning as the sun rose, my parents headed to the Care Center. I followed their every move. The car ride was almost as quiet as the night before. My dad looked extremely focused and kept his eyes on the road, while in the passenger seat my mother was stacking up pictures of me for Mom-Mom. When they arrived, they met Mom-Mom Joanna in her room. I remember how sweet and innocent she looked at the moment they walked in, wondering where I was.

"My mom hugged her with tears in her eyes. Mom-Mom said, 'What's wrong Vivian?'

My dad got on both knees and held Mom-Mom Joanna's hands and said, 'Diana's . . . . Diana's gone, Mom. She was hit by a drunk driver last night.'

"My Mom-Mom pleaded, 'No, no, no, no, not my grandbaby. She's not dead! God would not take her away from me. I know God would never do that. I already lost Barry I'm not losing Diana too.'

"I lost it when I saw Mom-Mom Joanna crying and trembling throughout those long hours. I thought about what my father had said the night before, so I repeated to myself that everything would be alright and that I would see them again. It was the only thing I could say or do without going crazy.

"Then, as my father sat there with a stone-faced look, Mom-Mom Joanna finally accepted the fact that I was gone for good. She suddenly stopped crying, grabbed my father by the chin, looked him in the eyes, and said, 'Barry Jr., stop it! You don't have to act all tough and strong for me.

It's okay. Let out your emotions. You just lost your daughter, and I just lost my grandchild. Acting all strong and keeping your emotions inside is not a healthy thing to do.' Then she patted his back and said, 'Let it out, baby, let it out. Don't hide your emotions like you did when your father died.'

"At that moment my father began weeping intensely. He shouted, 'MY BABY GIRL IS GONE, MOM! I MISS HER SO MUCH! OH, GOD, I MISS HER! I HOPE THE BASTARD THAT HIT HER GETS 100 YEARS IN PRISON! I'LL MAKE SURE OF IT!'

Diana sighed as she remembered everything that had happened that day. "I stayed close to them as they comforted each other. It really sucked knowing there was nothing I could do to make it better. And to make it worse, later that day my Dad got a call from the coroner telling him that my cause of death was a brain aneurysm and cardiac arrest."

Diana rolled her eyes. "Like they needed to hear that at the time, right? Talk about perfect timing.

"My parents planned my funeral right away. They just wanted closure, not a bunch of people at their home all week saying, 'I'm sorry for your loss.' Even though everyone means well, it can get pretty annoying hearing that over and over again from hundreds of people. So they contacted family and friends and announced that my funeral would be in two days. I watched Amber and Samantha spread the news all over *Gossip Place* like my parents had asked them to since they were helping out with the funeral arrangements. A bunch of people were posting "R.I.P. Diana" online, which was strange because I still felt alive; I was just alone.

"My funeral was held at the Silverside Baptist Church. There were so many people there. Like, hundreds. You would've thought the pope died. My parents' friends, my Mom-Mom's friends, and all of my family and friends."

Diana paused and sucked her teeth in disgust. "Including my ex and his current girl, who's the mother of his child. At that point I just wanted out. People were crying as the preacher spoke, my parents were distraught, and there was still nothing I could do. And staring at my own lifeless body in a casket was frightening and really freaked me out. The funeral was just filled with depressing and draining energy. I was about to walk out when my Mom-Mom stood over my lifeless body, held what used to be my hands, and said, 'Everything is okay, baby. I'll see you again. Now go on and have fun in Paradise, and say hi to your Pop-Pop when you get there for me.'

"After Mom-Mom Joanna spoke, a beam of light struck down upon me, and caused me to slowly float into its realm."

Noah was intrigued, "What was that like?"

Diana lifted her head from his chest and looked into his eyes. A single tear started rolling down her left cheek. "What?" she asked.

Noah gently placed his palm on her face and wiped the tear away with his thumb. "The realm," he whispered as he gazed into her eyes.

Oh my god, what's going on? I barely even know him, but I feel like we have a strong connection. He's really charming too! Aw crap! I forgot his question again, Diana thought.

Noah wondered, *Why is she so darn beautiful? This is a really sad moment, but when she looks at me all I want to do is kiss her. Is that wrong because she's technically dead? She's a spirit, so it's not like I would be kissing a corpse. Oh, forget it!*

As he leaned closer to Diana's lips, and she leaned toward his, Noah's alarm clock suddenly came on, interrupting the intimate moment and startling them.

"Shit!" Noah yelled. The clock said it was now six a.m.

Before he could say anything, his father burst through the door, midway through buttoning up his shirt for work. "Nope, can't have this thing waking up Nathan this morning," he muttered as he tried to shut it off.

After several failures, he finally tapped Noah on the wrist to wake him up. That instant contact caused Noah's spirit to zip right back into his body. He sat up abruptly as if he'd just woken from a nightmare.

"Whoa, you okay there son? Bad dream or something?" Mr. King asked.

Noah could see clearly again, and the dark blue tint in his room was gone. "Uh, yeah Dad, but I'm fine."

Mr. King handed Noah his alarm clock. "Well, do me a favor and shut this off, please, before Nathan wakes up crying." He walked out of the room.

"Gotcha, Dad."

After shutting off the alarm Noah plumped onto his pillow and looked at his ceiling. "What the hell just happened?" he whispered to himself.

8

WE NEED ANSWERS

About thirty minutes later, Noah finally stopped looking at the ceiling and questioning what had happened. When he came to his senses, he pulled out his phone and started researching. "Let's see here . . . what is astral projection?" he asked himself while plugging the question into the search engine.

"Astral projection is a form of telepathy where the soul is separate from the body and is capable of traveling around the entire universe. This act only happens when a person is laying down completely still, and becomes fully aware of their soul emerging from their body," Noah read aloud in a whisper, after finding himself on a lucid dreaming website.

In complete and utter shock, his heart started pounding heavily.

My soul was separate from the body! But I wasn't aware of it until later on. I just woke up like I would've from a normal sleep, and before I knew it I was already in spirit form.

He read on to find out more about this out-of-body experience. "There is no scientific evidence that proves that astral projection exists," Noah read.

Of course, because it's fake. Last night couldn't have been the first time I heard this term. I must've heard it a long time ago. I just can't remember where from.

Right after he read that sentence, Noah's cell phone began vibrating. When the caller ID popped up, he noticed that Mrs. Divine was calling him.

Strange—our follow-up session isn't for six days, he thought.

"Oh hey, Mrs. Divine, is everything all right?" he asked.

"Hello, Noah, and yes, everything is fine. I remember you told me to call this number whenever I have any questions or things on my mind that I would like to discuss with you."

Noah sat down at the edge of his bed and noticed that his rolling chair was still in the same position that Diana had left it in.

"Hello, Noah are you there?" Mrs. Divine asked with concern.

"Uhh, yes . . . yes, I'm here, Mrs. Divine; sorry about that. I got a little distracted. So, what's on your mind?"

Mrs. Divine took a deep breath and gathered up what she was going to say. "All right, well, last night the strangest thing happened."

As chills ran through his body, Noah's heart began to

race again in his eagerness to hear what Mrs. Divine was about to say next.

"Remember when I told you that I've been having dreams about Diana since the day after her funeral?" Mrs. Divine asked.

The suspense was killing Noah. "Yes, Mrs. Divine, I remember," he replied, gripping his phone tightly.

She slowly exhaled before revealing what she had to say. "Well, last night it didn't happen. I mean, I had the dream where I sit on my rocking chair and stare out into the lake while the sun sets, but this time Diana didn't show up. That's never happened before. Do you think it's a sign?"

For the first time in ten months Diana didn't appear in Mrs. Divine's dream. Yeah this has to be a coincidence.

For a few seconds, Noah thought about how to answer her question. "Ya know, maybe it's because you were completely satisfied with your session yesterday. Now that you're able to openly talk about Diana, it's probably improving your state of mind." Noah cringed, hoping that Mrs. Divine bought his idiotic statement.

"Yes, maybe you're right, Noah. It's either that, or she could've been busy going into someone else's dream," Mrs. Divine smiled.

Oh my god does she know?

Noah's eyes enlarged. "Well, that's another way to look at it," he replied, repeatedly tapping his feet on the carpet. "Mrs. Divine, I'm sorry about what I said a minute ago. I'm pretty sure you'll see Diana in your dreams again. You'll see her in no time," he added, redeeming himself.

"Aw, that's okay, you didn't say anything wrong. Thank you so much for speaking with me, Noah. I really appreciate you . . . I'm going to go now, okay? I'll let you know if anything else changes with this dream thing, and

I'll see you again this coming Saturday. Bye-bye, now!"

"Gotcha, Mrs. Divine. See ya later."

After hanging up the phone, Noah looked at his rolling chair again. "Diana, are you still here?" he whispered. There was no answer. "Diana, if you're here, make something move or show me a sign." Noah slowly crept around his room, eyes darting around. There was nothing but silence, and no sign of Diana.

I'm trippin' right now, I need to get it together. All of this is in your head man—it has to be.

Having heard Noah's worried voice, Mrs. King suddenly came into the room, where she caught him talking to no one. "Hey, is everything okay?" she asked, puzzled.

"Uh, yeah, Mom, everything is fine. Why?" Noah replied.

"Because I heard you talking to someone . . . as if someone was actually in your room . . . who's Diana?"

Dammit! I'm so damn stupid; why didn't I shut my door or pretend I was on the phone?

"Hello, Earth to Noah! Are you still with us?" Mrs. King teased him, waving her hand in front of his face.

Noah snapped out of his daze. "Yes, Mom, I'm fine . . . I was just repeating lyrics from a song I heard on the radio; that's all. I wasn't actually talking to someone or trying to talk to someone."

"Okay, whatever you say." Mrs. King bought Noah's story for now. "Hey! Do you still want to volunteer at the children's hospital this summer, and help out with the cancer patients? I think the kids will love you there."

"Oh yes, absolutely mom."

"All right, good to know well, breakfast is downstairs, okay? I made pancakes."

Noah smiled in relief.

Thank God that didn't escalate to another level of questions.

"Okay, thank you, Mom; I'll be right down."

~~~

During the afternoon, Noah spent hours just lying in bed thinking about what had happened the night before. He couldn't get over it. It was driving him crazy.

That couldn't have all been real, right? It had to be a dream. At the same time, though, no one just automatically has a vivid dream like that . . . or do they? I'm starting to think I may need a therapist.

"Hey Noah, I'm taking Nathan with me to the grocery store. Do you want anything?" Mrs. King asked from downstairs.

"No thank you, Mom, I'm fine. I'm going to get in the shower, then get some more sleep."

"Okay, hon, I'll be back soon," Mrs. King replied as she left the house carrying Nathan and her car keys.

After getting out of the shower and putting on sweats, Noah decided to put this astral projection thing to the test.

I gotta make sure I'm in my right state of mind here.

"Shoot! I need something to help me fall asleep. I should've asked my mom for some sleeping pills," he muttered, thinking about seeing Diana again.

"Let's see . . . let's see, I think music will help," he murmured, grabbing his aux cord and plugging it into his cell phone and stereo. When the music started, he slammed the side of his head down onto his pillow as he flopped directly onto his stomach. "Ah, you can never go wrong with '90s R&B."

Within an hour, Noah was well into a deep sleep.

Without warning, he heard the sound of a woman humming to the song playing on his stereo. Then he felt someone gently tap his left shoulder. "Hey, you have great taste in music," the voice said.

I remember that voice.

Noah sluggishly lifted his head and saw Diana standing near the left side of his bed. He also noticed that he was now lying next to his physical body, but that didn't seem to startle him like it had the night before. "Wow, so last night was real!" he proclaimed as he sat up.

Diana folded her arms across her chest and smirked. "Yeah, I told you that yesterday, silly." She then sat next to him on the bed. "And you did it again too, ya know."

Noah frowned. "Did what?" he wondered.

"You brought me here to your room again by constantly thinking about me. The only difference is that I actually don't mind being here this time. It's fun having someone around my age to talk to again."

Noah looked at his window and realized that his vision now had a blue tint like the previous night. It was much brighter this time since it was morning. He moved closer to the window to open it. "Hey, when you look around, do you still see a blue tint? It's almost like wearing blue sunglasses or something. Well, that's what my vision is like at the moment, anyway." Noah directed his eyes back toward Diana. "I mean, you and I aren't blue, but everything else is," he explained.

Diana understood. "Yeah, that's because the spirit dimension here on the first floor is all blue besides us . . . the spirits."

"Got it! I guess it's going to take some getting used to. So what happened to you this morning, after I got sucked into my body?" Noah asked.

"Oh yeah that was crazy." Diana snickered. "As soon as you got sucked back into your body, I instantly got sent back to the second floor. I had no control over it. I evaporated from here and appeared in the world I was in before, and then a few hours later, you brought me here again."

"Wow," Noah nodded as if he understood what Diana was telling him. "Let me get this straight: So last night, you said this was your first time here on earth since the day of your funeral, right?" he asked as he sat back down next to her.

"Correct," she replied.

"And somehow I have the power to bring you back down here when I think about you while I'm sleeping, or in the midst of astral projecting. Why is that?" he asked.

"You know what!" Diana twiddled her fingers as she pondered his question. "I have no clue, but that's what I've been trying to figure out. And sorry about last night. I didn't mean to get all intimate with you . . . I just haven't had real direct contact with anyone in ten months. It was all just—"

Noah quickly interjected. "It's okay, really." He smirked. "I—I honestly didn't mind it. A beautiful soul like yourself can cry on my shoulder any day," he smoothly added.

Jeez! He's such a flirt.

Diana began to blush and glow even more. "Well, aren't you quite the charmer." She paused. "Wait, you have a girlfriend, don't you? I know you do," she said, nudging Noah with her forearm.

Is she flirting with me? Noah giggled.

"Nah, uh . . . I actually don't. I haven't had one since my junior year of high school."

Diana gasped. "What! Get the hell out of here. You haven't had a girlfriend since your junior year of high school? Okay, now I'm curious, because I don't get how you're still single."

Neither do I.

Noah shrugged his shoulders and rubbed the top of his head. "Because I'm a nerd, that's why," he answered with embarrassment written all over his face.

Aww, well at least he's being honest.

Diana flipped her hair back behind her shoulders and gave Noah an endearing smile. "Who cares? You're a sexy nerd. You have a nice build, you're tall, you have perfect teeth, you smell good, and you're extremely handsome!"

She thinks I'm sexy!

Noah began repeatedly rubbing his hair, not knowing what else to do as Diana flooded him with comments. "Well, aren't you quite the charmer," he said mockingly.

That was such a corny ass response I gave her.

"Honestly though, I've been having trouble finding a girl I can connect with. Maybe it's because I don't go to parties and hangout with a bunch of people my age like I used to back in high school. I'm always busy with volunteer work or school work. Besides, after my ex did me wrong my junior year, I kind of just gave up on love and became very secluded," he explained.

Diana leaned forward, placing her elbow onto her leg. "Welcome to the club! I gave up on love too after my situation. So, what did she do?"

Noah looked muddled. "Huh, who?"

"Your ex! You said she did you wrong. What did she do?" Diana asked.

"Oh—her!" Noah shrugged his shoulders. "I really don't want to talk about it. It's too much to get into right now."

"Oh, come on, it's not like I'm going to tell the whole world about it. Besides Mom-Mom Joanna, you're the only person I talk too. So come on, spill the beans—please!" Diana begged, giving Noah puppy dog eyes.

I guess it wouldn't hurt to tell her.

Noah slapped his knee and deeply exhaled before beginning. "Okay, well, during our junior year of high school, my ex and I went to the junior-senior prom together. The night was going really well at first. We were talking with our friends, dancing together, and we even got our prom pictures taken in this Arabian Nights-themed photo booth they had. But later on that night, things took a turn for the worse. She suddenly wandered off, and none of my friends knew where she went. When I was finally able to spot her, I saw her cheating on me. She was kissing one of the senior all-star football players, Shawn Worthy, all sensually against the wall. I was fuming, so I confronted them. I remember asking Sheila—"

"Sheila?" Diana interjected.

"Yup, that's her name, Sheila. Why, do you know her?"

Diana chuckled. "Oh no, I never met anyone named Sheila before. I just can't picture you with a Sheila; that's all. All right, I'm done—go on!" she demanded.

Noah shook his head in confusion. "Okay, then I remember asking her what the hell was going on. She was drunk, and she told me she was done, that she'd found a real man who was going to be rich and successful and not some wannabe therapist. I was shocked—that was three years of a good relationship down the drain, just like that. Well, I *thought* it was a good relationship. I punched Shawn in the face and got escorted out of prom."

"You punched him!" Diana giggled. "Damn, well, look at you, macho man. That's okay though; he deserved it. I can tell that Shawn guy was probably a douchebag anyway, and Sheila is insane for letting you go. Some girls don't know when they have a good man right in front of their eyes, especially when they're young."

Diana displayed a look of total infatuation, but Noah didn't notice a thing.

He nodded in agreement. "True. That summer, Sheila got pregnant by Shawn and ended up dropping out of school. I also heard that Shawn left her a month before the baby was born, and he was also arrested for selling cocaine, which ended his upcoming college football career."

Diana shook her head. "Wow! It's true what they say—karma's a bitch; and surprisingly you and I have had very similar situations when it comes to our exes. Forget about them, though, what inspired you to become a therapist? I'm curious to know why you entered that profession."

"I just love helping people." Noah shrugged. "Maybe it's my calling. I believe it's a quality I get from my mother. Instead of physically saving people's lives, I do it on a mental and emotional level. That's why I enjoy volunteering at homeless shelters, providing gifts for the orphans during the holidays, and giving therapeutic advice to people who seek it."

Whoa! Who made this guy? Diana's mind was blown.

"You're amazing! I've never met anyone like you before." She expressed.

"Thank you but I'm nothing special, I'm just being myself."

"Well I love it! You put every guy I've met to shame, especially my ex."

Noah turned to Diana and squinted his eyes. "Oh really? So, what was your situation like?"

He just had to ask. Diana chuckled.

"Um . . . .What situation?" she asked sarcastically.

"I saw your picture with your ex on *Gossip Place*, Ms. Prom Queen!" Noah answered with a wide grin. "You looked happy with him."

Diana gasped, then laughed cheerily. "STALKER!" she shouted. "Okay, yes, the guy you saw in that picture with me was my ex, Tevin. We were together for four years. He cheated on me a lot, his basketball career never took off in college because he was never that good, he now has a child with someone too, as I mentioned before, and he's a deadbeat . . . there ya go!"

"Unbelievable! You and I did go through similar situations," Noah noted.

"Yup!" Diana laughed. "We sure did."

~~~

After a brief moment of silence, Noah started growing curious about what the second floor of the spirit dimension was like. "Hey, remember how last night you were going to tell me about what happened when you entered some realm after the light pulled you in during your funeral?"

Diana nodded. "Yeah I do, but there's so much to explain. You wouldn't understand a thing I was talking about unless I showed you."

An idea came to Noah's mind. "Do you think you would be able to show me this place?" he asked excitedly.

"Huh," Diana frowned. "Like right now?" she questioned.

"Yeah, I would love to see it now! This spirit dimension stuff sounds kind of cool," Noah insisted.

Diana sucked her teeth and stood up from Noah's bed. "Well, I would love to show you too, but ya see, there's a certain problem," she warned.

Noah just stared at Diana, clueless, expecting her to tell him what the problem was. "And what's that?" he finally asked.

"I'm stuck here! Remember what I told you last night? There's like some force field keeping me here. The last time I tried opening up portals to go through, it didn't work. Nothing worked until your dad woke you up. That's the only way I'm able to get out of here. It's when your soul gets sucked back into your body. It automatically launches me back to the second floor," she explained.

"So!" Noah shrugged his shoulders nonchalantly. "Try it again," he said.

He can't be serious.

Diana placed her hands on her hips, baffled by what Noah had said. "Did you comprehend anything I said a few seconds ago?"

"Yeah, but it might work this time. Ya never know . . . so you should try opening the portal thing again," he urged.

He's dead serious! Diana rolled her eyes.

"Oh my gosh, Noah, it's not going to work."

Noah stood up from his bed and put his hands in his pockets. "Wow, I didn't know you were the type of person to give up so easily. Oh well, I guess we are just stuck here for now," he said jokingly.

Diana bit her lip and squinted at him. "Shut up!" she said with a slight chuckle. "Okay then, I'll just prove it to you."

She went across Noah's room and placed her right hand on the wall. As she closed her eyes and concentrated on where she wanted to go, an oval-shaped portal opened up, displaying a view of a blue galaxy. Diana sighed in relief. "It worked," she whispered.

Noah was both astonished and frightened by what he was seeing. He couldn't believe it.

I didn't think it would actually work—I was just teasing her, he thought to himself.

"Wait!" Diana cried, backing away from the wall, which caused the portal to close.

"What's wrong?" Noah asked. "Oh wait, you know what, I'm probably thinking the same thing you're thinking. We don't have to go in there today. There's a lot going on right now, and I have things to take care of, so I'm changing my mind—we can worry about this spirit dimension stuff next time," he said, fearfully backing himself up into his dresser.

Diana began pacing back and forth in front of Noah, deep in thought. "If I can create portals here on the first floor to get to places on the second floor, then there could be a chance that I can get to places here on the first floor too."

Noah looked bewildered. "And what does that mean?" he asked.

"It means I can see my family again!"

"Cool, so I'm guessing there's a change of plans here?"

"Yes—I have to see them." She simpered. "I haven't felt them or seen them in forever, besides my Mom-Mom in her dreams . . . when it comes to the seeing part, that is. You already know that, though; I've told you about a million times already."

"Oh, okay, well I completely understand." Noah continued leaning back against the dresser as he stared at Diana. "Nothing means more than family, so you just go ahead and do you. I'll be right here in my room, and if you need me, you know where to find me."

"Wait, you aren't coming with me?" Diana despairingly asked, advancing toward him.

Noah struggled to come up with a direct reply.

"Are you afraid? Because if you are, there's nothing to worry about. You'll be with me the whole time," Diana assured him.

"What?" Noah waved her off, shaking his head. "No, I'm not afraid! I just didn't want to get too involved in your family matters, because that's private stuff," he explained, steadily backing away from Diana.

With every step Noah took back, Diana took another step forward. "Aw, that's sweet of you, but you pretty much know everything about us. You're my Mom-Mom's therapist, so you know more private things than I do," she declared.

By then, she'd walked Noah to the edge of his bed. He sat down as he continued pleading his case. "Diana, I don't think it's a good idea for me to go. That's all I'm trying to say."

In one swift motion, she grabbed him by his shirtsleeves and attempted to pull him off the bed. "I promise it won't be as bad as you think."

"Well, just let me think about it first!" Noah replied, throwing himself backward to halt their tug of war battle.

As Noah heaved himself all the way back onto his bed, Diana came falling right on top of him. When she lifted her head, she found herself staring right into Noah's mahogany eyes. During those few seconds they didn't say a word. They both wanted to kiss each other in that moment, but no one made a move.

"I could really use your help." Diana finally spoke.

Dammit, those hazel eyes got me again, Noah thought as he felt his mind changing while she laid directly on him.

I can't wait for him any longer. I have to see my family.

"You know what, I'm through with trying to convince you to come. I'm out of here!" she said as she pulled herself off of him and walked toward the wall.

Is he really going to let me walk away and go alone? Diana thought to herself.

Noah immediately stood up from his bed. "All right,

you win. I'll go with you."

Diana smiled like a child on Christmas Day. "Thank you so much!" she exclaimed. "Even though I would've gone without you anyway."

Yeah, right, Noah thought, following her to the wall.

Diana then placed her right hand back on the wall again, closed her eyes, and went into a deep concentration.

"Take me to Mom and Dad's place," she whispered.

Noah stood beside her, waiting for a portal to open. When Diana opened her eyes, though, she was astounded that nothing was there. "What the hell!" She tried again, quickly placing her hand on the wall in an attempt to open another portal.

Take me to Mom-Mom Joanna, her inner voice said. After about a minute, there was still just a solid wall. "I don't get it! So I can open up a portal to go anywhere I want on the second floor, but I don't have the power to go anywhere I want on the first floor. That means whenever I'm in this dimension, I'm just stuck in this stupid house. No offense, by the way—I didn't mean it like that," Diana said.

Noah smirked. "None taken."

Diana began pacing back and forth again as Noah continued looking clueless. Since he couldn't help her with her problem, he started to feel like a hopeless spectator.

"How can I see them again?" she asked herself, trying to come up with new ideas.

"Helping the dead is not an easy task," Noah muttered. "If I had the power to open portals, I would help you right away. It looks like a cool power to have, too."

Diana veered toward Noah, looking at him with a piercing gaze. *"You!"* she shouted, pointing at him.

Way to set yourself up, Noah, he thought. "What—what about me?"

Diana began tapping her foot against the carpet and biting her lip, thinking. "You probably have some type of power source or an energetic connection thingy that can open portals on the first floor, since you're still alive," she said, grabbing Noah's sleeve to pull him closer to her.

Noah laughed at this new idea of hers. "Diana, this probably won't work either," he said.

"You heard that—you said 'probably,' which means there might be a 50/50 chance that this *will* work. Besides, you already have the power to astral project, and the power to bring me down here into your room against my will. So come on, Noah, just give it a try—for me, *please*! It's the least you can do for me, since I didn't ask to be here," Diana begged.

Wow! She's really trying to guilt me into this mess. Noah sighed and gave in. "You know I'm not . . . like purposely forcing you into my room, and I'm not purposely thinking about you either. You're just, like, engrained in my mind at the moment, and that's something I have no control over. But okay, I'll try to help you out here. What do I need to do?"

Diana placed her fingers on her chin. "What time is it?" she asked.

"Hang on," Noah took a peek at his watch. "It's 3:27," he told her.

She nodded. "Okay, and it's Sunday, so that means Mom-Mom Joanna and my parents are together right now. Hopefully they're home or at the Care Center. All right, here's what you're going to do." She came around to his right side. "Do exactly what I'm about to tell you—okay?" she demanded, trying to make her voice sound soothing.

Fearful of what was to come, Noah nervously gulped and bobbed his head. "Okay," he agreed.

"Now place your right hand on the wall, close your

eyes, and take a deep breath. Think about my parents and my Mom-Mom, and imagine that you're about to go see them," she directed.

Noah followed her directives, and instantaneously a portal opened on his wall. "Whoa, it worked!" he blurted out.

This is a little petrifying, but don't panic! Especially not in front of Diana!

Diana joyfully clapped and jumped up and down. "You did it! See, I told you there was a chance this could work!" She wrapped him in a quick embrace. Surprised as he was by how he'd caused a portal to open, he was even more astonished by that hug.

Don't catch feelings, don't catch feelings, don't catch feelings . . . shit, it's too late; I caught them.

~~~

When Noah glanced through the portal, he could see Mrs. Divine along with Diana's father, Barry Jr., and her mother, Vivian, all sitting on a couch and talking with each other. As Diana laid eyes on them, she simpered and grew teary-eyed. "It looks like they're at the Care Center, in Mom-Mom Joanna's room. Come on, let's go!" she insisted, taking a step closer to the portal.

Noah was still kind of freaked out by the portal, since he was new to this whole spirit traveling thing. "Is it safe?" he asked with a brave face.

His mix of caution and curiosity made Diana smile. "Come here, silly, grab my hand," she said, holding out her left hand.

When their hands intertwined, a sudden warm and electrifying spark raced from their palms and began to surge all through their souls. Even though they both felt this magical connection, they didn't speak about it in that moment.

As Noah and Diana walked into the portal together, it felt like they were slowly walking into water without getting wet.

"That was amazing and weird at the same time," Noah said as he began warming up to this new experience.

Diana gleamed. "Yeah, eventually I got so used to doing it that I don't even feel it anymore."

After exiting the portal, they found themselves in Mrs. Divine's room. "Well, here we are," Noah said, gazing at Diana.

Distracted by the presence of her family, Diana unintentionally ignored Noah. She eyed their every move. Her mother and father were bringing in a box of pizza and a two-liter ginger ale. They placed it on Mrs. Divine's small dinner table. On the left-hand side of the room, Mrs. Divine was sitting at the end of her couch, writing in her journal. Diana was entirely overwhelmed with many emotions.

I can't believe they're right here in front of me. It's making me feel alive again!

"Mom, Dad!" Diana exclaimed, quickly moving toward her parents. "I miss you guys so much!" she said, trying to hug them.

But instead of hugging them, Diana went directly through her mom and dad. She was so upset that she was nearly about to cry once more.

I knew that wouldn't work, but I just had to try it, she thought.

"Why the hell did I have to die?" she shouted, stomping her foot on the ground.

Staring at the ginger ale and pizza on the table, she remembered that she had the power to grab objects. In an act of frustration, she attempted to smack the pizza box, hoping it would catch her family's attention. After watching her hand go straight through the box, and failing to even make it move, she lost all hope again.

"I can't even get their attention. Ugh, this sucks—I'm not getting this! I can grab objects when I want to in Noah's room. Why can't I do it here?" Diana said to herself.

"I have no clue," Noah replied, standing over Mrs. Divine's shoulder and watching what she was writing in her journal. "I can't seem to grab anything either, but it looks like your Mom-Mom is worried about where you are," he told her.

Diana squinted at Noah, then proceeded to walk over to where he was. "When did you wander over here? And what are you talking about?" she asked, before reading what Mrs. Divine was writing:

Joanna Divine's Journal

Last night I had the same dream I always have, but this time Diana wasn't there, and I was all alone sitting in my rocking chair. I wonder if she decided that it's time for her to enter the third floor, and finally go into Heaven for good. At the same time, I'm pretty sure Diana would've said goodbye first before doing that. There has to be a perfect explanation for whatever is going on.

Diana looked up at Noah when she finished reading what Mrs. Divine had written. "Oh my god, I missed my chat with Mom-Mom Joanna last night because of you."

"Oh yeah," Noah scratched his head, feeling sort of guilty. "This morning she called and told me that she didn't see you in her dream last night. She explained to me that this was the first time that this had ever happened since the day after your funeral."

"This is all *your* fault!" Diana snapped, pointing her finger at Noah. "Thank you for forgetting to tell me about my Mom-Mom calling you this morning too."

Noah blew out his cheeks. "You're welcome, smartass."

WHAT! Diana gasped in shock at his retort.

Noah then smiled at her, showing his perfect white teeth. "Just kidding . . . I'm sorry. I was trying to be sarcastic and brighten the mood around here. Everything seems so gloomy."

Diana turned her face away, but she couldn't help but grin from ear to ear. "You know what, you're lucky you're cute."

Noah chuckled, facing her. "Look, I'm just as lost as you are. I don't know why you can only touch things in my room, and I don't know why I'm the only living person that has the power to bring you here. I guess we both need answers, but I honestly don't know where to start looking for them. This shit is a puzzle."

After Noah finished, Diana remembered that there *was* someone they could talk to who could help them figure out whatever was going on. She walked up to the wall and placed her hand on it.

"Where are we going?" Noah asked as he watched the wall immediately turn into a portal displaying a view of a blue galaxy like before.

"The second floor—I think I know someone who can answer our questions."

Diana then turned around to look at her family one last time before entering the portal. "I miss you guys so much and love you all. I'll be back," she said. She then grabbed Noah's hand, causing that same warm and electrifying spark to come back again. "Come with me, silly!" she said as they stepped inside.

9

THE SECOND FLOOR

They were now surrounded by the galaxy. It was remarkably quiet and peaceful as they flew in the air.

Noah was speechless. He looked below him and saw nothing but stars and deep space.

Whoa, whoa, are we really flying right now? This stuff is crazy, man! I gotta be brave for her, though. Come on, Noah, get yourself together.

He looked back up, and regained his focus.

About a mile away, they could see a long narrow silver stairway floating in the middle of space. This stairway was much taller and longer than any skyscraper that human eyes have ever seen. It had sparkling silver steps, and it led all the way up to a golden circular portal.

When they were a few hundred feet away, Diana abruptly stopped in mid-flight. She and Noah hovered in space, staring directly at the stairway.

"This is where the light took me to," she said to him. "There were other spirits with me, too—hundreds of them." She pointed to the top of the stairway. "You see that really tall, bald-headed, pitch-black guy right there wearing all white?" she asked.

Noah looked in the direction Diana pointed in, and saw an extremely tall, bald-headed muscular man with jet-black skin. He was wearing a fitted white T-shirt, white slacks, and white dress shoes. His eyes were as white as snow, and he looked like an ageing adult due to the grey and white strands of hair in his mustache and beard. Noah noticed that the man had a very serious and stern demeanor about him as well.

"Yeah, that dude has to be about ten feet tall. JESUS CHRIST! I'm surprised he isn't wearing an ancient cloak." He teased.

"Maybe he likes to keep up with modern times." Diana put in.

"Who is he . . . God?" Noah wondered.

"No, not at all—this guy has a lower ranking position. I personally think God's a woman anyway, but um . . . yeah this guy said he's known as Father Time," Diana revealed.

"Oh, okay, good, so you've had conversations with him before?"

Diana swiftly shook her head, her eyes growing fearful as she squeezed Noah's hand a bit tighter. "Oh no! I've never spoken with the man directly. When I was brought from the light, he congratulated all of the spirits and said that we earned the right to enter the third floor. He explained that there are three floors in the spirit dimension.

"The third floor is commonly known as Heaven. The second floor contains stars, suns, moons, planets, and other galaxies. And you already know what the first floor is like.

"Now, the second and third floors are for spirits like me, but it's impossible for us to enter the first floor once the light decides to bring us up here," Diana explained.

"Oh okay." Noah bobbed his head. "Unless someone is powerful enough to summon the spirits back to the first floor."

Diana concurred. "Yeah, I was actually just about to say that."

Noah looked from side to side, curious about this whole spirit dimension thing. "Are there any evil spirits around here too?" He tugged Diana's arm, bringing her close to him. "I need a heads up, just in case I have to protect myself . . . or protect us, because I'll fight those bastards if they approach me."

"Boy, you're so crazy!" Diana nearly died laughing. "I haven't seen any dead evil people flying around here, like Hitler or Ted Bundy. I guess they have their own special place they go to that Father Time decided not to mention," she told him.

"Cool," Noah exhaled in relief. "All right—so, what else did Father Time say?"

"Well, he also explained to us that we always have the option to enter the third floor, a.k.a. Heaven, whenever we please. Other than that, we have the ability to explore this floor as long as we want," Diana said.

"It seems so lonely and empty here on the second floor," Noah remarked, observing nothing but deep space and the silver stairway.

"There *are* some cool places—well, one in particular. But other than that, you're right. The second floor is a lonely place. I'm assuming that's because everyone just walks into the third floor. Father Time said he's never seen anyone walk into the third floor and then walk right out. I've heard that once you walk into it, you won't want to leave because of how unbelievably beautiful it is. And apparently, you're greeted by many of your ancestors, relatives, and loved ones who passed away before you. Believe it or not, you even get the chance to meet people from different planets who've passed away. According to Father Time, there is nothing you can't love about that place."

"There are actual people living and dying on different planets? And we have the chance to talk to them about it when they get into Heaven?" Noah was amazed. "That sounds incredible—why didn't you go?" he asked.

"Trust me, I was sold on it, but once he told us that here on the second floor we could talk to our loved ones in their dreams and send down vivid memories to them, I knew I would rather do that than get distracted by the beauty of Heaven. At that moment, I decided I didn't want to leave my Mom-Mom behind because part of me still felt guilty about dying, and she had already lost my Pop-Pop a few years before. Me being permanently gone would've probably done much more damage. I knew that if I could somehow communicate with her, then she would be fine until we met again in this world. When you enter the third floor, you don't have that same power to communicate with your living loved ones, and I couldn't stand the thought of that," Diana elaborated.

After everything Diana had said, Noah understood why this ill-fated woman had made the decisions she'd made. "When Father Time finished explaining this to all of you, where did you go?"

"After he finished explaining everything to us, he said

we were free to ask him questions, enter Heaven, or go explore.

"And right then and there, I decided to go explore. During my expedition, I found this beautiful spirit world to settle in. I have to show you that place too; you'll love it. Other than that, I visited Mom-Mom Joanna every night in her dreams. Until last night, that is," Diana said, playfully rolling her eyes.

Noah caught on to what she was implying. "Again— sorry about that!" he said with a smile.

"It's all good; anyways, you're going to do me a huge favor and ask Father Time some questions for me before the next group of spirits arrives," she informed him as they softly landed in the middle of the silver stairway.

"Me?" Noah questioned, pointing to his chest.

"Yes, you!" Diana ordered, pulling Noah closer to her. "I'm scared of him! He has a scary voice, and on top of that his eyes are all white, even his pupils," she said.

"What happened to me not having to be afraid because I'm with you?" Noah joked.

"Unfortunately, he's the only thing in the spirit dimension I'm afraid of, and I'm still kind of new to this stuff anyway, so give me a break."

Noah sighed and looked at his watch.

Great! Now my watch doesn't work.

"Okay, okay. Well, luckily, to me he just looks like a retired NBA player who needs to wear sunglasses. How much time do we have left before the next group of dead people come?" he asked.

"I don't know," Diana shrugged her shoulders. "We don't have clocks or timers up here in the spirit dimension. There's probably a clock in Father Time's mind, but as you can see, he's free now, so let's take advantage of this opportunity while we can." She slightly shoved Noah to get him to start moving.

As they slowly walked up the stairway, Diana kept Noah's hand tightly clasped in hers. "All right, so what do you want me to ask him?"

"Ask him if there's any way you can contact your family while you're on the first floor," Diana whispered in his ear.

"Is that it?"

"Yeah, for now."

When they finally made it to the top floor, Noah gradually looked up at the ten-foot-tall man and took a deep breath.

"Um . . . hello, sir."

The man known as Father Time lowered his head, and detected Noah with his eerie white eyes. "What is it that you'd like to know?" he asked. His guttural voice made Noah and Diana's ears tremble.

Filled with absolute fear, Diana took a step behind Noah, pressing most of her weight against his back. With their hands still intertwined, Noah gently stroked his thumb over her hand to assure her that she was safe with him.

"I would like to know why I'm not able to contact my family while I'm on the first floor," Noah told him.

The bald-headed man smirked. "Who do you think you're fooling? I am Father Time! The Master of Information. I know that you, young man, are not dead. You're just magically astral projecting—and congrats, by the way; it looks like you've mastered it—though the girl behind you . . . oh, she's dead all right."

Diana remained behind Noah even though Father Time already had them figured out. He stared directly at Noah as if he could see the inside of his soul.

"Now, about your friend—even though she manages

to get back to the first floor from time to time because of you, she won't be able to somehow physically contact anyone, including her relatives."

"Ask him why not," Diana whispered in Noah's ear.

"Why not?" Noah relayed the message.

"Because, young ones, that is the way the universe intended it to be," Father Time answered.

Diana let out a harsh breath in frustration, then placed her hand around Noah's ear again and whispered, "Ask him how come I can physically touch and move things around in your room."

"Good question," Noah whispered back. "Well, how come she's able to physically touch and move things in my room?"

Father Time displayed his mugged grin. "You two first encountered each other in your room, right?"

"Yeah," Noah replied.

"Well then, there's your answer. Anytime the living and dead first encounter each other, like the way you two have, it causes high frequencies and vibrations to manifest in the spot or area where the encounter took place. This manifestation doesn't last long though; and one last thing: Tell your friend that her missing piece is finally with her. *Her missing piece is no longer missing.*"

Missing piece. Noah looked confused.

"What is that supposed to mean?" he asked Diana.

"I don't know. I'm just as clueless as you are," she whispered.

"If you two don't mind, I have new spirits that will be here any second now, so move along please," Father Time politely ordered.

After turning around to see the miserable look on Diana's face, Noah began to feel bad for her. "Is everything okay? I know you didn't receive the exact answers you wanted to hear," he said as he and Diana strolled down the stairs, still clasping each other's hands.

"No, but thank you for being here with me. I just don't know what to do now." Diana's frustration was potent. "This is so confusing for me. It's truly like a giant puzzle that I can't solve. Are you ready to—"

Noah had slipped out of her hand and been instantly yanked into a portal.

"Great, here we go again," Diana said sorrowfully as she watched Noah disappear.

The speed and pressure of Noah's soul getting sucked back into his body made him immediately sit up, exactly like the last time.

"Whoa, here we go again! Did you have another bad dream?" Mr. King asked, chuckling.

Noah gingerly stretched his neck until he was fully aware of where he was.

"You slept all through the afternoon and evening. It's eight p.m. now, and I just wanted to make sure you weren't in a coma."

Noah scrubbed the sleep out of the corners of his eyes. "Oh no, I'm fine, Dad. It was just a crazy dream, that's all."

Mr. King nodded and slowly backed into the hallway. "That must've been one hell of a dream," he remarked.

"It sure was!" Noah said, falling back onto his bed and drawing in a long breath.

Eight p.m.? Damn, I was gone for a while. Diana and I still don't have the answers we need either.

"Great, now I'm going to be up for a long time. I might as well get this freaking psychology project done and over with to kill time."

10

A CHAT WITH MOM-MOM

Back at the Paradise Home Care Center, Mrs. Divine was preparing to lie down in bed, hoping she would see Diana in her dream this time. "Come on, baby girl, I know you're still around," she mumbled as she dozed off to sleep.

Meanwhile, on the second floor of the spirit dimension, Diana was waiting patiently in the spirit world to be sent back to Noah again. Suddenly she saw a familiar yellow portal that revealed her Mom-Mom on the other side, sitting on a rocking chair.

Diana immediately entered the portal. *"Mom-Mom!"* she cried, racing to sit in the chair next to her.

"Hey, baby, where have you been?" Mrs. Divine asked.

"Uh, it's a long story," Diana responded, rocking back and forth in her chair.

"Well, you know I'm all ears."

"Okay! So I met your therapist—Noah."

Mrs. Divine was stunned. "Noah . . . you met him? How in the world did you do that?" she asked. "You entered his dream didn't you?"

Diana didn't answer that specific question right away, because there were other things on her mind. "Mom-Mom, why didn't you tell me you had a therapist or needed therapy?" she asked, holding back tears.

Mrs. Divine sighed. "Because I've been depressed lately, and I didn't want that to be a burden on you or your mom and dad."

"Aw." Diana's face was filled with gloom. "You'll never be a burden to us," she said, scooting her chair closer to her grandmother. "I love you, Mom-Mom, and I want you to know that everything is going to be fine, okay? I know it's been hard without me or Pop-Pop around, but we're all going to end up together again before we know it."

"Okay, yeah, I guess you're right, and I love you too, baby girl." Mrs. Divine smiled and wiped a tear from her face. "Now let's cut to the chase. Tell me about what's been going on between you and Noah."

Diana sat all the way back in her chair and began rocking steadily. "Noah's incredible! He is capable of having out-of-body experiences. Because of this special ability he has, he's able to communicate with me and travel to other dimensions with me. I've really gotten to know him over the past two days. I honestly don't know why this is all happening to us, but so far he's been helpful when it comes to figuring it all out," she explained, trying to hold back her grin while thinking about Noah.

Mrs. Divine noticed something different about her granddaughter. "Girl, you are glowing," she said.

Darn it! This woman doesn't miss a beat.

Diana shook her head and smiled. "I'm glowing because I'm a spirit, Mom-Mom," she countered.

"No, this is different. As soon as I mentioned that boy's name, you started smiling and glowing like there's no tomorrow! That's the look I give when we talk about your Pop-Pop."

"Oh no, see, you have it all wrong." Diana started laughing uncontrollably. "I'm just really happy to see you again; that's why I'm smiling. Besides, I'm dead and Noah's alive, so that would never work out."

"Okay, whatever you say, sweetheart." Mrs. Divine tittered and crossed her legs. "He definitely would've been perfect for you when you were alive, though."

Diana tilted her head and began to wonder. "You think so?"

"I know so!" Her Mom-Mom confirmed. "In fact, when I met him, a little part of me wanted you two to somehow end up together. And you might find this surprising, but your mother and father even like him."

"Wow!" Diana was blown away. "Well, if Mom and Dad like him, then I guess you're right. He's pretty remarkable, I guess."

"He sure is," Mrs. Divine agreed. "I think he's way better than that last guy you dated in high school. What was his name again?"

"Ew," Diana tossed her hair with a look of disgust on her face. "*Tevin*—anybody is better than that jerkoff," she spewed.

"You got that right, girl! I don't know what you saw in him."

While steadily rocking back and forth, Mrs. Divine caught a glimpse of Diana daydreaming. After a minute of silence, she called out to her granddaughter. "Diana!"

Snapping out of her daze, Diana instantly broke her focus from the lake and turned her attention to her grandmother. "Oh, uh, sorry, Mom-Mom; I was just uh—"

"Thinking about Noah," Mrs. Divine inserted.

"Um . . . no." Diana lied.

"Diana, trust me when I say this—I think you finally found your Prince Charming," Mrs. Divine stated.

Diana didn't really know what to think, but she thought it was too soon to jump to conclusions. "Aw, Mom-Mom, I know you're trying to make me feel better, but this thing you think Noah and I have doesn't exist and it never will. Shoot, even if that were the case it would literally be impossible for that to even work."

Mrs. Divine begged to differ. "Well, there has to be a reason why you two met up like this. I know you're dead and he's alive, but God never makes mistakes, honey. Everyone has a soulmate. *Shoot*, if you ask me, I think Noah just might be . . . your missing piece."

Diana's eyes broadened when she heard her Mom-Mom utter the words "missing piece."

Is that what Father Time meant? Was he talking about Noah? Is Noah really my missing piece? Diana thought to herself.

Mrs. Divine persevered as Diana sat there in deep thought. "Whatever is going on with you two, I'm pretty sure the both of you will figure it out. It's your destiny!"

11

JUST LIKE HEAVEN

By 6:00 a.m. on Wednesday morning, two days had passed since Noah last fell asleep. Throughout those days he did nothing but school work and stay home. Noah didn't tell anyone about Diana or his astral projection experiences. He reckoned no one would believe him. In the midst of his energy wearing down, Noah waddled upstairs into his room. He then staggered to his bed, collapsed onto his pillow, and—while thinking about Diana—fell into a deep sleep.

"NOAH KING!" a sudden familiar voice yelled.

Noah sluggishly sat up and saw that his body was in its

astral projection phase. Next, he noticed that Diana was standing right in front of his bed.

"Noah," she began worriedly, "I haven't seen or heard from you in two days. What happened?"

"Sorry. For some odd reason, I couldn't sleep. I've been up for two days straight, so I just put all of my focus into working on a school project until I fell asleep again," Noah told her.

After hearing that, Diana looked relieved and folded her arms. "Oh," she said. "Okay, just checking."

"Why? Did you miss me or something?" Noah asked with a flirtatious smile.

Diana waved him off and smirked, replying, "Oh, gosh no! For your information, Mom-Mom Joanna kept me company while you were gone doing your little nerdy assignment."

Noah swiftly approached Diana and bear-hugged her. This unforeseen gesture left her astounded.

Oh my gosh! Why do I feel like I'm actually starting to catch feelings for you?

The familiar warm and electrifying spark shot through their souls as they embraced. They both felt their connection growing stronger. "Well, it's great to see you again," Noah said, not bothering to let her go.

"You, too," Diana soothingly replied.

Aw, man, Noah thought, *Am I doing too much? I hope she isn't creeped out. Maybe I should let her go now.*

He smells so good, Diana mused, *And he's so sweet. He's just perfect! Please don't let go of me . . .*

As Noah slowly began to release her, Diana quickly grabbed his hand and walked toward the wall. "Come with me. I want to show you something," she said, opening up a portal.

I wonder what it is?

Immediately after entering the portal, Noah noticed that they were inside a different world. He looked up and spotted seven moons perfectly aligned on the eastern part of the sky; the western part displayed a large golden sun.

"Is this the spirit world you were talking about before?" Noah asked as he glanced at Diana.

"Yeah, this is it," she replied with a grin.

As they stood on a tall gleaming grassy hill, Noah observed his surroundings and paid close attention to every detail in plain sight. The view was magical. The green leaves on the trees were outlined in shiny gold. He even spotted the same shiny gold clinging to the edges of each blade of grass. As the warm spring breeze blew by and caused golden flurries to fly off the grass and trees, the leaves swirled into the air like snow before magically drifting away.

Out of nowhere, children of all ethnicities came running across the golden grassy fields and interrupted Noah's daze. They joyfully ran and played with lions, tigers, wolves, and all types of four-legged creatures.

No way! What am I seeing?

In the distance, a flock of winged people wearing casual outfits came flying behind the children and the animals. Noah was astonished. "Oh shit, are those—"

"Yup, they're angels," Diana interjected. "Before I ended up here, I didn't even think they were real."

What the hell! None of this feels real.

"What is this place?" Noah wondered.

Diana gradually swayed their intertwined hands back and forth. "When children pass away on Earth, this is the first place they go. The angels help them get adjusted to what Heaven is like. That way, the kids won't have to experience this brand-new journey lost and on their own like adults do. The angels end up taking the children to Heaven once they're ready. From what I can tell, I think I've only seen kids from the newborn age all the way up to the preteen age here."

Noah was still completely stunned. "Wow. Then how are we allowed to be here?" he wondered.

"Anyone on the second floor is welcome to stay as long as they don't try to take the children away or interfere with the natural order of things when it comes to the angels raising them. They really have an important job to do. Besides, the children won't really pay us any mind. They're absolutely obsessed with the animals and angels." Diana ended her response with a snicker.

"This is fascinating! How do you know so much?" Noah stupidly questioned.

"Well, for one, I witness these things take place every day here, and I forgot to mention that Father Time elaborated about certain spirit worlds. This was one of them," Diana answered.

Noah shook his head. "I know by now I shouldn't be mind-blown by this stuff, but I have so many questions."

Diana smiled and looked Noah in the eye. "It's okay. I have time to tell you whatever you want to hear. I just hope you won't disappear on me anytime soon."

"I'll try not to." Noah gripped Diana's hand a little tighter. "So, do you want to walk around and talk? I'd love to see more of this spirit world."

"Yeah," Diana grinned and began blushing. "I would love that."

Noah looked down at their intertwined hands and gave Diana a slight pull, gesturing for her to walk with him. "Well," he said, "I'm ready when you are."

While he and Diana wandered on the sacred land, Noah saw two people wearing hiking gear in the distance.

They were holding hands and walking aimlessly toward Noah and Diana. He could tell that the hikers were a couple from the way they were walking and talking with each other. "Do you know them?" Noah wondered.

"Who?" Diana replied.

"The two Asian people who are walking toward us right now." Noah then pointed at the couple. "They look like they're around our age."

Diana didn't recognize the couple. "No, I see random spirits wandering around here all the time. They're probably just exploring different spirit worlds for fun."

As the couple stepped closer and closer, Noah could tell that they were about to say something. "You're so lucky dude!" the man finally exclaimed.

"Extremely lucky! Enjoy it while you can!" the woman next to him added as they continued to walk past Noah and Diana.

Noah looked perplexed. "What are they talking about?" he questioned as he and Diana smiled at the couple.

"Oh, they just know that you're alive, that's all," Diana answered, nonchalant.

"How can you all tell that I'm alive? What's the difference between my spirit and yours?"

Diana scanned Noah's body up and down. "Your aura vibrates with the rhythm of your heartbeat and pulse, and we can all slightly sense the sound of your heartbeat, too. The aura around my spirit doesn't vibrate at all. It just stays still. Now that I think about it, you're actually the first astral projector who I've seen travel here."

"Wow. It seems like I'm making history every day!" He jested. "Hold on. I have to ask them something." Noah suddenly turned around and called out to the couple. "Hey!"

After the call, the couple instantaneously returned. "What's up?" the man inquired.

"I have a random question to ask you two," Noah declared. "I don't mean to offend you or anything, but what happened to you guys?"

The woman laughed, "Oh, it's okay! We died in a rock climbing accident."

The man nodded and snickered, "Yeah, dude. We forgot to tightly anchor our climbing ropes before going down the cliff. And I guess you can picture what happened after."

"Aw, sorry to hear about that," Diana said.

"It's all good. At least we can hike forever now. So what happened to you?" the woman asked Diana.

She huffed. "Hit by a drunk driver."

"Wow. Sorry to hear that. . . . We're about to check out a new spirit world soon. Do you guys want to come?" the woman offered.

"No, thanks." Diana declined. "I'm actually showing him around. It's his first time experiencing a place like this."

"Alrighty. Well. You're going to really like it here. Later, guys!" the woman replied as she and her boyfriend waved and walked away.

"See ya!" Diana waved back. "Why did you ask them that?" she whispered.

"I don't know. I guess I just had to know. Maybe it's the therapist in me."

While continuing to walk and make small talk, Diana and Noah suddenly found themselves in the center of a redwood forest. They decided to stop by a small creek.

"Let's sit here," Diana insisted as she let go of Noah's hand and plopped down onto the shimmering grass. She observed him while he looked up at the trees, and she could tell that he was still deep in thought. "What else is on your mind, silly?"

Noah took his concentration off the trees and began to focus on Diana.

"I remember you told me that you found this world during your expedition, after Father Time talked with you and the rest of the spirits, but how did you manage to get here exactly?" he wondered.

"Well, honestly, after he spoke with us, I was determined to get back to Earth," Diana explained, "So, when I saw some spirits entering the third floor, I decided to walk back down the stairway until I reached Earth again. Unfortunately, after walking for like twenty hours . . . well, it felt like twenty hours, anyway. There weren't any more stairs left, and I ended up at a dead end of nothing but deep space and stars. I just went ahead and flew downward into space, even though I was scared to death of where I was headed. At first, there was still nothing but dark-blue space and stars, and then I suddenly saw this planet appear that was surrounded by a bunch of moons. I could tell that it was the world Father Time had been talking about. At that point, I knew that trying to get back to Earth would be like beating a dead horse, so I decided to enter the planet and give it a look. Now this place is like a second home to me."

Seconds after Diana finished speaking, a small white portal appeared floating by her side. "Check this out! It's my Dad . . . . He's thinking about me. He looks really sad, too," Diana said as she gazed into the portal. She could see her father staring at a picture of them hugging each other at her college graduation. He was completely teary-eyed, and his heart was filled with devastation.

It's okay Dad, I'm about to take some of that pain away.

Diana placed her hands together with her palms facing

up. Instantly, a white ball of energy formed hovering above her hands. She then blew the white ball of energy into the small portal, causing it to close. "For some odd reason, my mom and dad never have lucid dreams. I can never find their dream portals."

"I think that's normal. Not that many people have lucid dreams. I know I don't. To be honest with you, I don't think I've ever had one . . . and what just happened?" Noah wondered. "I can't sit here and pretend that I didn't just see white powers forming from your hands like some kind of telekinesis. That was crazy!"

Diana found Noah to be remarkably humorous at times. He could cheer her up at any given moment. "You're hilarious," she insisted. "But, yeah, that was a memory you saw coming from my hands. I sent my father a vivid memory of the moment after my graduation ceremony when he hugged me and said that he loved me." She raised her chin, and stared into the golden sun. "It will only soothe his pain temporarily, though."

"At least your able to help out in some way." Noah thought that a life in this particular spirit world wasn't so bad after all. "Well, I guess ten months of this and talking to your Mom-Mom in her dreams isn't so bad," Noah mentioned while nudging Diana.

Man, I really should just keep my mouth closed sometimes, he thought, realizing that being dead and not seeing her parents was already hard enough for her.

"Damn, I'm sorry. I know that didn't come out right."

Diana gave a mirthless laugh and stared at Noah. "It's okay, silly. I know you didn't mean any harm by it. Even though I sure would give anything to be alive right now. I just miss everything about life in general, like waking up in my own bed, going to sleep in my own bed, hugging my parents, burping—"

"Burping?" Noah interjected.

"Yes, burping!" She guffawed. "You end up missing weird random things like that when you're dead."

"My, oh, my, that's kind of funny," Noah remarked.

"You know what's funny?" Diana asked as she raked her hands through her hair and showed her lovely smile.

"What?"

"I was in this same exact spot the day I evaporated from here and got pulled into your room."

Noah placed his head down and began laughing. "Well, as I mentioned before, I'm truly sorry about that," he said.

"Don't be." Diana clutched his shoulder and laughed. "I'm glad it happened."

~ ~ ~

Suddenly, Diana saw an outline of a body appearing across the creek. At that moment, a male angel with tan skin and black hair flew down and landed near the outline. Both Diana and Noah noticed that the angel was wearing a brown leather jacket with black jeans and black boots.

"Aw, Noah, watch this. I love when this happens," Diana spoke softly as she leaned her head onto Noah's shoulder and pointed across the creek.

The outline of the body formed into a redheaded little girl wearing a hospital gown. She looked all around her and seemed entirely dumbfounded. "Daddy? Daddy, where are you?" the girl shouted frantically. She was on the verge of balling her eyes out.

Poor girl. She has to be about eight years old.

"Should we do something?" Noah questioned. "I think we should go over there and help."

"No, we can't interfere, remember? Don't worry. The

angel guy has this under control," Diana clarified, immediately clutching onto Noah's arm. "Just slow your roll Superman."

"Hello, little one. Don't be frightened," the angel said as he knelt down in front of the redhead.

The sound of the angel's voice instantly calmed the little girl. She then wiped away her tears.

"Hi, mister. I don't know where I am. Earlier, I was lying on my bed in the hospital, and my dad was crying and sitting next to me holding my hand. Then, I heard a loud beep, and my eyes shut. . . . Now I'm here," she explained, starting to wail again.

"It's okay, it's okay," the angel soothed, trying to calm the little girl down once more. "Do you want to see your mommy?" he asked.

The little girl was startled by his question.

"Mommy? But my Daddy said she died at the hospital when I was born. That was a long time ago. I never met her before. I've only seen pictures of her," she explained.

The angel smiled. "Your name is Lindsay, right?"

"Yes," the girl answered.

"Well, Lindsay, you will see your Dad again. Trust me. But in the meantime, I'm going to prepare you to see your Mom. I know she's waiting for you. And don't worry. I'll be with you every step of the way. My name is Miguel," he explained, holding his hand out and gesturing for her to give him a high-five.

Lindsay automatically smiled and high-fived Miguel. "Hi. It's nice to meet you, Miguel."

"It's nice to meet you, too. Do me a favor, Lindsay. Feel the top of your head," Miguel insisted.

Lindsay listened and touched the top of her head. She felt her full thick red hair and was amazed. A huge grin grew upon her face. "My hair! It's back! I don't have a bald head anymore!" she rejoiced.

Lindsay noticed that Miguel had wings sticking out of the back of his brown leather jacket. "Miguel, are you an angel or something?" she wondered.

"Yes, I am, and so is my friend Sarah. You'll meet her really soon. She's going to get you into some new clothes," Miguel said as he held Lindsay's hand and magically flew them away.

"Did you see that? Oh my god, when the kids meet the angels for the first time, I always end up crying," Diana said as a few happy tears rolled down her face.

"A few weeks ago, if someone told me that I would be in some spirit world with a spirit girl watching magical moments like that take place, I would have said they were crazy as hell," Noah declared, gently wiping a tear from Diana's face.

My heart melts when he does that. Well, if I still had a heart, it would melt, Diana thought as she grinned at Noah.

Man, I've done this twice to her already. I hope it isn't too much. I can't help it. She's just too alluring. Besides, as a kid I would see my Dad do the same thing to my Mom all the time whenever they would watch sad movies.

In that moment, Noah and Diana heard two voices laughing across the creek. When Noah turned his attention to the voices, he saw a little cocoa-skinned boy holding hands with a mahogany-skinned female angel who had a perfect jet-black afro.

"That's Hakeem with his guardian angel, Tiffany," Diana announced.

"Oh, okay. So, what's Hakeem's situation? Did he pass away from cancer like Lindsay did?" Noah wondered.

"We don't know for sure if that little girl had cancer,"

Diana replied while glaring at Noah.

"She told the angel she used to have a bald head, and she was wearing a hospital gown. I'm 100% sure it was cancer. Which sucks because I know that the drug companies have found a cure by now. They're just using temporary treatments to milk money out of people," Noah expounded.

"Okay, silly nerd. I'll agree with you on that." Diana then sighed, "But, no. Hakeem didn't die from cancer. Sadly, he was beaten to death by his horrible stepfather. Hakeem tried to protect his little sister from being abused by that evil bastard."

"Oh. Damn. I think I actually heard about that story on the news last summer. They said his sister is okay now, and his stepfather was charged with the death penalty, too," Noah elaborated.

"Good. He deserves it," Diana responded as she watched Tiffany speak with Hakeem across the creek. "This might be Hakeem's last day here," she revealed.

Noah was curious. "Really? . . . Where is he going?"

"Oh my goodness! Noah, do you listen to anything I say? He's going to the third floor! You'll see," Diana answered as she focused on Hakeem's and Tiffany's every move.

"Alright, Hakeem. Are you ready to see your big brother Darnell and your grandmother Pam?" Tiffany asked.

Hakeem grinned from ear to ear. "I sure am!" he replied while hugging his guardian angel. "Are you going to stay with me?"

"Of course, I'll be there by your side for as long as you need me."

"Awesome! Okay, now I'm ready!"

"Okay, hon. Then away we go!" Tiffany said merrily as

they shot up into the sky faster than a bullet.

"Whoa!" Noah exclaimed as he watched them take off.

"Pretty cool, right?" Diana loved the expressions on Noah's face.

"Yeah. It feels like I'm in some type of fantasy world," Noah told her. 'I can feel, hear, see, and smell this place; but I'm having a hard time taking this in as reality."

"That's because you're new to all this, and I understand where you're coming from." Diana briefly admired the sparkling creek. "You're expecting to wake up from this dream that's too good to be true at any moment. At the same time you're thinking, how can a place like this be filled with so much peace and love, while the Earth is filled with so much evil and hate."

"Exactly! You took the words right out of my mouth." Noah gazed deeply into Diana's hazel eyes. "I'm just glad I'm able to lay my eyes on the most beautiful thing this universe has ever created."

Diana blushed and directed her attention elsewhere. "You haven't seen anything yet. Just look at that!" Diana declared as she pointed to a random child riding quickly past them on a tiger.

"Now that's really out of this world. There are a bunch of wild animals freely roaming around here, but they're all harmless and kind as ever. All of this stuff is freaking mind-blowing!" Noah continued.

Diana pleasantly watched Noah as he talked.

Why couldn't I have met you in high school? she wondered. *My life would've definitely been way better with you around.*

Noah looked up into the sky. "And this view here is just breathtaking. I can't believe I'm seeing seven moons all at once, and right across from them is a massive golden sun hovering in a sky filled with different shades of blue and gold. It really is like a dream I wouldn't mind having over and over again," Noah mused.

Diana stood up and brushed the golden flurries from the grass off her pants. "Oh, you think this view is great? Wait 'til you see what I'm going to show you next," she said as she walked toward a redwood tree and placed her hand on the trunk. "It's remarkable!"

Noah got up and followed, wondering, "Okay, so where are we going now?"

"You'll see," she said as a wide portal opened up toward the base of the large tree. Diana looked back at Noah and winked. "Just follow me," she ordered, walking with him into the portal.

12

IN THE STILL
OF THE NIGHT

As they exited the portal, Noah noticed that they emerged out of a thick palm tree.

"Do you like the beach?" Diana asked, stepping suddenly onto the sand and staring out into a calm dark-blue ocean.

Noah raised his head and noticed that it was nighttime in this particular world. While continuing to scan the sky, he saw millions of white stars and nothing else but a massive blue, ringed planet in the center of the black expanse. As he gradually returned his gaze to the surface of the ocean, he realized that only water, sand, and palm trees surrounded them.

Diana was right, this place is remarkable! I don't even know what to say right now.

"Take off your shoes and socks! The sand feels great!" Diana insisted as she threw off her black kitten heels.

"Okay!"

After removing his own footwear, Noah gently held Diana's right hand. As they touched, their chemistry grew stronger than ever before. They began to steadily walk toward the ocean. With each step, the soft golden sand hugged their feet, gradually releasing with each step and not leaving a single particle clinging to their skin. The smooth grains beneath their soles felt cool until they waded into the warm still ocean.

They came to a brief standstill. The glistening stars and the light from the blue, ringed planet reflected onto Diana's captivating eyes. Noah couldn't stop staring at her angelic essence. When Diana caught Noah staring, she displayed a radiant smile that instantly gave him butterflies.

"What?" she asked innocently.

Noah awoke from his daze. "Oh . . . nothing . . . I just noticed that the sand didn't stick to my feet as we walked in here."

Diana held back her laugh and uttered a titter instead, "Yeah. Well, that's only one of the magical elements about this world. The water won't stick to us either. If you take your foot out right now, you'll see it dry up in a millisecond."

As they stood in the very shallow part of the ocean, Noah lifted his right foot and saw that it immediately dried, like it hadn't been in the water at all. "Jesus! I can't even say I'm surprised by this stuff anymo—"

Diana cut him off by throwing a handful of water into

his face, preventing him from finishing his sentence. Although his face instantly dried, he was still startled by what she'd just done. While Noah stood there with a baffled look on his face, Diana was hysterically cracking up.

"Oh, okay. I see how it is. Two can play that game!" Noah said, quickly chasing her away from the shallow water.

Diana screamed joyfully as he grabbed her by the waist and lifted her onto his shoulder. He walked deeper into the ocean.

Oh, my goodness. And he's strong, too, Diana mused.

"Put me down, Noah," she demanded playfully as he came to a sudden stop.

Don't put me down! You can hold me forever, her thoughts continued.

Unexpectedly, Noah tossed her into the water, creating the only splash and waves that the still ocean had probably ever experienced.

"Noah!" Diana gasped, quickly popping up for air.

"Why are you gasping for air if you're dead already?" Noah questioned while steadily approaching her.

"HA-HA, I don't know," she responded. "Maybe it's just a natural instinct."

Noah continued to inch toward her. He lightly treaded his hands through the water, causing tiny waves to brush against his fingertips. "So, you never tried breathing in this water before?"

"Nope, I usually just come here to stargaze." Diana blurted as she looked Noah up and down. "And why are you coming closer and closer towards me?" She asked hoping that he would kiss on her.

"No reason." Noah answered with a mischievous look.

"You better not try to throw me in the water again,

silly." Diana demanded as she gleamed.

"I won't I promise!" Noah lied. He quickly grabbed hold of her and fell back into the ocean, causing both of them to fall in.

While submerged underwater, Noah attempted inhaling to see what would happen.

Holy shit! I'm breathing in the water. I can't believe I'm actually breathing in water, he thought.

"It works!" Noah shouted as he popped his head above the surface.

You little liar!

Diana was now focused on getting him back. "Alrighty Mr. King!" She gave Noah a flirtatious scowl. "My turn!" she said as she started swimming after him.

"You're too slow to catch me! I'm out!" Noah declared as he rapidly swam and then ran out of the water to sit down on the sand.

"You're lucky I don't feel like running," Diana said, gradually exiting the ocean and strutting toward Noah to sit down beside him.

My God why is she so divine! Shit, why is God even teasing me like this? I know this girl doesn't feel the same way I do. She probably just sees me as the friend type. . . .Ugh, forget it man! Just focus on something else. Noah shifted subjects in his head.

"So, is it always nighttime here?" He asked as he observed the dark sky overhead.

"Yeah, this world has no sun at all. It doesn't even have a moon. The only light it gets is from the stars and that huge blue planet right there that looks like Saturn." Diana explained, lying back on the sand to enjoy the view of the enchanting sky.

Noah loved being in Diana's presence; even though they'd only known each other for a short time, he couldn't imagine what his life would be like without her. "Hey, I know this is an erratic question, but when do you think you're going to decide to go . . . y'know . . . into Heaven?" he wondered.

Diana gently bit her lip and thought about what to say. "I think I'll decide to go in once I know the time is right. . . . Why? Are you going to miss me or something?" she joked.

Noah laid down directly to Diana's right. "Honestly, yeah," he answered, placing both of his hands behind his head and gazing up at the stars. A random shooting star passed by in the night sky, briefly catching their attention.

Diana started to blush. "Aw, aren't you sweet," she said relishing the moment they were having together.

After hearing that, Noah wanted to disappear.

Yup, she friend zoned my ass. He continued to overthink.

~~~

The night was tremendously peaceful and silent. After a while, all Diana could hear was the sound of Noah's heartbeat. The beat that conjoined his body and soul and gave him life was the thing Diana missed the most and yearned to have again. "Oh my. Your heart is pounding," she said, taking advantage of the excuse to touch Noah's chest.

Yeah, that's because I was embarrassed, but now I'm nervous and confused as hell. Is she into me or not? I'm getting mixed signals here.

Finally, Noah uttered, "Really?"

"Yeah, it's kind of nice though. I haven't felt or heard a heartbeat in a long time," Diana admitted as she went ahead and rested her head and hand on Noah's chest.

Come on, come on, place your arm around me, silly, she thought to herself as she scooted her body as close as possible to his.

While continuing to look at the stars, Noah wrapped his left arm around Diana and began to slowly stroke the lower part of her shoulder.

Yes, he did it! Diana mentally cheered.

Alright, there goes my first move, Noah's mind conveyed. *I had no choice but to go for it.*

The flowery lavender scent of Diana's aura was driving him crazy. At that point, Noah just wanted to turn to her and kiss her glistening lips, but his fear of her reaction got in the way of taking things to that level.

Diana gradually tilted her head toward Noah, breathing softly on his neck and causing him to tremble.

His cologne or his body wash that's infused with his aura is driving me wild. Whatever it is it sure does smell great on him, she cogitated.

Okay . . . so does she want me to kiss her or not? Maybe I'm thinking too much. I should really make another move soon, but I need to wait a few minutes to think this all through.

Noah was sure that he was going into full panic mode.

Out of nowhere, Diana began to flirtatiously giggle.

"What's so funny?" Noah wondered.

Diana sighed, placing her arm around Noah's waist and admitting, "Oh, nothing. I believe my Mom-Mom thinks that if I were alive today, then somehow you and I would have connected, and would have possibly been a couple or something . . . . She's funny."

At that point, Noah gained full confidence in himself.

Yup, she's feelin me!

He turned his face toward Diana and gazed intensely into her glimmering eyes. "You as my girl . . . I think I would've loved that," he stated.

Diana didn't know what to say. She was so flattered that all she could do was smile and bite her lip.

I would've loved that too, her mind hopelessly wondered.

As their spirits grew warmer, Noah gently stroked Diana's hair, turned her on her back, and leaned in for a kiss.

With their lips just millimeters away from connecting, Noah was drawn back into his physical body.

"WHAT THE FUCK?!" he shouted as he jolted upright in bed.

"Noah!" Mrs. King exclaimed in shock. She happened to be standing in his room.

"Oh. My bad, Mom. I was . . . fighting someone in a nightmare," Noah lied to make everything seem fine.

After that, he noticed that his mother was standing a pretty good distance away from him and that it would have been difficult for her to wake him up from so far away from his bed. "Did you wake me up?" he asked.

Mrs. King shook her head. "No, Nathan did. Can't you feel him grabbing your hand now?"

When Noah looked down, he felt and saw his baby brother grabbing his hand and smiling at him. "Oh. Hey, little bro! Sorry. Didn't mean to startle you, and I'm pretty sure you didn't mean to startle me," Noah said.

"Thank God you didn't hit him. You know my poor baby is growing up and walking all over the place now. I watched him wobble all the way across the hall and into your room to wake you up. He slapped you right on the wrist. If you hadn't gotten up, I would've assumed you were in a coma," Mrs. King laughed. "Oh, dinner is ready if you want some," she added.

Did she say dinner?

Noah rubbed his eyes and looked at his clock, but he quickly learned that his clock was off; he spotted that it had been unplugged. "Dinner? What time is it?" he asked before he thought about checking his watch.

"It's 7:45 p.m.! Noah, I wish I got as much sleep as you've been getting lately. If you weren't already a 4.0 student, I would be worried, but this is honestly normal for young adults like yourself who are working and going to school."

Noah yawned, "Well that's good to know, Mom. Thanks for the fun fact. I'll see you all downstairs."

~~~

Meanwhile, back in the spirit world, Diana remained at the enchanting beach, lying on the sand and looking up at the glistening stars, wishing that Noah was still there with her. "Dammit, Noah!" she shouted, punching the sand with the back of both fists. "Next time, I'll just make the *real* first move."

13

THE GHOST FEED

After dinner, Noah went upstairs and plumped down on his pillow. But try as he might, he couldn't fall back to sleep. He got up, exercised, showered, and brushed his teeth, but still didn't feel tired. Desperately wanting to make up for what had happened in the spirit world, he looked for sleeping pills in the medicine cabinet. Finding nothing, he shut it and looked into the mirror with disgust.

"Damn, I'm such an idiot. Why didn't I kiss her when I had the chance?" He frowned at his reflection.

The entire night, Noah just stayed up thinking about what he would do when he saw Diana again. As the night transitioned into morning, he was still wide awake.

I can't believe it! It's been several hours and I'm nowhere close to being drowsy.

Growing worried, he pulled out his phone to find out if astral projection ever affected anyone's sleeping patterns. But after hunting for a long time, he grew frustrated and gave up.

"I can't find anything about what I'm going through." He muttered, tossing his phone onto the bed.

That moment, his mother crossed the hall to put Nathan's clothes in the hamper.

"Hey, Mom!" Noah called, trotting over to her.

"Yes?"

"Since you're a doctor I want your opinion on something."

Mrs. King looked worried and stopped what she was doing. "Okay . . . my opinion on what?"

"I'm having trouble sleeping. I was up all night, and no matter how many times I tried I just couldn't fall asleep. And a couple of days ago, I was up for over twenty-four hours!"

Alleviated, Mrs. King rested a hand on her hip and smiled. "Oh, Noah, that's just because you've basically been sleeping for the entire spring break. You've practically only been awake on the days you had work. It's good for you to get eight hours of sleep a night, but you've been getting closer to twenty on average."

Noah shot his eyes at the calendar on his wall. "Wait, twenty hours? Today's Thursday, right?"

"No, honey," Mrs. King chuckled. "It's Friday night!"

Friday night!

Noah's eyes widened.

I was sleep for a day and a half.

"Okay, well can't you check my pulse or something to

make sure my health is all good?" he begged knowing that his mother always kept her stethoscope with her.

Mrs. King smirked and shook her head as she took her stethoscope from her pocket. "Noah, I really think you're fine, but all right, let's see . . . your heartbeat is fine . . . your pulse in fine. Now look from side to side . . . okay, your eyes are good. Your ears are fine too. You're perfectly healthy, son. You have nothing to worry about."

She observed Noah like one of her patients. "Your body is just well-rested. I mean *extremely* well-rested, so I wouldn't be surprised if you were awake for forty-eight hours. When you go back to school Monday, your sleep will get back on track in no time."

Noah tightened his lips and tapped his foot on the carpet repeatedly.

"What's wrong now?" his mother asked.

"I actually have class Saturday afternoon, right after my therapy sessions. Hopefully my sleep cycle doesn't decide to kick in then. Maybe you could prescribe me some sleeping pills. Or I guess I can just go buy some at the drug store."

"Absolutely not!" Mrs. King frowned. "People overdose on those things all the time, and my son will not fall victim to that. I know you're grown, but I'm a doctor who is also your mother, and like I said before you're just a young adult going through normal young adult problems. You'll be fine. Trust me." And with that, she walked away to take care of Nathan.

"I hope I'll be fine," Noah muttered. "Because Saturday is tomorrow."

And it looks like I'll be missing out on another day with Diana.

He picked up his phone from his bed and started browsing the internet again.

There have to be other people who have met spirits. I can't be the only one . . . right?

"Hmm . . . Are there people currently interacting with spirits?" Noah spoke out loud while typing the question.

The first link that popped up was a site called TheGhostFeed.com. He clicked. As it loaded, Noah saw that the site gave off a dark and demonic vibe. There was artwork of the Grim Reaper, of demons, gargoyles, ghosts, and other ghoulish figures in a repeating cycle at both ends of the page. At the top center it read

Welcome to the Ghost Feed

This is a community where mediums, psychics, and other ghost communicators share their stories. Anyone is welcome to talk about their paranormal experiences here. We are all family.

There are thousands of group chat rooms, and even private one-on-one chat rooms for you to join. So don't be afraid to engage.

If you want to join in the chat rooms, you have to sign up.

Anyone who is reported or appears to be trolling then will be banned from this site forever.

Noah considered signing up, but the page's theme of darkness bothered him. But after a few seconds of deep thought, he concluded that he had no other way to communicate with people who were like him. He drew in a long breath and went for it.

"I can't believe I'm about to make an account. What the hell am I getting myself into?

"Username . . . my username should be something random like . . . SpiritGuy7.

"Okay. There's no turning back now."

He submitted his information. The website abruptly informed him that the username "SpiritGuy7" was already taken.

"What! Seriously? Who would make a name like that?" Noah smacked his forehead and thought. "I guess I'll try SpiritMan20#." He continued.

This time his username and password were approved. He started by searching for a chat room that fit his situation.

"My Demon Buddies," he read on one of their titles. "Oh god, no, definitely not that one." He scrolled until another caught his eye.

"Bring Out Your Darkness.

"Exorcism Is Life.

"Satan's Lovers."

What the hell are these people into? I'm only going to look for one more chat room. If the next one doesn't seem to fit my interest I'm logging off for good.

"I'm In Love With The Dead," he read with contentment. "Now this might be the one. It doesn't sound great, but it's worth a shot." He clicked on the title, and at once a member named Gothgirl98 sent him a private message.

[GOTHGIRL98]
Hello

[SPIRITMAN20#]
Hey

[GOTHGIRL98]

So I see you're in love with a ghost
too

[SPIRITMAN#20]

What?

How do you know that?

[GOTHGIRL98]

Duh, because you are in the "I'm In
Love With The Dead" chat room

[SPIRITMAN20#]

Okay well I'm kind of new to
this entire experience.

[GOTHGIRL98]

That's fine!

We all have to start somewhere.

So how long have you known the ghost?

[SPIRITMAN20#]

She doesn't like being called a ghost.

She likes being referred to as a spirit
because ghost just sounds eerie.

[GOTHGIRL98]

Lol whatever dude!

So how long have you been having
this fling with spirit girl?

[SPIRITMAN20#]
It's not a fling!

It's a real connection, and
I've only known her for a few days,
but it feels like I've known her my entire life.

What about you?

What's your situation?

[GOTHGIRL98]
Wow just a few days and she already
has you whipped and sprung all over her!
LMAO

My ghost boyfriend's name is Todd and
we've had our little on and off fling for
about two years now.

[SPIRITMAN20#]
Fling?

Listen.

I'm really not in the mood for
jokes here.

I'm trying to....
....you know what

Never mind that.

Do you ever astral project
when you see him?

Astral project?

What the freak is that?

. . .

I just looked up the term you mentioned
and that stuff is fake dude.

So, the answer to your question is no.

I've never astral projected before.

And I've never seen Todd.

I can actually feel him though.

My friends think it's just my imagination,
but I know I can feel him when he gives me
the deed.

Ya know like at night ;)

~~~

Noah quickly exited the private chat.

"Ew! She doesn't actually know a spirit, she's just a freak. I should've known that as soon as she said astral projection was fake." He tapped his fingers on the bedsheets. "Maybe I should log off now. This site is filled with weirdos."

Suddenly, another private chat bubble popped up on Noah's phone.

[DIMENSION_LOVER]
Hey, so I see you've encountered a
spirit you took a liking to.

Welcome to the club!

[SPIRITMAN20#]
Hang on.

Quick question before I get too engaged.

Have you ever astral projected?

[DIMENSION_LOVER]
Yeah I have!

I still do it from time to time.

[SPIRITMAN20#]
Awesome!

Great to know that I'm not alone in this.

Do you ever stay up all day and night
because of how well rested you are
after the whole process.

[DIMENSION_LOVER]
Yeah it used to affect my sleep honestly,
but then I got adjusted to it after my spirit
partner and I came up with a plan.

[SPIRITMAN20#]
Oh wow really!

What did you two do?

[DIMENSION_LOVER]
Life is what we did

[SPIRITMAN20#]
What?

[DIMENSION_LOVER]
I brought him back to life

[SPIRITMAN20#]
Stop joking around!

You're playing with me right?

[DIMENSION_LOVER]
No I'm serious I found a way
to bring him back to life

[SPIRITMAN20#]
Oh come on now I'm not buying this.

But let's say part of me believes you

How did you do it?

[DIMENSION_LOVER]
It's a long story

[SPIRITMAN20#]
Well I've got nothing but time
and I'm pretty sure you do too.

[DIMENSION_LOVER]
Ha-ha okay well let's break it down.

Ask me specific questions so I can
put it together piece by piece

[SPIRITMAN20#]
Alrighty so did he go back into his body or
did he go into someone else's?

[DIMENSION_LOVER]
Neither!

When I summoned him back
he had a brand new body that
looked exactly like his old one.

[SPIRITMAN20#]
What?

Something sounds fishy here.

So where did the new body come from?

And who is he?

I want to see if this guy really died or if he even
exists.

[DIMENSION_LOVER]
Hey we're supposed to be a family in
this ghost-talker community remember,
so you should trust me!

I've been to spirit dimensions
just like you have buddy.

So we actually have a lot more
in common than you think.
From the looks of it I can tell
you actually need my help.

[SPIRITMAN20#]
Okay sorry I trust you, and yes I do need
your help because bringing my spirit
friend back to life can do a lot of good.

She really misses her family!

And I really want to help her!

If I could just somehow help her
communicate with them again,
then that would be perfect.

What was this guy's name by the way?

[DIMENSION_LOVER]
Awwww, that is so heartwarming!

I can tell you really care about this girl

And oh.

I can't give you his name or what it used to be because I'm keeping his identity safe from the government.

I can't take that risk of him being investigated and used as some government experiment.

[SPIRITMAN20#]
Okay I see.

So did you physically see his body appear from somewhere?

What exactly did you have to do?

[DIMENSION_LOVER]
The answer to your first question is NO.

Now what I did was perform a summoning ritual in my closet.

Five minutes later he inexplicable opened the door and was in human form happy and ready to start a new life.

[SPIRITMAN20#]
A summoning ritual?

I don't know about that it sounds pretty creepy.

[DIMENSION_LOVER]

Oh it's fine I summoned him from the good part of the spirit world.

I don't interfere with bad energy or bad spirits.

You can trust me remember?

[SPIRITMAN20#]

Okay well that's a relief.

You have to excuse me this is still kind of hard to believe.

Does this ritual thing always work?

[DIMENSION_LOVER]

Oh yeah!

But it only works for people who have the power of astral projection like me and you

[SPIRITMAN20#]

I see so how do I perform this ritual?

What do I have to say and what materials do I need?

[DIMENSION_LOVER]

Yeah here's the thing

> To find out more that's going to cost ya
> $500

[SPIRITMAN20#]
What the hell?

Are you serious?

I thought we were supposed to be
a community and a family in this!

> **[DIMENSION_LOVER]**
> We are but I still have to make a living.
>
> So do you still want to find out how to
> bring your spirit lover back to life or not?

[SPIRITMAN20#]
Hell no I'm not paying $500 for something
I'm not sure will work

> **[DIMENSION_LOVER]**
> Alright then your loss pal

[SPIRITMAN20#]
....

> **[DIMENSION_LOVER]**
> I guess you don't want to live a
> life with your true love in the picture
>
> And I guess you really
> don't care about her.
>
> If you truly cared about her

you would do everything in your power to help her be with her family and friends again.

[SPIRITMAN20#]
Wait, Wait, okay I'll pay.

You're lucky I'm desperate.

[DIMENSION_LOVER]
☺ Glad to see that you've come to your senses.

You can send the money to my account through this website. Just click on my account then click in the [SEND MONEY] tab.

[SPIRITMAN20#]
Alright I sent it

[DIMENSION_LOVER]
Okay got it! Thank you ☺

[SPIRITMAN20#]
Okay so what do I need to do?

[DIMENSION_LOVER]
Here are the steps:

3) Find a piece of clothing or jewelry your spirit friend wore while they were here on Earth.

2) Find an object that contains their DNA

So that means find something like a
strand of hair, a tooth, or a piece of skin,
you get my drift.

So if you have to go back to their grave
to recover some DNA then do it.

3) Place all of the items you found
into a closed off space like a
closet or bathroom.

(You at least need two items
but if I were you I would use three)

You then light two candles inside of
this closed space and repeat this séance:
So-n-so I summon you
So-n-so I summon you,
So-n-so I summon you

If you say it three times like that then
they'll appear.

[SPIRITMAN20#]
So-n-So? Who's that?

[DIMENSION LOVER]
Your spirit partner's name LOL.

I was just using So-n-So as an example
of a name.

I'll use a better name for my example
this time: (Jenny I summon you)

You get it now?

[SPIRITMAN20#]
Oh okay yeah I get it now I just copied and
pasted the steps to my phone.

Thank you!

This better work!

[DIMENSION_LOVER]
It will trust me!

Have a goodnight SpiritMan20#
Oh yeah make sure that your spirit partner
is there with you when this takes place.

~~~

Noah logged off of the website and plugged his phone
in beside his bed to charge.

"Now I have to find a way to execute this without
messing up or getting caught. I hope she was telling the
truth and that this ritual thing isn't some demonic shit."

14

SHE KNOWS

The following morning at the Paradise Home Care Center, Noah listened to Mr. Wise rant for two hours. The entire time, all he could think about was how Mrs. Divine would act during her follow-up session.

I wonder if Diana told Mrs. Divine about us. God I hope not!

After the session with Mr. Wise was over, Mrs. Divine strolled in happily, cheesing harder than ever.

"Wow! It looks like someone is having a good day today!" Noah said.

Mrs. Divine sat on the couch cheerfully. "Yes, I am! I know your little secret!" And she pointed at him.

Noah couldn't believe what he had heard. His heart

dropped, and he took a sip of water to calm his nerves. "Uh, I don't know what you're talking about, Mrs. Divine."

"I know about you and Diana," she revealed. "Yes, I knew it! My dreams are real . . . and I can tell she really likes you, too!"

"Mrs. Divine," Noah giggled nervously. "Maybe this is part of your dream—because I've never met Diana." He felt himself breaking into a sweat.

"Oh, Noah!" Mrs. Divine could see right through his cover-up. "You don't have to put on this act for me. I know you traveled to the second floor with her, I know she's been in your room, and I know she was with you when you put your baby brother back to sleep. She thought that was so cute, too!"

Noah didn't know what to do. His palms were sweaty and his legs were shaking anxiously. "Um, I'll be right back, Mrs. Divine. I just have to go to the bathroom really quick." He stood up and swiftly left the room.

As he shut the bathroom door, he whispered to himself, "Shoot! What am I going to do? I'm sure this breaks doctor-patient confidentiality."

Suddenly he remembered his conversation with Diana that night on the sand in the spirit world.

Oh—that's what she meant when she said her Mom-Mom thought we were a cute couple. They actually talked about us. I'm so freaking stupid, how did I miss that? I should have told her not to say anything!

"This is going to be a long session." Noah wiped the sweat from his face and neck. "Okay, man, get yourself together. You've got this. Just go with your gut."

Mrs. Divine stared Noah down as he reentered the room. "So I know how she feels about you. But how do you feel about her?" she asked.

Noah sat down slowly and struggled over how to

respond. His heart was pounding. After checking to see that the office door was closed, he finally spoke. "I had no idea she told you about us." He paused a moment, glanced up at the ceiling, and let out a harsh breath. "Isn't all of this kind of weird to you?" he asked.

"Is what weird, Sweetie?"

This entire situation!

Noah took another breath and finally just said how he felt. "That I have the ability to see Diana . . . that I enjoy spending my time with her . . . that out of all the women in the world, I happen to like your . . . your dead granddaughter." He dropped his face into his palms. "That's weird, right? This sort of thing doesn't happen to your average Joe. This whole situation is just strange." He looked up at Mrs. Divine.

The uncertainty on Noah's face made Mrs. Divine smile. "Honestly, I don't see anything strange about it. I know that you're alive, and I know that she used to be alive here on Earth, but now she's alive in a better place. You're around the same age, you both have the power to see, hear, and feel each other, and let's not forget, you're bonding in a special way. It's actually quite lovely. It's not like you're developing intimate feelings for a dog, or a tree, or something completely unlike you—now that would be strange."

After hearing that, Noah felt considerably better about his situation; especially because he could finally tell someone about it without feeling like a creep. "Well, when you break it down that way it doesn't seem so bad," he noted. "Did you see Diana last night?"

"I most certainly did! She entered my dreams three times this week. From what she tells me, the nights I don't see her are the nights she's with you. So tell me, Noah. What was it like when you two first met? Diana told me, but I want to hear your side of the story too."

At that moment, Noah realized that their professional relationship had been thrown out the window. Mrs. Divine was now more like family to him.

"Okay, well, that day when you showed me the most recent picture of Diana, I couldn't stop thinking about her. Mrs. Divine, your granddaughter is the most beautiful and angelic woman I've ever laid eyes on.

"Anyway, that same night Diana appeared in my room. I was terrified . . . y'know—because she's dead. I thought I was having a nightmare. But once I looked into her eyes, I couldn't turn away. It was as if she put a spell on my mind. Seeing her face-to-face was magical! It's kind of hard to explain, though, because a lot of indescribable things happened that night." As Noah spoke, the image of Diana was fixed in his mind.

Mrs. Divine blushed. "Oh, you two are so cute. She lights up the same way you do when she hears your name or talks about you."

Wow, she does?

Noah smiled and started twiddling his fingers. "Hey, uh, Mrs. Divine I don't think we should tell anyone about this. Okay?"

"Really? Why not?" Mrs. Divine gave him a worried look.

"Because I could be fired if your family or anyone at the Care Center thinks that I'm putting all of this into your head. No one will believe us, and it will just make things worse."

For a moment he thought about telling Mrs. Divine about his plan to bring Diana back to life, but the moment passed just as quickly. That would be way too much information for her to take in all in one day.

There was a sudden knock at the door.

"Excuse me," Noah said. He hopped off his chair.

When he opened the door he found Diana's parents, Barry Jr. and Vivian. Between them was a desirable and voluptuous woman with a dark chocolate complexion. She was on the short side, standing about five feet three inches tall. She wore a red flowered sundress and had a blonde buzz cut. The look fit her.

"Hi Noah. This is Amber," Barry Jr. revealed. "She was Diana's best friend since elementary school."

Before Noah could respond, Vivian added "She works in the fashion industry with her mother and me. She's been designing some incredible outfits lately. She even put together that dress she's wearing now."

Noah presented his bright smile and gently shook Amber's hand. "It's nice to meet you, Amber. Your dress looks amazing!"

Sheesh! This girl is extremely attractive. I know you and Diana were probably breaking hearts left and right.

"Thank you, it's nice to meet you too," Amber said, looking at Noah seductively.

Noah darted a glance in the direction of the office. "Do you all want to come in?" he asked.

Barry Jr. intervened. "We won't be long. Vivian and I just came in to talk to my mom about something for a moment. We'll be out quickly. You two can talk out here while you wait. If that's okay with you, of course?"

Noah was a little confused, but he went along with it. "Oh—okay, sir, that's fine." He watched Barry Jr. and his wife walk into his office and sit down with Mrs. Divine.

Amber broke the awkward silence. "Now, Ms. Vivian said you were cute, but she didn't tell me you were *fine*."

"Ha-Ha, thanks." Noah timidly rubbed his shoulder. "But you're absolutely jaw-dropping. I know guys are lining up to approach you 24/7."

"Yeah, but for some reason it's always the wrong type of guys. You know what I mean?" Amber speculated.

Noah seemed to understand. "Yeah I know what you mean."

He looked to see if Diana's parents were finished with Mrs. Divine.

Oh god, they're still talking. I think they're trying to set me up with this girl! That would be wrong on so many levels. Barry, I'm your mother's therapist, for crying out loud! We have to keep things professional, and my social life private. I can't get involved in this...

... Shit—maybe I'm just as bad as they are by keeping this whole thing with me and Diana a secret.

Noah turned his attention to Amber again. "So, you were Diana's best friend, huh?"

Amber pinched her lips and nodded. "Yeah. I miss that girl. She brought out the best in me, even though I didn't deserve to be in her presence." She spoke sadly, then brightened. "But hey, you're a young therapist, and I hear you're almost done with school. No kids, either! That's what I call the perfect package!" She said as she reached forward to play with Noah's tie.

Whoa! This girl's fast, Noah thought while displaying a fake smile.

Amber seemed to sense his uneasiness. "Oh, sorry. I'm not coming on to strong, am I? I'm just excited to finally meet the perfect guy the Divines have been telling me so much about." She took a step back to give him more personal space.

"Oh, no, it's not you." Noah felt bad for giving off an awkward vibe. "Sorry, I'm a bit of a nerd. My social skills aren't up to par." He hoped Amber fell for his half-truth.

She suddenly licked her lips and smiled. "Aww, you're cute . . . Look, I know this is random as hell, but um—Mr. Barry bought us two tickets to the Silverside Art Museum tomorrow. Do you want to go?"

Damn, they are setting me up. But this just isn't right, I have to turn her down. . . . . . . Still, this would be the perfect way to find out if she has anything that belonged to Diana—way easier than breaking into the Divines' house. All I know is that I have to retrieve items for this ritual, ASAP.

He smiled. "Sure, I'd love that! I need to get out more anyway."

"Awesome, then!" she exclaimed. "It's a date!"

~~~

In the office, Mrs. Divine wasn't too happy with her son and daughter-in-law. "What are you two up to?" she grilled them.

"Nothing, Mom. We're just letting Noah and Amber get acquainted with one another," Barry Jr. replied happily.

"Yes. And look, aren't they precious together?" Vivian inserted with a wide grin.

Mrs. Divine rolled her eyes and sucked her teeth. "She looks like a little homewrecker if you ask me."

Vivian gasped. "Momma Divine! That wasn't nice! Amber isn't like that at all," she proclaimed.

Mrs. Divine momentarily sealed her lips as she watched Amber flirt with Noah in the hallway. "Well, she looks like one to me. Look how she's dressed! Who wears a sundress that small? Her butt is hanging all out like some stripper."

"Mom, would you relax! You know this was your granddaughter's best friend, right?" Barry Jr. reminded her.

Mrs. Divine shrugged and frowned at her son. "So? That doesn't give her the right to go and steal my grandbaby's man!" She instantly realized she had slipped up and broken Noah's wish. But a part of her felt she was doing what she had to do for Diana.

"*What?*" Vivian gushed.

Barry Jr. looked at his mother in astonishment. "Hold on, Mom—are you saying that *Noah* is Diana's man? Like her boyfriend or something?"

"Never mind what I said, child!" Mrs. Divine rolled her eyes again and waved them off. "What else do you two have planned between Amber and my innocent Noah?" She knew that if she moved on, Barry Jr. and Vivian would let her slip-up get swept under the rug.

"Oh, gosh, okay Mom," he said. "Well, I bought them tickets to the art museum, so if everything works out right they should be going on a date tomorrow."

"Yes, I could even see them being a power couple like you and Poppa Divine were!" Vivian suggested.

Mrs. Divine had had enough of their shenanigans. She stood up from the couch and grabbed her purse. "Excuse me!" she said as she quickly stormed out of the office.

Barry Jr. looked worried. "Where are you going, Mom?" He followed suit.

Mrs. Divine briefly turned to him and whispered, "I'm going to go take a nap. Just remember, that girl over there isn't your daughter. Diana cannot be replaced."

As she passed Noah and Amber in the hallway, Noah spoke. "Hey, Mrs. Divine, what about the rest of your session? We still have plenty of time left."

She reached the elevator and pressed the button for the top floor. "That's all right, Noah. Don't worry about it. We can catch up next week, Sweetie Pie. I'll be sure to let Mr. Manning know you did a great job today," she replied as she entered the elevator.

"I wonder what's wrong with her," Amber said.

"Yeah, so do I. We've never ended a session early before," Noah responded.

Amber shrugged and smiled at Noah. "So, do you have

a phone?" she asked.

Noah reached inside his left pocket. "Yeah, I do," he answered innocently, not realizing her intentions.

"Well, can I see it, please? I want to give you my number."

He blinked in comprehension and then handed his phone to Amber.

Remember, you're only doing this to bring Diana back.

"Awesome!" She typed her number in and handed the phone back. "I'll see you tomorrow, okay?"

"Okay, can't wait! See you tomorrow, Diana—uh, I mean Amber. Sorry about that!"

Noah immediately began to panic in his mind.

Aw, fuck! Did I really just call her Diana? I hope it looked like an honest mistake.

"Um, that's okay." Amber looked baffled. "See ya later," she responded hesitantly while walking toward the exit.

Barry Jr. and Vivian had overheard the end of their conversation. "That's fine, man. I know my mother talks about Diana all the time, so you were bound to call someone Diana at some point, ha-ha." Barry Jr. patted Noah on the shoulder.

"Yes, I even think Momma Divine somehow wants you to be romantically involved with Diana," Vivian laughed.

Oh boy, if only you knew the truth!

"Mrs. Divine means well," Noah told them, hoping that they bought his professional act. "It's just hard for her to cope with everything. But she's making progress. And from what I hear, your daughter was a lovely person."

"She sure was!" Barry Jr. agreed, "I wish you two would've met. I have a feeling she would've really liked you."

Well you're right about that.

"And maybe you're right about my Mom! Thanks again, Noah. We know you're doing the best you can, and all we can do is hope for the best."

15

CAN'T CATCH A BREAK

About an hour after saying his goodbyes to Diana's parents at the Care Center, Noah headed straight to school. As soon as his class started, he turned in his psychology project to Mrs. Wright while everyone else was taking notes on how to do it correctly. Mrs. Wright was still getting herself ready to teach the class.

"Here ya go, Mrs. Wright! Sorry, I know I finished it a little early. I just had a lot of free time on my hands."

Right after Mrs. Wright finished twisting her dreadlocks into a bun and applying cocoa butter on her arms and hands, she placed Noah's type-written project on her desk.

"That's absolutely fine, Noah! You truly are a remarkable student. Mr. Manning has been telling me that you've been getting incredible reviews and that you're going to go far in this field." She beamed.

"Thank you. I'm just glad everything has been working out the way I intended it to, but I wouldn't be in this position without you," Noah told his professor.

"Aww, Noah! Thank you. I appreciate that, but you should take the credit for your success and accomplishments!" Mrs. Wright protested. "And it looks like this is the last assignment of yours I need to grade, since you finished everything else on the curriculum this semester. Now, all you have to look forward to is the final online exam and graduation day."

"Can't wait! So am I free to go?" Noah wondered.

Mrs. Wright giggled, "Yes, you're free to go. I have nothing else for you to do."

Suddenly, a cute, freckle-faced woman with a caramel complexion approached Mrs. Wright's desk. "Hello. Sorry, Mrs. Wright, I couldn't help but overhear that one of my classmates has already finished the psychology project," she whispered while playfully twirling her finger through her curly, reddish-brown hair.

"Oh, hi Claudia. Yes, that classmate of yours is Noah King." Mrs. Wright pointed at Noah, who stood there glancing awkwardly between them.

Noah put on a fake smile. "Uh, hey Claudia."

Claudia smiled happily. "Hi, Noah. I've always noticed you sitting at the front of the class, but I never actually took the chance to introduce myself. It's nice to finally talk to you," she unveiled while shaking his hand before turning her attention back to her professor. "Mrs. Wright, when class is over, do you think it would be okay if Noah helps me out with my project? That wouldn't be like cheating or anything, would it?"

Oh god no. Give me a break! I have way too much going on already.

"No, that wouldn't be cheating at all. I don't see a problem with him helping you out, but that's all up to him. Noah, it would be nice to see you finally getting acquainted with at least one of your classmates," Mrs. Wright cheerfully acknowledged, obviously hoping he would say yes. "He's a little shy," she added.

Great, now you now sound like my mom.

Claudia turned to Noah and rocked back and forth on her heels. "Aw, don't worry, I don't bite," she flirted. "So what do you think, Noah? Can you help me—just for today?" Her emerald eyes gazed into his imploringly.

Aw damn—all these girls would come out of nowhere now that I've met Diana. Just my luck, right? Noah reflected while nodding.

"Yeah, that's no problem at all. I can help you," he approved.

After class, Claudia met up with Noah in the hallway. "You wanna go to the library?" she asked while swaying her rainbow-colored backpack from side to side.

"Sure, that's fine with me," Noah answered.

While they walked down the stairway toward the library, Noah observed Claudia's outfit. She was wearing blue denim overalls and a light blue t-shirt with white and blue sneakers. "You're a big fan of the color blue, I see," he offered.

Claudia squinted at him. "What?" she asked, giggling like a shy child.

Noah pointed to her outfit.

"Oh—yeah! I do like blue. I like a lot of colors, actually. I'm an artistic person."

He nodded slowly. "Okay. Cool."

"Why? You don't like my outfit?" she worried.

Noah could sense she was slightly nervous. "No, I like it a lot! Blue looks good on you," he answered, trying to keep the conversation pleasant.

"Thank you! I'm digging the white collar-shirt and black tie you're wearing, too," Claudia conveyed.

"Thanks! These are just my work clothes, though. I have a bunch of white collar-shirts," Noah clarified.

"Yeah. Before I left class, Mrs. Wright told me you've been interning as a therapist at a Care Center. No wonder you dress different from a lot of the guys in our class." Claudia moved a little closer to Noah as they continued to stroll down the school's stairway. "I think I want to be a therapist too, but for children."

"Okay. So you love kids?"

"Yes, I absolutely love kids—and I'm great with them," Claudia replied. "I also always wanted to model. It just seems like a fun gig."

"Cool," Noah responded unenthusiastically. His mind was completely focused elsewhere.

When they finally entered the library, they found a private study room to sit in. After an awkward moment of silence, Claudia tilted her head and smiled at Noah as she unzipped her backpack. "Why are you so quiet?" She could tell something was on his mind.

Noah lifted his shoulder in a half shrug. "I'm not that quiet. I just usually keep to myself that's all."

"No, you are *that* quiet," Claudia disagreed emphatically. "I never ever hear a peep from you in class; and so far you've been giving me nothing but one word answers."

Because I have to hurry up and make it home to see Diana. That's all I can think about right now.

"Okay," Noah laughed. "You win—I'm as quiet as a mouse. I guess it's just one of those things I can't help. Are you ready for me to show you the steps of the project?"

"The project!" Claudia smacked her forehead. "Oh yeah—duh, Claudia, that's what we're here for." She pulled out her papers and slapped them onto the table. "All right, so I know our project is about the human brain, right?"

"Yup: this is a Cognitive Psychology assignment. Our job is to research how humans think, how we understand, how we perceive, and how we make decisions. You have to write at least two pages for each question. Then, after that, you have to write a one-page conclusion about what you learned and how the human brain functions overall," Noah explained thoroughly. "What helped me was observing random people and their body language in a variety of situations; or at random places like the park or the mall. For this part of the assignment, you can use your family, friends, random people, and even films or the internet to help you. Just make sure you cite your sources if you do use the internet."

"Oh my god—okay, I get it now. Wow! I either need to pay more attention in class, or you're just really smart," Claudia said as she began writing ideas down for her project.

Within seconds, Claudia stopped writing and placed her pen on her notepad. "Do you have a girlfriend?" she wondered out of nowhere.

I've been asked that before, but this time it's actually a good question, Noah began contemplating. *I honestly don't know. I really need to ask myself: What is Diana to me? Is she a friend who just happens to be a spirit, or are we more than friends now?*

"Well, right now it's complicated. I really don't know what's going on," he finally answered.

"I see." Claudia slowly bobbed her head. "Now I understand why you're acting so distant." She set her palms down flat on the table and jiggled her feet. "Let me guess! .

. . . So—you like this girl, but you don't know if she likes you back the same way," she guessed uncertainly.

Noah wished he could say what was really on his mind. *It's more like this: I like her and I'm pretty sure she likes me, but I'm alive and she's not—so that's . . . that.*

Starting to feel a little drowsy, he decided to answer Claudia the best way he could. "Yeah, that's it, but sprinkled with a little more complication. Listen, I would love to stay and chat with you some more, but I really have to go home and get some sleep." He yawned and began to gather his things. "I've had a long day. It was really nice meeting you, Claudia."

"Aw, okay, I understand. I know you're a busy guy. It was nice meeting you too, and thanks so much for your help. Don't be afraid to shoot me a message sometime. I just followed you on *Gossip Place*!" Claudia answered.

"Got it! I'll follow you back," he declared as he left.

16

ANOTHER CHAT WITH MOM-MOM

That evening, as Mrs. Divine napped in her room at the Care Center, she rocked back and forth on her chair at a faster pace than usual. In her dream, she was waiting for Diana again.

When Diana suddenly appeared, she could see the concerned look on her grandmother's face. "Hey, Mom-Mom, what's going on? You look worried."

Mrs. Divine grimaced. "You won't believe what you're mother and father are up to," she complained.

Diana seemed unsettled. "What are they up to?"

"I still can't believe it myself." Mrs. Divine dramatically leaned a bit closer toward Diana, as if she was about to tell her the biggest secret of her life. "They're trying to set Noah up with your friend Amber. They even have some date thing planned."

A date! . . . . WITH AMBER!

Diana was put off by this news. "WHAT?!" she shouted out. "But Noah's not even Amber's type! She likes wild bad boys—unless her taste has recently changed."

"Well, guess what she was drooling all over him, honey." Mrs. Divine gripped the arm of her rocking chair. "She even came to the Care Center today dressed like a homewrecker, wearing a small sundress that barely passed her buttocks."

Diana suddenly thought about Amber's past.

If you only knew what I knew, Mom-Mom, you would really dislike her. . . . But who am I kidding. Deep down I know Amber is a better person now.

She laughed to cover up her feeling of dismay. "Oh Mom-Mom, Amber isn't a homewrecker. She's just very social, that's all. Do you know if Noah agreed to the date?"

"Darn it!" Mrs. Divine clenched her teeth. "I'm not sure—I was so angry with your Mom and Dad that I just left to go take a nap."

"Well, I'm pretty sure he turned down the date," Diana said, trying to make herself feel better and not pay the Noah and Amber situation any mind. She flipped her hair behind her shoulders and smiled. "You know, the other night, Noah and I almost kissed before he disappeared on me. I feel like our chemistry gets stronger and stronger every time we meet."

"Hmmmm," Mrs. Divine looked as if she already knew everything Diana was telling her. "I could tell something was up with you two," she confirmed. "Noah's eyes light up every time he talks about you. He even told me to my face that he likes you, but girl, I think he's actually in love with you."

In love? With me?

"Wow. So he had no problem talking to you about us?" Diana wondered. "And I don't know—love is a pretty strong word to use right now, Mom-Mom."

"It took him a while to finally admit that he met you, but I got to him, and eventually he came around and revealed what happened during your magical encounter. And I think love *is* the right word, honey, I know love when I see it," Mrs. Divine replied confidently.

"Mom-Mom, what if I'm holding him back?" Diana asked, suddenly having mixed feelings.

Mrs. Divine looked directly into Diana's eyes. "Holding him back from what?"

Diana fidgeted. "You know, from having a real life— especially a real love life with someone who's alive like he is," she answered, depressed.

"Baby girl, listen to me." Mrs. Divine scooted her chair closer to her granddaughter. "I know that this isn't the ideal situation two young people like yourselves would want to be in, but you have to realize that there is a special connection here. Although this relationship may be indescribable at the moment, I can tell you two were meant to be together. Miracles like these cannot be taken for granted. Just do me a favor and embrace the magical bond you two have while you still can," she pled.

"Okay, Mom-Mom, I will." Diana gave a slow huff. "I love how you're always right!" she said, wishing desperately that she could hug her grandmother at that moment.

"That's because I've lived a long life, and—" Mrs. Divine suddenly stopped. "Oh my god, your birthday is just two days away!" she exclaimed. "I can't believe I almost forgot! Do you think Noah has anything special planned for you?"

"Does he have anything special planned . . . . for me?" Diana snickered and shook her head. "No, not that I know of. He probably doesn't even know or remember when my birthday is. I told him when we first met, but I wouldn't be surprised if he forgot."

"I guarantee you he knows!" Mrs. Divine reclined in her chair. "Great guys like him always have something *special* planned for the women they love. Just you wait and see."

17

MIND BOGGLED

That same evening, after showering and putting on lounge wear, Noah stumbled to his bed completely drained. After two nights of being fully awake, he was exhausted and finally ready to get some sleep.

When Noah dozed off into a deep sleep with Diana heavily on his mind, she instantly appeared in his room.

"Hey there," she whispered delicately into his left ear.

After adjusting to his spiritual body, Noah stood up and greeted her. "Hey. I've been thinking about you all day."

Diana clutched his left hand straightaway, causing that familiar overwhelmingly warm impulse to shoot through their souls once more.

"I know you have, silly! Come on, let's get out of here," she said after gazing at him for a second.

She quickly opened a portal to the spirit world they'd visited before with the enchanting night sky and peaceful beach. Although other things were on her mind, she was hoping that they could recreate that magical night.

"Okay," Noah said softly as they went through the portal. "I'm right behind you."

When they entered the spirit world, however, Diana grew unusually quiet. Her mind kept switching from happy thoughts to jealous ones about Noah and Amber.

I hope he tells me about this Amber situation, and I hope he turned down that date, she thought while waiting for Noah to say something.

Paying Diana's suspicious behavior no mind, Noah sat down on the sand and began making himself comfortable. When she just stood there staring at him with a scowl and looking as if a bipolar switch had been flipped inside her body, Noah snickered. "Aren't you going to sit down?" he asked, patting the sand. "I have something special planned for your birthday on Monday. Most of what I've planned is a surprise, but I can give you a couple clues," he added with a grin.

Aw, Mom-Mom was right—he remembered my birthday and did plan something special for me . . . but that's beside the point for now. Diana was conflicted. *Noah, please tell me you aren't going on a date with my best friend.*

Finally deciding to speak her mind, she said, "So . . . my Mom-Mom told me that you met my friend Amber today."

Noah immediately stood up in shock.

Shit, I forgot to tell her about that first.

"Oh yeah, she's really cool. I was going to—"

"Mom-Mom also said that my parents tried to hook you

two up, and are planning for you and Amber to go on a date tomorrow," Diana interrupted. "They're crazy. She doesn't even know you. When did they start hooking people up with strangers?"

Folding her arms, she turned her back to him. "You know what, I'm sorry. I don't mean to seem all upset. I just want—" Diana's emotions were all over the place; she couldn't possibly spew out everything she was thinking at the moment. "Uh, never mind. Forget that I even mentioned it."

As Diana looked out across the still, dark blue waters, Noah gradually approached her and gently hugged her from behind. He could tell that she was extremely bothered. *Let's just enjoy this magical night like the night before,* he thought while placing the side of his face against hers.

Look Diana, this is clearly a sign that he's really into you and that he most likely turned Amber down; so stop acting like a jealous little girl and get over it already, her mind implied as she slowly turned back to Noah and smiled.

Noah smiled back and leaned in for a kiss.

Ugh, but I just have to know.

She gently shoved Noah away before their lips touched. "All right, I'm sorry. I changed my mind: I just have to know," she said.

Noah knew exactly what she was referring to. He clenched his teeth and exhaled. "Yeah, about this date. I—"

"You aren't going, are you?" Diana interjected. "I mean, I love Amber and all because she's my best friend, but if you agreed to go on a date with her and you two began to develop a strong connection and get into a relationship, then what happens to us? Noah, what are we, exactly? Like, what is this thing going on between you and I?"

As she babbled, she placed her hands on her hips and

swayed back and forth.

"Diana, I'm trying to get to the point! Just let me explain," Noah said, moving closer again.

At that particular moment, Diana's energy did not feel welcoming at all. Her hair had started to blow in the wind, but Noah noticed that there was no actual wind: Diana was creating it herself. Her spirit was also glowing brighter than usual as wrath enhanced her spiritual energy.

Raising his hands above his chest slightly in fear, Noah said, "Please don't flip out. Uh . . . yes, I agreed to the date, but it's for a good—"

"You did what?" Diana interrupted again, freezing and feeling her spiritual energy begin to drain away. The wind blowing in her hair instantly stopped, and she felt like dropping to her knees and sinking into the sand. "Why didn't you tell me that first? I—"

"LISTEN, DIANA!" Noah shouted. "I agreed to the date because I have a plan. That plan involves bringing you back to life, and I'm going to need Amber's help to do it." He took a deep breath. "I was going to reveal all of this to you on your birthday, but you obviously spoiled the surprise."

After calming down, he added, "It's okay, though. I guess it's better that you know now, anyway."

For a solid minute Diana was speechless and had a blank stare. "What, bring me back to life?" she finally asked. "That's impossible. Does Amber even know about what you're trying to do?"

"Are you kidding me?" Noah shook his head. "Oh god, no! She would think I'm crazy and report me to the authorities. I'm not telling anyone about this until I bring you back, and even then your family would have to keep quiet so the wrong people don't find out."

"So it sounds like I'm going to be living like a fugitive if this actually works." Diana raked her hands through her hair and looked skeptical. "I don't know, Noah—this seems really fishy and hard to believe."

Noah palmed the front of his forehead in frustration. "After everything you've seen when it comes to this spirit dimension stuff, this is the thing you find hard to believe?" he wondered incredulously. "I must admit, I thought it sounded fishy too at first—but, Diana, anything is possible! Hell, most people would find it hard to believe that I travel to a spirit world almost every other night and that I'm falling in love with a woman who happens to be a spirit, but it's the truth and it's currently happening."

A cozy rush ran through Diana's soul.

Oh my god, did he say 'falling in love'? I don't even know what to say back, and dammit now I can't stop smiling, she thought while grinning uncontrollably from ear to ear.

Damn, did I just say love? I mean, it's true I'm falling for her, but I don't think this was the right time to say so. She looks pleased, though. She probably didn't catch everything I said. Just keep talking as if you never uttered those words, Noah advised himself.

"We just have to hope that it works," he said aloud.

"Okay. So we obviously have a lot to address," Diana agreed, "But right now, let's talk about this plan of yours. And I'll do my best to believe in whatever you're talking about. So how did you find out about bringing spirits back to life?" She still felt highly skeptical.

For a moment, Noah fiddled with his watch, trying to come up with an answer that didn't sound ridiculous. "I had to pay someone $500 to reveal these secrets to me. I found them on this website called TheGhostFeed.com. Apparently, this person had a relationship with a spirit and found a way to bring them back. All I have to do is follow the steps she gave me for this ritual."

Diana shook her head in instant denial. "Um, $500? I

know you just talked about having hope, but now I really don't know about this, Noah. I think you got ripped off."

That was something Noah didn't want to hear, especially from Diana, since he was doing everything he could for her. He frowned. "Do you want this to work or not? Because it seems like you could care less," he said in frustration.

Diana stomped her foot into the sand. "Of course I want this to work! I absolutely would love to be alive again, even though this time around it seems like I would be living like a damn fugitive based on what you're saying. It just all seems too good to be true. And let's get something straight here—I want to be alive just to be with my family and two close friends again. That's it. Other than that, I would gladly walk into heaven to see my Pop-Pop."

Oh really.

Noah noticed how Diana purposely didn't mention him when it came to why she wanted to be alive again. "Okay," he said as he began to walk away.

Where the hell is he going?

Diana chased after him. "Hey! Where are you going?" she demanded.

"Home!" he answered as he approached the thick palm tree.

That's it! That's all you have to say?

Diana was irritated by Noah's sudden one word answers. "You can't open up portals here on the second floor," she protested. "You need my help to do that—so you aren't going anywhere until we finish this conversation." She kicked sand at his legs. "And what do you need Amber for if she doesn't need to know about this ritual thingy?"

Noah's demeanor remained calm. "After watching you open up portals to the second floor in my room, I'm pretty sure I can open up portals to the first floor while I'm up here in your territory. I'm alive, remember. And, to answer your question, I have to see if Amber has some important memorabilia of yours that I can use to perform the ritual. This plan could really work. I know it can!"

Pausing, he snickered. "My original plan was to find a way to break into your parents' house and take whatever I could find. I didn't think that particular plan out too well."

"Oh, wow!" Diana tried to keep a straight face and remain angry, but she couldn't help it and started laughing. "Well, yeah, there's no need to go with the original plan. The security system at my mom and dad's house is top notch, so that would never work. And lucky for you, I actually have two shirts and a brush at Amber's house—but how would you plan on getting those things?"

"Easy. I'll just say your Mom-Mom knows about some of your belongings being there and would like them back to help her cope with your death," Noah explained.

"Okay, that works." Diana slowly bobbed her head. "So you really don't have to go on that date with her, then. Just tell Amber that you have to collect my things from her because my Mom-Mom needs them, and then you can cancel the date altogether."

Noah sighed. "Diana, I can't stand the poor girl up. I could tell she really wanted to go on this date. And your dad went out of his way to buy us tickets. I don't want her or your parents to think that I'm some type of douchebag because I bail on her out of nowhere," he explained.

"Really Noah!" Diana was growing upset again. "They won't care, and I'm pretty sure you can come up with a good excuse. It seems like you're already good at doing that anyway!" she accused. "And honestly, when did Amber start liking good nerdy guys?" she quietly added to herself.

Noah attempted to hug Diana to help her relax, but she

stepped away from him when he approached her, showing that she didn't want to be touched.

He sighed again. "Nothing is going to happen between Amber and me, trust me. It's not like I'm going to up and forget about you. For this plan to work perfectly, I have to go about it this way. Besides, why are you acting all jealous? Amber is supposed to be your best friend. What's the deal with you and her?"

Diana cringed as unpleasant memories came to mind. "Nothing . . . nothing at all," she lied. "Just leave me be for now. I want to be alone."

Even though Diana was upset, all Noah could really focus on was trying to bring her back to human life in time for her birthday. "As you wish! I promise, by the time your birthday comes around, you'll be alive in the flesh again."

Touching the palm tree, he opened a portal that led back to his room.

Wow, he was right—he can open portals back to the first floor. . . . . .

I have to stop him!

Her mind began to play tricks on her as she thought about Amber and Noah together as a couple.

He's going to end up falling for her, just like the last one—I know he is!

Running toward, the palm tree, she stood in front of the portal to block Noah's exit. "Listen, don't go on that date, okay?" she pled.

They were now face to face, staring each other dead in the eyes. "I already told you, I have to!" Noah protested. "Will you relax?" He tried to move around her.

Diana did her best to hold back her tears. "Well, you know what? Since you won't listen to me, go ahead—just know that I'm never going to see you again after tonight. You can forget about that ritual, and you can forget about me!" she threatened.

Noah could not take Diana seriously, and he couldn't help but laugh. "Not if I can help it. I have the power to transport you directly into my room when I think about you in my sleep, remember."

Diana frowned while continuing to hold back her tears. "Don't you even bother trying to think about me, either."

Noah shrugged, then smiled. "I can't help it if you're always on my mind," he replied charmingly while reaching for her hands.

Diana quickly moved her hands away by folding her arms across her chest. "Whatever. Whenever you do summon me back into your room, just remember that I won't be talking to you."

"We'll see," Noah said skeptically. "So, are you going to step out the way now? I have a lot of planning to do for you, and I need to get an early start."

As Diana kept her strong stance in front of the portal, she and Noah could not stop looking in each other's eyes. "I'll move when I feel like it," she stated, continuing their stare-down.

"Once again, two can play that game," Noah said, wrapping his right arm around Diana's upper back and his left behind her lower thighs to lift her off the ground.

Diana tried to ignore the enhanced sexual tension between them. As he placed her down a few feet away from the portal and gave her a kiss on the cheek, her soul was suddenly stimulated with warm passion that made her knees feel weak.

"I'll see ya tomorrow, okay? Unless you want to come with me right now while we still have time," Noah said softly as he stepped halfway into the portal.

Diana just ignored him; her emotions were spinning and racing everywhere like a roller coaster. It was like she wanted to see Noah and not see him at the same time.

"My oh my, women," Noah muttered, smiling and entering the portal.

18

THIS MAGIC MOMENT

Diana sat down on the sand and looked up to the stars, with her vision blurry due to her eyes being filled with tears.

She suddenly heard a voice behind her. "Diana?"

As she slightly turned around, and rubbed her eyes she saw that it was Noah twinkling at her. The sight of his face with the engaging starry night behind him gave her butterflies.

"You know I couldn't leave you here all by yourself like that. I care about you too much," he willingly confessed as he reached out for her hand.

Diana took his hand as he delicately pulled her up onto her feet.

She wondered, *Why can't I stay mad at this boy?*

As the enchanting blue planet and starry night sky reflected upon Diana's angelic face, Noah once again observed the essence of magic in her captivating eyes. He did not want to regret his actions by not making a move this time. As he caressed her face, he leaned in for a kiss just like the last time.

It's going to happen this time. I can feel it, he thought.

Diana smiled, but turned her face away from his lips.

"What did I do now?" Noah charmingly asked.

Diana's smile still lingered. "I'm still mad at you, silly. You'll get a kiss when I know it's the right time."

Noah bit his bottom lip and softly swayed his left foot in the sand. "Although that part may be painful for me to bear right now, I'm still glad that I'm able to be by your side."

"Hmm!" Diana quickly kissed Noah on the cheek, which suddenly stimulated his soul with warm passion. "Well, so far, you earned that!" she said.

"That's a start!" Noah conveyed as he and Diana held hands. "Hey, let's go to that spirit world you like so much."

Diana flared her eyebrows and asked, "Okay, but why?"

"Because I have an idea," he replied as they approached the thick palm tree.

"You're always up to something." Diana then opened the portal to her favorite spirit world, filled with angels, animals, and children. When they entered it and stepped onto the shimmering grass, she turned to face Noah. "All right, we're here. So, what now?"

In the near distance, Noah spotted a group of what seemed to be four children all playing together with a full-grown male lion with shining golden brown fur. He began to approach them while pulling Diana with him.

"Noah, what are you trying to do?" Diana questioned with a smirk on her face.

"You and I are going to have some fun today and enjoy this place together while we still can. Let's have a stress-free time and play with the children over there. It looks like they're having a blast!" Noah was eager to try to something new, but deep down he and Diana didn't know what to expect.

Seconds later, Diana turned her attention toward a female angel with pale skin and long blonde hair. She was wearing a blue denim jacket with black pants, and was hovering above the children watching their every move. Diana figured that the angel would be very overprotective. "Uh. Noah, I don't think we're allowed to," she whispered.

"Sure we are! Remember, you said as long as we don't try to take the children away from here, or interfere with the angels raising them, then we're all good. All we're going to do is play with them." Noah didn't seem to have the same fears as she did.

Diana looked up at the blonde-haired angel again. "Yeah, but I don't know how she's going to feel about that."

Noah turned toward Diana and saw that she was staring directly up above them.

"Oh, I see," he said as he observed the angel watching over the kids. "Well, what's her name?"

Diana shrugged. "I don't know," she whispered.

"You knew who that one angel lady was. What was her name again—Tiffany? Yeah, Tiffany. That's it," Noah whispered back.

"Yeah, that's only because I just so happened to hear Tiffany reveal her name to the little boy Hakeem when I was sitting by the creek one time. Other than that, I don't know anyone else's names," Diana divulged.

"Okay, fine." Noah laughed. "I'll just ask her. We have nothing to lose." Diana admired Noah's bravery. He was always completely sure of himself. Although, they've never spoken to angels face to face before, Noah had no problem with breaking the barrier. He looked up at the angel and asked, "Hey Miss, what's your name?"

The angel smiled as her wings steadily flapped, keeping her in place in mid-air. "Sarah," she answered.

"Hey, Sarah. You don't mind if we play with the kids, do you? I promise we won't do anything malicious," Noah humorously told the angel.

Sarah chortled and nodded. "I know you won't. I can tell that you're kind people. Go ahead and have fun!" she insisted.

Diana was amazed.

I can't believe he charmed his way into this. Well actually . . . I can believe it.

Noah intermingled himself with the four children, looking like a giant among them. The pure and innocent sight caused Diana to feel a warm tingling feeling inside.

And of course he's good with kids, too, her mind wondered.

"Hey. So, what are you guys playing?" Noah asked the kids.

"We're about to play tag in the forest over there," a tan chubby kid answered.

"Cool! Can my friend Diana and I play with you guys?" Noah begged them.

The chubby kid randomly started tucking his orange shirt into his khaki shorts and bobbed his head once he was finished. "Sure, you two can play," he said. "But Oden is it," the kid added while pointing at the large lion.

"Whoa," Diana uttered.

"Whoa is right" Noah began to tremble. After seeing

the lion he was about to curse but he held his tongue. "That huge full-grown lion is it?" He pondered.

"Yeah, we're starting in thirty seconds so you better prepare to run," the kid warned while getting into his running stance.

Diana clutched the top of Noah's shoulder. "Hey, look on the bright side. At least the animals are harmless," she whispered.

The kid shouted as everyone took off into the magical forest. "Ready, GO!"

"I hope you don't mind this." Diana quickly leapt onto Noah's back a second before he began to run. "I just don't feel like running in these freaking heels," she said.

Noah chuckled. "Nah, I don't mind it, even though your feather-weight behind is going to slow me down a bit."

As Noah dashed into the forest with Diana on his back, he immediately found a gleaming green and gold spruce tree to hide behind. In the midst of hiding, they saw the lion softly trying to tap two of the children with his paw, intentionally missing them so that the game could go on longer. Eventually, all of the children got away and hid with Noah and Diana.

"Noah," Diana called, tapping his shoulder. "You guys, let's go hide in the tree house right there," she whispered as she hopped off Noah's back. Moments later, they all began to creep toward the sparkling cedar tree that held a large tree house built for the children.

"Diana, you climb up the ladder first so that you can pull the kids up when I hand them to you," Noah ordered.

One by one, Noah lifted each child into Diana's grasp so that she could pull them into the tree house. After Noah climbed inside last, he dusted his hands off and looked at all of the children joyfully hiding next to Diana in the corner. They were attached to her sides as if she were their mother.

Even the kids are bonding with her. I'm not surprised! How can you not love that girl?

"Are you all having fun?" Noah asked them.

A little curly-haired brown girl replied with a grin, "Si, lo soy!"

Noah smiled and rubbed his chin as if he understood the little girl. He then gave her a thumbs up. "Okay, I'm going to pretend like I know what you just said. It seems like you're really happy though," he joked. "I'm really sorry I don't speak Spanish."

Diana was unable to restrain her laugh. "She said, 'Yes, I am,' silly."

"What!" Noah was flabbergasted. "I didn't know that you could speak Spanish."

"In actuality . . . ." Diana commented while scratching her head. "I can't, but for some odd reason I understood her."

A little girl with braided hair wearing a Kenyan Maasai dress interrupted, "Oden yeye kuja."

"I understood her too." Diana turned her attention to Noah. "She said Oden's coming."

She can understand Spanish and Swahili? I guess the magic of the spirt world is helping her understand them. I'm assuming since I'm still alive, I don't have this luxury.

"Hey, there's no way that lion is making it up here. He would have to climb the tree or jump really high, and neither is happening," he finally uttered with pure confidence.

"Wow, you seem pretty sure of yourself," Diana said as she continued to sit in the corner with the children.

In a sudden moment of silence, they saw the tree house's curtains slightly blow in the wind. Suddenly, the lion sprung into the open window and through the curtains, causing Noah and Diana to holler at the same time.

"HOLY CRAP!" Noah shouted while exhaling heavily. "I didn't know he could jump that high," he admitted after the lion gently tapped him on the leg, gesturing that he was now it in the game of tag.

Laughing, a boy with a white baseball cap said, "Oh, wow, you two were scared of Oden!"

"Who me?" Noah waved the boy off. "Nah, I wasn't scared. I was just playing around with you all. I was just trying to make the game more entertaining by acting like I was afraid," he lied.

The children all gave Noah a blank stare.

Diana paced over toward Noah and whispered, "It looks like they've caught onto your fib."

"I see," he whispered back. "Look, kids. I'm all for building up suspense and all, but you guys are giving me a *Children of the Corn* vibe right now. I don't need to go get Sarah, do I?" Noah playfully teased them through irrepressible giggles.

"Well, I was scared," Diana confessed while cracking up at Noah's foolishness.

The chubby boy said, "At least she admits it!"

"Okay, okay. I was scared. You have to excuse me, but Oden looks like Aslan from *The Chronicles of Narnia*. So, I think I have the right to be afraid of him."

An instant burst of deep, loud, and hearty laughter came from the children. "Your boyfriend is silly!" The chubby boy told Diana.

Did he just call Noah, my boyfriend?

He just called me, Diana's boyfriend . . . I hope she doesn't correct him, and just goes along with it.

"I know. He really is, isn't he?" Diana said while displaying her ravishing smile and eyeballing Noah.

She went along with it!

"He isn't so bad, though. I can see why you like him," the Kenyan girl voiced her opinion.

"Yeah he's all right, I guess," Diana replied softly nudging Noah's side.

"Hang on! Wait a minute! So, you can actually speak English!" Noah said in surprise.

"We can when we want to," the Latina girl mentioned.

"Wow, way to go girls, you two sure had me fooled," he conceded.

"Come on, guys. Let's go ask Sarah if she and her friends could take us across the bridge again," the boy with the white baseball cap suggested.

The little girls were happily jumping up and down. The Latina girl exclaimed, "Si, me encanta el puente!" The Kenyan girl joyfully added, "Mimi pia!"

"And now they're back to their native tongue, I see. What did they say?" Noah whispered to Diana. The nerdy side of him just had to know.

"She said, 'Yes, I love the bridge,' and she replied to her by saying, 'Me, too,'" Diana divulged while pointing at the little girls.

After figuring out what they were going to do next, the children climbed down the ladder.

The tag game is over already? Noah wondered as he watched the children leave. He slowly turned to the lion, and abruptly asked him, "Are you done playing the game, too?" Oden just turned away and jumped out of the tree house window, lightly pouncing onto the ground.

Diana laughed as Noah stood there waiting for an answer. "Well, I guess that was a 'Yes.'"

"Yeah, I guess so." Noah peeked out the treehouse window to see where the children were headed. "Where is this special bridge that they were so excited about anyway?" he asked Diana.

"I've seen it before when I first came to this world. It's inside of a cave, but I never actually attempted to walk inside the cave or across the bridge before. I remember where it is. It's a pretty good distance away from here," She explained.

Noah wanted the fun to continue. "Gotcha! Let's just go follow the kids there while we still have the chance," He urged.

After making their way out of the tree house, they saw that the four children, the angel Sarah, and the lion Oden were gone. There were now a bunch of other kids, angels, and animals in a crowd playing in the forest.

"They're gone!" Noah turned to Diana. "Oh, well. You're sure you know where it's at, right?" he inquired.

"Yeah, I know where it is." Diana claimed. "But I can't tell you what to expect once we walk inside."

"Okay, that's fine by me. We'll just be creating new experiences together," Noah professed placing his arm around her as they walked out of the magical forest.

"You see, this is why I thought you had a girlfriend. Because you can just charm your way through any and every situation," Diana told him as she mildly held onto to his forearm.

Noah satirically shrugged. "I can't help it if I was born with this—charm that you say I have."

Diana sighed. "I guess you're right!" She replied while rolling her eyes. A random thought instantly came to her.

"This is unbelievable, I can't believe I've never really attempted to explore the rest of this world before," she mentioned as they walked onto a hilly road plastered with bright multi-colored crystals.

Noah couldn't believe it either. "So, you've really just sat at that creek for ten months and entered your Mom-Mom's dream portals repeatedly, huh."

In that moment Diana beamed as she thought about it. "Yeah, I never really had a reason to go anywhere else till now. You've actually made me enjoy it here a lot more. So, I guess I don't mind exploring the rest of this place—now that you're here."

~~~

Moments later, they spotted the starting point of a brown narrow bridge that immediately led into a cave. "There it is," Diana said as she pointed toward it.

"Alrighty. Let's go inside!" Noah commanded.

As they walked onto the bridge and entered the cave, their view went pitch black. Diana held onto Noah tighter since they could not see where they were walking. The brief seconds of darkness quickly turned into illuminating wonder as they walked deeper into the space. There were hundreds of glow worms and fireflies that spellbindingly lit up the entire cave. The combination of the bright yellow and green lights reflected upon their faces.

"Oh my god, Noah. It's so beautiful in here," Diana said as they gracefully continued to walk across the sturdy bridge.

"Yeah. It's a beautiful view all right, but I don't think anything is as beautiful as you are," Noah suddenly expressed, grabbing Diana below her waist with his arm and lifting her up.

Diana took the compliment as a joke. "Aw, whatever you say, silly," She replied with her elegant smile, wrapping her arms around his neck.

"I'm serious," Noah contended.

When he looked into her eyes, he could see the magical reflection of the bright yellow and green lights in the cave.

At that instant, Diana felt the need to randomly bring up their conversation from hours ago. "Noah, you never answered my question from way before," she began.

He seemed confused and gently placed Diana on her feet.

"What question?"

"Remember when I asked you what are we, and what is this thing going on between us?" She continued.

"Oh, yeah. I remember."

After hearing his answer Diana shrugged. "Sooo," she said, prolonging the word.

Noah took a deep breath. He asked, "Well, what do you think we are? . . . . And you heard what the boy said about us in the tree house, right?"

"Oh my god!" Diana giggled and shook her head. "I want to hear it from you, silly."

"Okay. Well, I want you to be my girl and all. I really do, but—you keep playing games," Noah revealed. "Sometimes I feel like you keep giving me mixed signals."

Diana blushed and anxiously ran her fingers through her hair. "Ha, ha. I'm playing games, but you're the one who wants to go on a date with my best friend," she responded.

"Ugh, I already gave you the reasoning behind why I have to go on that date," He told her.

Diana playfully shoved him. "And I already told you there's another option."

Noah didn't want to have another argument with her, so he said what he knew she wanted to hear.

"You know what, Diana? You're right! I won't go on that date with Amber. Okay," he quickly said easing the tension.

She was surprised. "Really?" Diana queried.

"Yes, really," Noah assured her.

Diana displayed her sudden joy with that beautiful smile and slowly approached him. As she placed both of her hands behind his head, she swiftly kissed him on the cheek. "You earned that one, too," she whispered to him right before walking away further into the cave.

After feeling his soul grow warmer, Noah bit his lip and watched her as she advanced into the enchanting cave. "See, this is exactly what I'm talking about. You play too many games."

Diana heard his echo travel throughout the cave. "Well, now that I'm your girl, you can definitely earn a lot more than that—depending on how you make me feel that is."

Noah rubbed his hands together. "Oh, wow. So, this is official then! Sweet!"

~~~

After a few minutes of traveling down the bridge, they spotted light at the end of the tunnel and heard the sound of water splashing onto something. As they approached this light, it led them all the way to a clearing that was also a dead end. At this impasse, they observed that they were high above the surface. There were two tall waterfalls, to their left and right, and an array of white clouds in the center. When the clouds cleared a minute later, they could finally see what was in between the waterfalls. There were blue waters that led to a more expansive ocean once they had surpassed the active vigorous crash of the waterfalls.

Noah gulped. His eyes widened in fear at the unfamiliar

sight he was seeing. "Whelp, it looks like we're turning back around," he said as he turned his body from the dead end and attempted to walk away.

Diana immediately reached for his left hand and asked him, "Don't you want to see what the kids are so excited about when it comes to this particular spot?"

Noah wanted no parts of that. "Nah, I'm cool. I'm not dropping to my death today."

"Oh god!" Diana briefly covered her mouth as she laughed. "Noah, you can't die here. Everyone's already dead," she clarified.

"Yeah, everyone except for me, and today would be the day that it happened if I decide to do whatever you're trying to make me do. And hey, maybe the kids were specifically talking about the bridge and this cave," he replied while observing their surroundings.

"You won't die! Your spirit will be fine, Noah! And I feel like there's more to whatever is out there," she disclosed.

Diana instantly thought of a clever way to have Noah come with her. "Oh, my! Come here really quick. Look at that!" She exclaimed out of nowhere while pointing out of the tunnel toward the ocean.

"What—what is it?" Noah asked as he stepped up to take a peek out of the cave.

"Oh, nothing!" Diana said breezily while quickly grabbing hold of him and slowly leaning forward off the cliff.

"Yo! What the hell! Diana, chill! Are you crazy? WAIT! STOP!" He shouted while closing his eyes and tightly holding onto her as they fell.

When he suddenly opened his eyes, he realized that they were floating in the air way above the ocean. "Oh, lord! Thank God we're okay," Noah uttered in relief. "I see that we're flying again like before."

"I told you nothing would happen to you. Now let's go see what all the fuss is about," Diana declared while clinging on to Noah's arm as they flew above the immense waterfalls.

When they finally reached the expanse of the ocean, they witnessed a multitude of angels each holding onto a child while flying above the ocean's surface. It was breathtaking. There were also numerous children riding on humongous whales, dolphins, and sharks that were rapidly swimming in and out of the ocean. Right next to Diana and Noah, a flock of various gigantic birds appeared. Each giant bird had a child sitting on its back.

What in the world! There's no way in hell I'm actually seeing this. Am I really witnessing a bunch of children flying on the back of giant eagles, seagulls, toucans, and swans right now?

"Now I see what all the fuss is about!" Noah yelled, shouting over the thunderous roar of the waterfalls crashing into the ocean.

"Yeah, this is pure magic that we're watching take place!" Diana affirmed.

In a flash, they detected an enormous high rock cliff topped with gold and green grass floating in the air above the water. The cliff was surrounded by nothing but sparkling blue ocean water. No one was on it.

"I'm going to take us over there," Noah said as he flew him and Diana on top of the floating cliff. At this point, he had gotten a little more comfortable with his flying ability. Flying made him feel free, powerful, and more at peace. He absolutely loved it, but being in the presence of Diana made it a hundred times better.

As they softly landed and sat on the grass, Diana sat in between Noah's legs and laid her back against his chest. Noah wrapped his arms around her while they stared out into the bright sun, listening to the waves crash, the birds chirp, and the children laugh.

"Noah. Are you sure you want this?" Diana unexpectedly asked as she continued to stare at the magnificent view.

Noah looked down at Diana as the golden sun rays shined upon her face, and as the wind from the ocean blew her hair back. "Am I sure I want what?" he answered with a question.

"Are you sure you want me as your girl?" she wondered aloud while subtly caressing his forearm.

"Absolutely! More than anything in the world," Noah proclaimed.

Diana smiled happily and snuggled closer to him as she felt the affection of love travel all through her soul.

Right after that tender moment they shared, Noah suddenly felt something vibrating near the right side of his hip, but when he looked down he saw nothing there. He asked Diana, "Hey, do you feel that?"

She looked unclear as to what he was referring to. "Feel what?" Diana said quizzically.

"Like, something vibrating. I feel it right here. It—" At that exact moment when Noah reached for the vibrating motion on the side of his hip, he immediately zipped back into his physical body.

When he disappeared, Diana instantly fell on her back since his presence was no longer there to hold her.

Not again! I hate it when that boy is away from me, she thought while smirking and sniffing the sleeves of her sweater that still lingered with Noah's clean scent.

19

THE DATE

When Noah entered his body, he woke up and saw that he was holding his cellphone near the right side of his hip. As it vibrated again, he swiped the screen to see what was going on. "Damn!" he swore as he noticed that he had three unread text messages from Amber.

(Amber)
Hey Noah it's me!

Just letting you know that
I will be at the Museum by
6pm alright. See ya there!

(Amber)
Noah?

Just checking on you
because I haven't received
a response from you yet

Is everything okay?

(Amber)
Hey it's 5:48pm now

Are we still on?

(Noah)
Hey Amber I'm so sorry

My phone died and I
couldn't find my charger

And yes we are still on

Just give me about 15 minutes
And I'll be there okay

(Amber)
Awesome!

And aw that's okay it's
no rush at all I know this
art isn't going anywhere

See ya soon!

"5:50 p.m.—damn, I was gone for over 24 hours this time!" Noah said as he quickly checked the time on his phone.

After cleaning himself up and getting dressed, Noah rapidly drove to the art museum to meet up with Amber.

When he rushed into the building, he spotted her in the center of the front hallway. "Hey Amber, it's good to see you again. Sorry for being late," he greeted. Wanting to make sure things started out smoothly and observing her violet wrap dress, he added, "And you look great, by the way."

"Aw, that's okay. It's good to see you too! And thank you! I'm loving that brown blazer and black tie you're rocking! You've definitely got dress game!" she replied merrily as she hugged him.

"Well, ya know—I try!"

As they started walking through the halls and looking at the art on the walls, Amber began to make small talk. "So, Mr. Noah King, what type of art do you like? I'm a big fan of portraits," she revealed as she pointed to the paintings on the wall that displayed different faces. "It blows my mind how a painter can replicate what someone looks like on a canvas. That takes raw talent."

Noah pinched his lips and bobbed his head. "Yeah, portrait paintings are incredible, but, to be honest with you, I'm a fan of conceptual art because it has no boundaries. The artist can create any weird and crazy thing they want. As a person who studies the human brain, I always wonder what's going on in the artist's mind."

Noah pointed to a conceptual art piece he saw across the hall. "Like here, for instance." He and Amber began walking toward it. "There are a bunch of clothes scattered all over the floor, with a perfectly waxed chair sitting directly in the center." He slowly scanned the art. "Like, what was going on in the artist's mind here? I'm fascinated to know how his or her brain was working."

Amber thought Noah's concentration on the art piece

was charming. "Hmm," she murmured. "I'm fascinated to know what you think this artist was thinking."

With one arm folded across his chest, Noah placed his fist on his chin and tilted his head. "Well, I think the scattered and messy clothes represent malfunction, disorganization, and chaos. And the shiny waxed wooden chair represents cleanliness, organization, and peace. Now, maybe he or she grew up in a terrible household and had a terrible childhood, but remained hopeful, intact, and a beacon of light throughout all that chaos, which helped them strive for success."

Unexpectedly, a waiter appeared holding a tray of wine glasses. "Would you like wine, madam?" he asked Amber.

"Yes, thank you," she answered gratefully as she grabbed the wine glass and took a sip.

The waiter then turned to Noah. "What about you, sir?"

"No, thank you." Noah raised his hands slightly. "I don't drink."

Amber smoothed down her skirt and whispered, "I didn't know they served wine here."

"Me either." Noah wished the waiter was serving lemonade or water. He would've gladly taken those beverages instead.

"It's pretty good. Too bad you don't drink." Amber took another sip. "I have to admit, the way you broke down that art piece was kind of sexy. It's like there's some sophisticated 45-year-old man living inside you," she joked.

Aw, man!

Putting his hands in his pockets, Noah let out a moderate chuckle and bowed his head.

Amber's curiosity soon sparked another question. "So, how long have you been Mrs. Divine's therapist?"

He raised his head again. "Um, for about three weeks now."

"Oh, okay. She's such a sweet lady. It's a shame, what happened. I can tell losing Diana has really taken a toll on her . . . " Amber paused. "Her death took a toll on all of us, actually."

Noah slowly nodded. "Yeah, I'm sorry to hear about the loss of your friend. I know that was hard for you to endure."

BACK IN THE SPIRIT WORLD

At that moment, Diana was sitting near the beautiful creek she loved when she saw a small white portal appear by her side. Through the portal, she could see that her friend Amber was heavily thinking about her, but she could also see that Noah was with Amber and surrounded by artwork.

"What! No way! He still went on that date with her," she said to herself, clenching her hands into fists with an instant and unfamiliar surge of rage.

I trusted him.

After watching how happy Noah and Amber looked together, she decided not to send Amber a vivid memory and quickly waved off the portal, causing it to disappear.

"I can't believe he lied to me," she said under her breath.

BACK AT THE ART MUSEUM

"Thank you! Right after college, Diana was going to professionally model the outfits I designed, and we were basically going to go into the fashion business together. She was the sweetest person you could ever meet. People loved being around her because she just had a way of making everyone feel better about themselves. Everything about her was calming and exciting at the same time. It's kind of hard to explain. You know what? Some days, I even feel like she's still alive." Amber's heart was filled with abundant pain, but she did a substantial job hiding it.

Well in a way your friend is still alive. Kind of! She's just in another dimension, and there's no way you would believe that if I told you.

"Hey, do you happen to have two shirts and a brush that belonged to Diana?" Noah randomly asked.

Amber's eyes widened in complete surprise. "Yeah. Um . . . how do you know that?"

Noah gulped before spewing out his rehearsed lines. "Mrs. Divine explained to me that Diana told her about the things she left at your house a few months before she passed away. I guess she wants whatever she can have of Diana's . . . She really misses her, ya know. I know you do, too, but Mrs. Divine has been suffering from depression lately. So would it be possible for me to retrieve those items from you?" Noah smiled politely. "I could give them to her during her session."

Amber seemed to sincerely and fully understand Noah's explanation. "Oh. Yes, of course you can! I know Mrs. Divine is going through a much tougher time than I am. You can follow me back to my to place after we leave here, and I'll hand you everything there," she answered.

Noah was relieved to know that the first part of his plan was working. "Thank you so much. I know Mrs. Divine will appreciate this," he replied gratefully.

"No problem—anything for the Divine family," Amber responded as she began scanning Renaissance paintings while she and Noah strolled through the halls.

"Hey—I think Diana would have really liked you, by the way." she randomly put in.

Noah grinned and caressed the back of his neck.

I hope Diana finds a way to forgive me after going on this date with you. For some reason, I feel like she knows that I'm here right now. I can just feel her staring right at us!

"Wow! Believe it or not, Mrs. Divine actually told me the same thing ," he replied aloud.

Gazing at him, Amber knew that it was just a matter of time before she revealed everything that was on her mind. "Yeah, I believe it! I don't know what it is. There is just something about you that screams out MR. RIGHT. You're the type of guy a girl can take home to her parents," she admitted truthfully.

"I'm glad you feel that way, but I'm just being myself. I honestly just do my best to treat everyone with love and respect in any situation. In return, I hope that I receive that same energy back. It's all about staying positive and spreading positivity. Of course, it's impossible to be like that 24/7, because I definitely have those days where I'm upset. You just have to make sure your good days outweigh the bad ones," Noah explained thoughtfully.

"Well, yeah—see, that's the thing. I love how you just kept it real right now. It's genuinely hard to find that in a lot of people, especially with certain guys." Amber suddenly sucked her teeth. "Speaking of certain guys; I remember when Diana dated this a-hole named Tevin in high school. And my goodness, because of him, she and I almost ended our friendship for good . . ." She took another sip of wine. "Well, the majority of it was because of a mistake I made."

Noah was intrigued by this sudden news. "Wow. What happened, if you don't mind me asking?"

At first, Amber was hesitant to answer, but she finally went ahead and spoke. "It's a long story, but I'll start by explaining the type of guy her boyfriend Tevin was so you can get the full picture."

No, I just want to know what you did wrong. I don't care about knowing who this Tevin guy was, Noah thought as he began to feel a little envious.

"Tevin was an all-star basketball player at Bay Valley High, and because of his success and popularity at school, he was really cocky and a big flirt."

Yeah, Diana sort of told me that already.

"Matter of fact, he was a big cheater, and I mean a big-time cheater."

I know that too!

"I don't know how and why Diana put up with him for so long," Amber went on to explain.

Good point—because this Tevin guy definitely didn't deserve her at all.

"I soon realized that the reason every other girl put up with his nonsense was because of how charming and witty he was. I can't lie—the guy was extremely attractive, six foot six, dark skin with wavy hair and a beard. On top of that, he was always the life of the party, so eyes were always on him.

"And speaking of parties, one night during senior week, all of our little cliques were at Tevin's beach house, and for some reason that night after he saw me in my bikini, he kept following me and trying to dance with me. I guess you can say my curves captivated his horny ass. It was really annoying, and Diana didn't even notice what was going on because she was busy being bombarded by our other friends asking her to sign their yearbooks.

"Later on, after having about three beers, I was completely buzzed, and that buzzed part of me was falling for Tevin's charm. I was no longer ignoring him. I really feel bad saying this, but I was actually enjoying the attention he was showing me. When Tevin finally had the chance to corner me, he placed his arm against the wall and pretended like he and I were having a friendly conversation. He then asked me if I could come with him to his room. I immediately told him no, but Tevin didn't give up that easily. He just kept saying, 'You know you want to,' and then he eventually leaned closer to my face and kissed me..." Amber took a deep breath and paused for a moment. "Now, here's where it gets worse.

"When he kissed me, I didn't pull back. Like, I didn't even attempt to. I enjoyed it and put my arms around him and we kept kissing, using tongue and all. When the crowd noise died down, I stopped and saw that Diana and all of our friends had witnessed the whole thing. I could see the humiliation written all over her face, and I felt like the scum of the earth when I saw her reaction. There was nothing but awkward silence, while everyone continued to stare at us. Diana quickly grabbed her things and told Tevin it was over, doing all she could to keep herself from crying. Tevin didn't seem to care, though, and he asked me again if I wanted to come to his room. At that point, I came out of my drunken stupor, pushed him out the way, and chased after Diana as she ran out of the house. What kind of best friend was I?"

Not a great one. Noah thought.

"By the time I made it outside to go talk to her, she had already driven off. I remember trying to apologize to her every day, but she avoided me and blocked my number. This was a very low point in my life because I had no one to reach out to. All summer, I felt isolated. The only good part about all of this was that we didn't have to return to high school to face the embarrassment of what transpired that night.

"After what I'd done, I felt like I needed a new identity; so that summer, I got a buzz cut and dyed my hair blonde. That sort of helped me feel better, but Diana didn't talk to me for like three months until we met up in college again. She liked the new look, too. Thank God she was nice enough to forgive me and move on from it all. After we had a long talk about how dumb I was for doing what I did, we seemed to automatically click again. And you know what's crazy, she never even told her parents or her Mom-Mom about what happened between us. I don't think she's ever told anyone. Apparently, that summer when her parents would ask her where I was, she would just tell them that I was busy with fashion stuff. I'm pretty sure Diana never really got over it, though, because things always felt awkward between us whenever we hung out after that," Amber revealed.

Oh—now I know why Diana didn't want me to go on a date with you. Diana is still affected by the past. She was afraid that you and I would hook up like you and Tevin did. She probably believes that I would end up falling for you, too.

Noah noticed that Amber hadn't mentioned her friend Samantha yet. "So, was there another friend that you and Diana had that helped bridge that gap of awkwardness?" he asked intelligently.

Amber smiled. "Yeah, Samantha! Meeting her in college was perfect timing for Diana and me. She was more like the glue that held everything together, but Samantha hasn't really been the same person after the accident. She still blames herself for everything that happened. She just sits at home depressed all day . . . but I think that's enough sadness for now. I'm sorry, I just don't want to start crying while I'm in this museum. Are you ready to get Diana's things?"

Noah nodded. "Yeah, sure. We've pretty much seen all the artwork, so I'm ready when you are."

~~~

After following Amber to her house, Noah parked out front and watched her walk up her steps. "Wow, she lives in a nice-looking mansion. Damn, this neighborhood is full of them," he said to himself while checking out his surroundings.

Suddenly, Amber turned back around and approached Noah's car.

Aw, what now?

"Hey, do you want to come in?" she asked welcomingly.

"Uh, that's okay. I don't want to hold you up or anything. I can wait here," Noah answered.

Amber unleashed a sultry giggle, "It's okay, you won't hold me up. Come on in!" she begged.

Great—now I don't have a choice, he thought as he followed her to the front door.

"One moment—just gotta unlock the two locks on my door really quick," Amber said, searching through her purse to find her keys.

As they walked into the mansion, Noah observed a circular white staircase that led to the top floor, where a glassy chandelier hung. The floor in Amber's mansion was entirely covered with marble, which complemented the white leather couches in her living room.

"This is a really nice place!" Noah indicated while turning from side to side.

"Thank you! Is this your first time in a mansion?" Amber wondered.

"Yes. Surprisingly, it is!" He laughed, then followed it up by asking, "Diana lived close to you, right?"

Amber was a bit thrown off, but she answered anyway. "Um, yeah, the Divines' home is about a mile away from mine. You know how you saw the number 94 on my mailbox out front?"

"Yeah, I saw that."

"Well, if you head directly down the road and see a mailbox with the number 110, then that means you'll be right in front of their mansion."

Noah made sure he remembered Diana's address, but he acted as if he didn't care about where she lived so he wouldn't blow his cover. "Oh, okay! So are these your parents right here?" he asked, looking at a family picture of Amber with two people he assumed to be her mom and dad that was hanging above her gold fireplace.

"Yes, but they aren't home right now," Amber specified with a smirk, obviously hinting that she wanted to do more than just talk about her parents. "Come with me! Diana's stuff is in my room," she ordered as she trotted upstairs.

Aw man, she's not giving up at all.

When he followed Amber into her room, she promptly turned to him and smiled. "Thanks for everything today! You're a great listener."

Noah nervously looked around the room, trying to avoid Amber's seductive eyes. "You're welcome. It was great hanging out with you today. Thanks for inviting me to the museum. I really enjoyed it!"

As Noah finished, Amber was slowly approaching him. "You're welcome, but let's skip all the small talk for now," she said, her eyes loaded with total desire.

No, please stop!

Amber could no longer contain herself. When she got close enough, she leaned in for a kiss and attempted to wrap her arms around Noah's waist, but he quickly moved out the way before any of their body parts could touch.

Amber immediately grew frustrated. "What the fuck is wrong with you, Noah?" she demanded. "I don't get it! Do you not like girls or something? Or do you think I'm ugly?"

Noah giggled slightly. "Yes, I like girls, and no, I don't

think you're ugly at all. You're really attractive—and I mean *really* attractive. If my heart wasn't somewhere else, I would be all over you right now. It's just that I'm still in love with someone," he divulged.

Amber folded her arms, frowned, and shifted from one foot to the other. "What? The Divines didn't tell me that you were in a relationship or that you were seeing anyone."

Noah knew that lying to Amber was better than telling her the truth about him and Diana. "Um, it's my ex—she died a couple years ago, and I'm still not over her. The Divines don't know about that part of my life; so can we just keep this between us, please? It's been a tough couple years for me." He gave her a sincere look.

Amber instantly felt bad. She began handing him Diana's things one by one, saying, "Oh, you poor thing. I'm so sorry for your loss. Now I know why you weren't showing me any signs of being interested. I feel horrible! If you ever need or want to talk about anything, just let me know, okay? I can't imagine losing someone you were in a relationship with."

Thank God that worked.

Noah was getting closer and closer to completing his plan. "Thank you for understanding, Amber, and I'm sorry for wasting your time."

"Oh no, don't worry about it. I'm glad I got the chance to meet you and talk with you. If you're ever up to it in the far future, we should definitely hang out again."

"Yeah, that'll be great!"

"Ugh, I feel so bad now," she said honestly. "Let me just give you a hug. Can I give you a hug?"

I don't see why not.

"Sure," Noah said as he and Amber embraced.

"Thanks for the comfort, Amber. I'm glad this worked

out well."

"You're welcome. I'll never come on to you like that again, but I would really like to be your friend. I think we both have a subject we can sort of relate to now, and I would love to talk to you on the days I'm feeling low." Amber said as she released him. "And, of course, it won't be like actual therapy sessions. I don't want you to feel like you're at work. I just want us to have a heart to heart."

"Sounds good," he replied. "I would like that!"

~~~

After retrieving Diana's items, Noah drove down the road to take a look at the Divines' home. "Here it is, mailbox 110," he said to himself while pulling up to a silver mailbox on the side of the road.

When he looked up, he noticed that he was in front of the mansion and near the top of a long driveway. He observed that the green grass on the wide lawn was freshly cut and saw an angel fountain in the center of the yard with engraved words reading *'Dedicated to our beloved daughter Diana Divine'* on the base.

"You'll be back here soon, Diana . . . I promise," he whispered as he drove away.

20

BAD TIMING

About an hour later, Noah headed to the drug store to purchase candles for the ritual. While shopping, he went ahead and grabbed some sleeping pills just in case he needed to see Diana if anything went wrong.

I know my mom doesn't want me buying these things, but I'll most likely need to use them tonight.

While searching through random aisles, he unexpectedly ran into Claudia. He noticed she was wearing a black and white striped shirt, shoes, and leggings.

Wow, this girl loves patterns and obsessively matching, he thought.

"Well, look who it is! Hey Noah, you're looking dapper today. What are you doing here, and why are you dressed so sharp?" she asked joyfully.

"Hey, Claudia. I'm just here looking for candles, that's all. My mom needs them for the house. And I just came from a friend's showcase at an art gallery," Noah answered, coming up with a quick lie.

Claudia simpered and took it upon herself to take a piece of lint off of Noah's blazer. "Sorry, you had a little something stuck on your clothes. And aw, that's cool. You should invite me next time!" she teased. "So, you live around here?"

"Yup, all my life."

"Wow, I didn't know you were commuting. I wish I was! My family and I are from the east coast part of the map—New York City!" Claudia explained.

"Yeah, New York City is a long way from Silverside, California!" Noah stated factually.

"I know, right? But I don't mind it. Silverside is a beautiful place!"

After a brief pause, it was clear that Claudia thought Noah could use some help shopping. "Does your mom know what particular scent she wants when it comes to the candles? Because I could help you find some," she hinted, turning her shopping cart toward him.

Thanks, but that's probably not a good idea, Noah thought.

"Sure, that would be great! Thank you!" he said aloud.

Why am I so nice? I hope she doesn't get the wrong idea like Amber did.

"My mom didn't tell me to pick a specific scent. I think she's fine with whichever one I choose, as long as it doesn't stink," Noah joked as they walked down the candle aisle.

Claudia gave a cute laugh. "Well, I'll make sure that

you'll pick the ones that smell good!" she said as she walked toward a shelf. "Okay, so they have cinnamon scent, lemon scent, red apple, summer night, Hawaiian love, honey spring, and winter forest. Those are all my personal favorites," she informed Noah while pointing at the candles.

Noah slowly observed each candle she talked about. "Hm, I'll go with two of the honey spring ones since it's spring time," he said as he collected the candles.

Claudia smiled. "Great choice! You take sleeping pills?" she wondered suddenly, catching a glimpse of what was inside Noah's grocery basket.

Caught off guard, Noah quickly pulled the grocery basket to his side. "Uh, yeah. I need it sometimes after a long day of work."

"Oh, I understand." Claudia nodded. "Based on what Mrs. Wright has told me, I can tell that you're a work-horse."

Noah looked from side to side, not knowing what to say. "Yeah, I'm addicted to work. I can't help it. Sooo um, how has your day been going so far?"

Why would I ask her that? I have to make it home ASAP!

Mildly blushing, Claudia used both her hands to briefly fluff her curly hair. "It's been fine so far. I'm buying food and drinks for a party tonight. My sorority is hosting it! If things still aren't working out with that girl you should come."

"Cool, thanks for inviting me! I'll truly think about it, okay." Noah sincerely told her.

"Okay!" Claudia winked. Her emerald eyes were filled with hope.

I have to go now. Like right now!

"Uh—I want to thank you for helping me, Claudia, but I have to go purchase these candles and hurry home now."

They were slowly walking out of the aisle and toward the self-checkout line. Claudia smiled at him. "You're welcome, Noah. I owed ya one. It was the least I could do after you helped me with the psychology project. I hope your mom likes the candles, and hopefully we run into each other again. If not by tonight then *hopefully* by the time I'm finished with school."

Noah waved at her, quickly checking out his three items, "That's definitely a possibility. With graduation happening and all, we'll see each other again," he said.

"Alrighty, can't wait! See ya, Noah!"

Man, oh, man! Amber and Claudia are really nice and attractive girls, but my heart is somewhere else. This was all just bad timing in the universe's space-time continuum.

21

MRS. DIVINE KNOWS BEST

That night, at the Divines' place, Barry Jr. was really bothered by the fact his mom wouldn't talk to him. "Mom, what's your deal with Amber? Does she upset you so much that it's causing you not to talk to me or Vivian? Because you haven't said a word to us all day," he complained.

Mrs. Divine remained quiet and continued not answering her son. However, Vivian suddenly came speed-walking into the living room with a joyous look on her face. "Guess what? I got a call from Amber, and she said the date went great. She thinks Noah and her will be going out again soon!"

Barry Jr. was delighted to hear this. "That's fantastic! It

looks like you and I are good at setting people up."

"Mm-hm," Mrs. Divine hummed.

"After hearing that just now, I can only guess how my mom is about to react," he said as he faced his mother.

"She doesn't look pleased," Vivian noticed. She could see the distaste on her mother-in-law's face.

"Sorry, Mom, but I have to ask you something," Barry Jr. announced, knowing that questioning his mother would probably cause an even bigger argument.

"Ask me what?"

"Do you have a crush on your therapist?"

At that point, Mrs. Divine had had enough and could no longer keep silent. Pressing her hands to her cheeks, she yelled, "GOD NO, Jr.! What in the world! The boy is old enough to be my grandchild. How could you possibly even think that?" She let out a huff. "I'm just sick of you two trying to act like Amber is your daughter. It's like you're trying to replace Diana and throw poor Noah into your twisted little fantasy by grooming him to be your pretend son-in-law."

Vivian approached Mrs. Divine and sat down by her side. "Aw, Momma Divine, we would never try to replace Diana. That's our blood. At the same time, Amber has always been like a daughter to Barry and I, you know that. Now, I don't know why you feel like she's some sleazy girl, but she is honestly a great woman. We just thought it would be nice to set up two young single people who are both on the journey toward success. There's no harm in that," she explained, trying to reason with Mrs. Divine.

Barry Jr. was appalled by how his mother could think that he and Vivian would ever attempt to replace Diana. "Mom, how could you honestly believe that I would try to replace my own daughter? And, as a matter of fact, what about you?"

Mrs. Divine grimaced. "What about me? What the hell do you mean *what about me?*" she replied

"This thing with you and Noah. You just tried to call out Vivian and me about us wanting him to be a pretend son-in-law, but I haven't forgotten about your little comments and the way you acted at the Care Center. You were so on the defense about him going out with Amber that you even brought your deceased granddaughter into the situation. I just don't get it! Thank God I know you don't have a crush on him now, but if I didn't know any better, I would go on to say that you somehow think Noah is your actual grandson-in-law," Barry Jr. explained.

Mrs. Divine shrugged. "Well, he sort of is," she said confidently.

"WHAT?" Barry Jr. and his wife Vivian shouted at once.

"You heard me!" Mrs. Divine no longer cared about keeping this secret just between her and Noah. "That's right, Noah and Diana are together—or at least they're destined to be together, from what I've witnessed."

Vivian rose from her seat and clutched Barry Jr.'s arm. "Maybe these therapeutic sessions weren't such a good idea after all. Momma Divine, do you hear yourself?" she asked. "Noah can't possibly be involved with Diana. She's—she's dead!"

Mrs. Divine nodded with a stubborn look on her face. "I hear myself just fine, thank you," she answered. "And she's actually alive in the spirit dimension, and that's how Noah communicates with her. I think he's able to travel to the spirit dimension every night."

"Listen, Mom." Barry Jr. knelt down in front of his mother and held her hands. "I know that you miss Diana and that she and Noah would've most likely made a great couple, but going around pretending like they're together isn't healthy for any of us. You have to understand that she's gone, Mom. She's gone."

"Now, wait just a minute." Mrs. Divine looked her son piercingly in the eyes. "Barry Vincent Divine Jr., don't talk to me like I'm some senile old lady. I am not playing pretend here. In my dream, Diana personally told me that she met Noah and that she likes him. That girl was glowing and blushing as soon as I mentioned his name."

"That's exactly what these are, Mom! They're dreams, and they're not real!" Barry Jr. snapped.

"They are real!" Mrs. Divine snapped back. "Noah even admitted to meeting her too. That young man really has a gift that allows him to see spirits and travel through spirit dimensions like I mentioned before. Now, I don't know exactly how he does it, but I'm telling you the truth. And he really loves your daughter too, and God has made them soulmates whether you like it or not."

Barry Jr. and Vivian looked extremely baffled. "This woman has gone mad! We have to talk to Noah as soon as possible," Barry Jr. whispered to his wife right after leaving his mom's side.

"Yeah, you're right, but let's wait until tomorrow morning to give him a call. I don't want to bother him tonight with all of this chaos," Vivian answered. "Do you think she talks like this in front of him?"

"Most likely! And the poor kid probably has no choice but to ignore her or go along with whatever she says."

Watching Barry Jr. and Vivian whisper to each other, Mrs. Divine could tell that they were talking about her. "When Noah finally decides to tell you the truth, don't get angry with him, Barry Vincent Divine Jr., or you're going to have to deal with me. He's an incredibly sweet young man, and I'm going to let you two know this right now. I believe your daughter is genuinely happy with him, and you wouldn't want to take away her happiness, now would you?"

Barry Jr. shook his head, "Yeah, I doubt he'll admit to whatever you're talking about, but okay, Mom, I'll play along with this little game of yours for now. If Noah just so happens to tell the truth as you call it, then I won't get angry with him or try to hurt him. I promise you it will be a pleasant conversation and that I'll be on my best behavior," he explained, hoping that this would end their conversation.

Mrs. Divine knew that her son and Vivian weren't convinced that her story was real. She could tell that they were just starting to see her as some deranged old lady; so she tried to open up their minds by taking a much smoother approach with her words this time. "Vivian, do you have faith that you'll see Diana again someday?" she queried.

Vivian slowly nodded, "Yes, Momma Divine, I know I will." she answered.

"Okay. And what about you, Barry? Do you have faith that you'll see Diana again someday?"

"Yes, Mom, I do."

Mrs. Divine sat back against the couch comfortably and shook her head. "You two didn't sound confident at all. What happened to the hope and faith you used to have? It seems like you've lost it. If you truly had faith in seeing your daughter again, then you would believe me. That's okay, though, because I know you two will see her again— and so will I, trust me. One day, she'll send you a sign proving that she was always with you and is still always with you. And thanks to Noah, that sign may come pretty soon! Just watch and see!" she said as she finally put an end to their discussion.

22

THE STORM

That same night, when everyone was asleep at Noah's house, he turned off the lights, gathered all of Diana's belongings along with the lit candles, and placed them in his closet. When he shut the closet door, he took a deep breath and prepared to do the ritual.

"Okay, here goes nothing," Noah said, placing his hands on the closet door. "Diana, I summon you, Diana, I summon you, Diana, I summon you."

After waiting for about three minutes, Noah heard nothing.

Where is she? I'm pretty sure I did it right.

Losing patience, he opened the closet door and saw nothing but the items he'd placed there.

"What the hell!" He scanned the closet, hoping that something would appear.

"Oh yeah, that's right—I need her spirit here with me to perform the ritual. How did I forget about that part?" Reaching into his bag, Noah grabbed the jar of sleeping pills he'd bought at the store.

Sorry, Mom, but desperate times call for desperate measures.

He swallowed two pills.

"Come on, kick in already! I need to see Diana right away," Noah said as he paced around the room, impatiently waiting for the pills to subdue him.

After forty-five minutes of pacing, Noah's eyes began to grow heavy and he was losing control of his balance. He suddenly dropped face-first onto the floor and fell into a deep sleep.

Moments later, he heard footsteps drawing near him. As he lifted his face off of the carpet and stood up, he saw that his physical body was planted face down on the floor which assured him that he was astral projecting.

Man, those pills do work! I didn't even make it to the damn bed.

When he pivoted to his right, he saw Diana storming toward him. Her hands were infused with a white glowing substance that resembled fire.

Aw damn, she looks pissed. I'm assuming she knows about Amber and I.

"Hey, I—"

"LIAR!" Diana instantaneously cut him off by striking him with a deafening blow to the chest.

Noah went soaring into the air, crashing onto the wall and then tumbling to the ground. He didn't feel any pain at all, though. It just felt like a forceful wind had overpowered him.

Oh god! Maybe I deserved that, he thought while plastered to the carpet.

Seconds later, he heard a thump on the opposite side of his room.

When he timidly peeked above his bed, he saw Diana sitting on his rolling chair with her arms folded across her chest. The white fire on her hands seemed to have dissipated.

"Hey, I didn't know you could do that. You never told me about that power specifically."

She ignored him.

I didn't know I had it either, but I'm glad I do, she thought. *It felt good knocking you on your ass.*

"Look, I know I deserved that, and I'm sorry for breaking my promise, but I think I found a way for the ritual to actually work. I just needed you here with me first . . . I think," Noah said with a lack of confidence as he slowly approached her.

Diana didn't answer him, just giving him a serious straight-faced look. Her bottom lip was slightly tucked into her mouth, her glistening hazel eyes locked onto his.

"Oh, so you're not talking to me, huh?" he said soothingly.

Diana continued to ignore him, her soul still filled with the desire for vengeance.

Noah exhaled with frustration. "Okay, you don't want to talk? Fine . . . I'll just sit right here directly in front of you then and continue to talk your head off," he said as he sat down on the side of his bed, facing her.

"Okay, I know you're pissed about the date. I'm sorry, all right! How many times do I have to say it?"

Still, there was no peep from Diana.

"Just letting you know—nothing happened on that date with Amber and I."

Diana rolled her eyes and briefly looked in another direction.

Noah was not giving up on trying to get her to respond. "She gave me your two shirts and your old brush. And that was what I needed to execute the plan. Everything worked out smoothly."

All of sudden, Noah's computer screen brightened as a message popped up on his *Gossip Place* account. The message was from Claudia.

DAMN, not now!

Noah wished he could've somehow distracted Diana from seeing the message, but he knew it was too late. Diana instantly turned her attention to the computer screen, since she was sitting right next to it. She then observed what the message said:

Gossip Place

[Claudia]

Hey Noah it was great running into you today!

Let me know how your mom likes the candles.

And I would honestly love it if you could find a way to make it to the party tonight!

I know you told me about your funny situation and all but if that girl isn't showing you any love she doesn't deserve your attention.

I'm sorry.

I don't mean to keep bringing it up.

I just want you to know that you're
an amazing guy!

Have great night! ;)

Diana unleashed a slight chuckle that automatically grew into huge laughter. "Oh wow, based on her profile pic here, I can tell she's really pretty!" she said, finally speaking. "I guess you really are *quite the charmer*, huh? So who's Claudia?"

At that moment, time stood still for Noah. He moderately shook his head. *Unbelievable! Now she wants to talk? And how the fuck am I going to explain my way out of this situation? Thank you, Claudia! Thank you very much for this awkward moment!*

He slowly huffed. "Claudia is just a girl from school. I barely even know her. I just helped her with her project the other day, that's it. I'm not interested or anything, if that's what you're thinking." He prepared to reveal even more. "That same day, she asked me if I had a girlfriend. This was before you and I were official, and I told her it was complicated. She assumed I liked a girl who didn't like me back. I really didn't know what to say back to her. I couldn't tell her the truth about me being involved with a spirit. You understand that, right?"

Really—then why is she sending you winky faces? You probably flirt with her all the time.

"Whatever," Diana responded as she rolled her eyes again and looked away, pretending like she didn't care.

"You're a liar! You still went on that date with my best friend when you told me you wouldn't, and you never ever mentioned this Claudia girl 'til you got caught just now. I should've never fallen for your charm. You're just like the rest of the guys I've known in the past."

Noah instantly pulled Diana's rolling chair closer to him. "Amber told me about that situation that happened with her and your ex Tevin."

Diana was surprised. *She did?* she thought as she chose not to respond.

"I know what happened to you that night was horrible. Trust me I know the exact feeling. But you really don't have to worry about Amber taking me away from you, or Claudia for that matter, if that's what's eating you up inside. I want you to know, I'm nothing like that asshole Tevin, and I'll never be anything like him. Diana, the main reason why I want this ritual to work is because I want nothing else but you! Can't you see that?" Noah was explaining this whole-heartedly. "Look, you complete me, okay! Every time I see your face you make me feel whole and rejuvenated, like I was just granted a brand new life. No woman has ever made me feel that way before. I guess it's that *magic of romance* thing your Mom-Mom always talks about."

Diana flipped her long flowing hair back behind her shoulders and stared directly into Noah's eyes. Although her face displayed no emotion, the words coming from his mouth was like music to her ears. Watching him pour his heart out to her made her feel like a princess who had just found her prince charming.

Why do you have to be so damn perfect, Noah King?

Noah sighed after Diana continued to sit there and stare at him. "Okay, so now we're back at this again, and you're still not going to talk—"

Diana quickly grabbed Noah by his tie, yanking him close to her. She leaned her face into his and passionately kissed him. Once more, that warm and electrifying spark surged through their souls, but this time something was different. They felt more of a rush, as if it was blood racing through their souls the same way it rushes through a person's veins.

In the heat of the moment, they both stood up with their lips still pressed against one another. Noah then firmly grabbed Diana by her waist, causing their kiss to grow even more intense. As their mouths sensually connected, their souls began to shine brighter than ever before. The energy and passion they felt just from kissing felt better than sex in the flesh. Unable to contain herself, Diana started stroking her hands all over Noah's body. As her hands went exploring inside of his shirt, she relished feeling each crevasse and muscle on his fit frame. Diana then gave Noah a slight push, causing him to sit on his bed. She climbed on top of him and hugged him intimately.

At that exact moment it began to rain in the city of Silverside. Paying no mind to the sounds of the raindrops splashing against the windows, Noah started to gently caress his fingers through Diana's hair and down her back. He kissed her up and down her neck, causing her to whimper. Acting on impulse, Diana unlaced Noah's tie and threw it to the ground. Subsequently, they took off each other's clothes one by one until their spiritual bodies were no longer covered. Diana then laid her back directly onto the bed, and Noah followed suit, climbing on top of her. The pace of the rain was now growing immensely, showing possible signs of a storm to come.

When their spirits finally intertwined, Diana moaned breathlessly. It was the most intimate and passionate feeling they'd ever felt. The sensations Diana was feeling caused her eyes to glow as bright as the sun. The light coming from both her and Noah's spiritual auras began to swirl and twirl around the room like confetti at a New Year's party. A storm was now raging in the city of Silverside. The storm eventually grew louder and shook the skies more vigorously than ever before.

After the intense climax, Diana and Noah's spiritual energies steadily began to simmer down. At that exact moment, the booming storm automatically calmed. With their spirits drained and now in the process of recharging, they lovingly cuddled underneath the comfy blankets.

While Diana's back was up against Noah's chest, he smoothly wrapped his arm around her, and Diana repeatedly kissed their intertwined hands until she fell asleep. Noah, on the other hand, smelled Diana's flowery lavender-scented hair until he zonked out. That warm and electrifying spark they would occasionally feel prior to what transpired was now there to stay; establishing a connection that their souls would forever feel whenever they were around each other.

23

HAPPY BIRTHDAY DIANA

The next morning when the sun rose above the city, Noah woke to an amazing sight. He and Diana were now face to face, even though she was still asleep. The sunlight beamed through the window behind him and reflected onto the white pillow and blanket that Diana was sleeping on, complementing her glowing, medium-brown skin.

Although Noah's sight still had a blue tint, the sunlight gave him a captivating view.

Unbelievable! Her beauty stays intact even when she's sleeping.

He caressed her face and subtly kissed her lips. Right after Noah's kiss, Diana opened her eyes and smiled. Her radiant smile and angelic look made his soul flutter. "Happy Birthday, Diana," he whispered.

"Thank you, handsome!" she replied, stretching her arms and yawning with no shame, since her breath was permanently minty.

"I would buy you a cake to eat, but it would just fall right through your body," Noah joked.

Diana laughed so hard she ended up snorting. "You're such a goofball," she said. Rubbing his facial hair, Diana came to a sudden realization. "Oh my god, this is the first time I've slept in over ten months!" she exclaimed.

Noah was intrigued. The thought of spirits sleeping or being permanently awake had never crossed his mind before. "Interesting. Did you dream about anything?" he asked as if he were Diana's therapist.

"Nah, I was just resting and saw nothing but darkness."

"Yeah, me too: I didn't dream about anything either. It's probably impossible for spirits to dream . . . Maybe falling asleep for spirits isn't normal," Noah replied.

"It's probably normal. I think it all depends on how much of our energy we consume, especially in something like what we did last night," Diana explained with a smirk.

"Hmm, I guess you're right. You would know more about this spirit stuff than I do."

Randomly, Noah began to wonder about her past relationship. "Hey, Diana," he began, "so, umm, what did you ever see in that Tevin guy?"

"Wow! That question came out of nowhere. Why do you want to know?"

"Because I can't picture a great woman like you with a guy like that," he explained. "Like—what were you even thinking?"

"Hey, I wasn't some perfect angel, okay?"

"You could've fooled me."

Diana rolled her eyes. "I was more attracted to him physically than emotionally and mentally. He was the class clown, always in detention, flirted with all the girls because they all wanted him, and he made sure everyone felt his presence. He was the quote-unquote 'bad boy' and the cutest guy in school. Unfortunately, a lot of young girls go through phases where they fall for guys like Tevin."

Noah snorted. "Wow, that explains it."

"Hey! Not so fast—it's not like I was the only one who had a bad relationship and chose the wrong partner. What did you see in Sheila?"

"My oh my, where do I start?" Noah contemplated the question. "Well, I was recommended to be her study partner to help her pass our science class. From then on, we were good friends, and eventually we connected. We loved being around each other, so our friendship grew into a relationship. But like I told you before, that all ended during our eleventh-grade prom. Sheila was everything to me . . . I just wasn't everything to her."

By the look on Noah's face, Diana could tell that his ex really tore his heart apart. She couldn't understand how someone could do that to such a pure soul. "Aww well, forget her—because now you're my everything."

"I couldn't have said it better than that! So how do you feel, birthday girl?"

"I feel brand new and replenished. This has definitely been one of my favorite birthdays so far, I can tell ya that much."

"Well, it's about to get even better," Noah said as he gave her a quick kiss. Sitting up on the bed, he started to put on his clothes. "Now, when you get a chance, I'll need you to get ready—because I'm going to help you see your family again, and you'll be with all of us for good this time."

"I really hope this plan of yours works. You seem really confident about it," she said as she got dressed underneath the bedsheets.

"It will! I know it will!" Noah couldn't wait any longer. "Are you ready to try it out?" he asked eagerly.

Diana gave him the most hopeful smile ever and climbed out of his bed. "Yeah, let's do it."

Noah approached his closet door and opened it. "Okay, so your only job is to stand in here by these candles and your old belongings."

Before Diana entered the closet, Noah gave her a tight hug like it was last time he would ever see her.

"Boy! It's okay, you're going to see me again. I'm just going to be here in the flesh this time around . . . I hope," Diana said wistfully as Noah slowly released her.

"Yeah, I know I'll see you again, and you're right—this time, things will be different; so head on in," Noah answered.

He watched her walk into the closet before closing it. "All right, I'm about to perform the ritual now. Are you ready?" he asked, leaning his ear against the door to hear her response.

"Ready," Diana answered.

Please work, Noah thought to himself.

"Okay, here it is. DIANA, I SUMMON YOU. DIANA, SUMMON YOU. DIANA, SUMMON YOU," he chanted.

What? That's the ritual? What kind of ritual is that? It sounds like a five-year-old made it up, Diana thought to herself.

After waiting for a few minutes, Noah grew curious. "Do you feel or look any different?"

Diana looked down at her semi-transparent hands. "No, I don't feel any different. And I'm pretty sure I'm still glowing," she told him from inside the closet.

Noah hurriedly opened his closet door. "SHIT!" he yelled when he saw that Diana was still in spirit form.

He panicked, quickly slamming the door and repeating the ritual. "DIANA, I SUMMON YOU. DIANA, I SUMMON YOU. DIANA, I SUMMON YOU!"

Diana still felt nothing; no human flesh appeared on her body, and she was still glowing. "Noah, I don't think it's working," she informed him.

"You've got to be kidding me," he said while opening the door once again.

Frustrated, he pulled out his phone from the pocket of his physical body where it was lying on the ground and logged onto TheGhostFeed.com website. "I have to contact this 'Dimension Lover' girl. I paid her a lot to receive information about this ritual."

Diana frowned. "You really shouldn't have paid her $500 for this crap! Noah, I know we argued about this before, and I don't want to get into a heated debate again, but I honestly feel like this woman scammed you."

Noah walked away from Diana, since he was still frustrated and angry. "You're not helping," he said under his breath while searching for the Dimension_Lover account.

After minutes of searching, he could not find her account anywhere. He logged onto the "I'm In Love With The Dead" public group chat.

[SPIRITMAN20#]
Hey has anyone heard or seen from
Dimension_Lover?

[GHOSTBUSTER3]
Nope I haven't heard
from her in awhile

I wonder whatever happened
to her because she was supposed
to reveal some secret to me about
bringing the dead back to life

[BLOODSUCKER*]
No, I've been searching for that
crazy woman all day!

She owes me money!

I knew something was off
about her

[DEAD-RESIDENTS]
Man she owes me money too

I paid $500 for a ritual that didn't work

Now I'm trying to find a way to sue her

[BLOODSUCKER*]
OMG yes she told me I could
bring my grandmother back to
life with the same ritual she possibly
told you all about

But guess what?

The damn ritual never even worked!

[DEAD-RESIDENTS]
She told me I could bring

my best-friend back to life

[CasperGirl]
You guys!

Dimension_Lover was banned
from the site recently for
ripping people off

Apparently she's scammed hundreds
of people over the past year

And you guys are idiots for
paying someone $500 for
some fake ritual

Who in their right mind would
do that

[The3rdEyeGuy]
Unfortunately she swindled me too

I just found out she's been doing it
for more than a year

This has been happening for at least
three years on different sites.

[Bloodsucker*]
Thanks for the news but you
don't have to be a name calling
ass-hole about it

[THE3RDEYEGUY]
Who me?

[BLOODSUCKER*]
No not YOU!

I'm talking about CasperGirl

We just lost a bunch of money
and she wants to call us names

It was so uncalled for

[CASPERGIRL]
Whatever if you don't like me
being truthful then just leave
the chat room

[GHOSTGIRL98]
Hey Spiritman20#

Where have you been?

You never replied back to me

Message me back baby

;)

~~~

After reading most of the comments in the chat room, Noah logged off. "SON OF A BITCH!" he shouted, tossing his phone onto the bed.

Diana placed her hands on her hips and shook her head.

"I told you it was a scam! You should've known that by the way you chanted the ritual."

Noah was pissed. "You know what, Diana, you're really not helping the fucking situation!" he snapped.

Excuse me! Diana thought, her jaw dropping.

She shifted her weight to her right side, keeping her hands on her hips. "I'm sorry, but may I remind you that I'm the one who believed in you and supported however you wanted to execute this ridiculous plan. We should've— I mean you should've been more logical and realistic about it," she answered in an uncouth tone as she walked away from Noah to sit on the bed.

"Nothing about this shit is logical! Hell, it doesn't even seem realistic at times!" Noah squealed. "I honestly don't even know how this is going to work."

"Wait—you don't know how what's going to work? What are you talking about?" Diana asked, looking disheartened.

"I'm talking about us! I don't know how this relationship between us is going to work."

"Don't say that. I'm going to pretend like you didn't just say that," she answered, trying to keep her composure.

Thinking about his and Diana's situation, Noah began to laugh maniacally, as if he were in an asylum.

"Oh my god, look at what's happening right now!" Still upset about the ritual not working, he was going to continue taking out his frustration on her and saying things he didn't really mean. "I'm talking to a freaking spirit, I'm having an out-of-body experience, and I can't even talk to people about what I'm going through because they would think I'm a damn lunatic. Diana, let's face the facts! You're dead and I'm alive! This whole thing is crazy, and you know it. Like, why are you even here? And what are we even doing? What the hell am I supposed to tell people when they want to know why I'm not going on dates or don't plan on getting married and having kids? What do I say then? Should I say: 'Oh no, sorry, I can't do any of those things because I'm in love with a damn ghost, and that's that!'?"

All of Noah's harsh words struck Diana right in the soul. She was so stung, she couldn't work herself up to respond beyond letting irrepressible tears run down her face.

"Do you expect me to have an explanation for that? Like I said before, they would just look at me like a damn lunatic and put me in a mental institution," Noah continued to rant.

Suddenly, Diana stood up. Her spiritual energy was filled with rage, her hair beginning to blow briskly in the wind she was creating. The white fiery substance reappeared on her hands, and the room went chill.

Noah's folders, posters, papers, and books began to fly all around his room like a tornado. *HOLY SHIT!* he thought.

Seeing what was happening, Noah's anger simmered down. He instantly regretted the harsh things he'd just said. "Diana, calm down! You're destroying my room!" he protested.

It was too late, though: Diana had already lost it. She approached Noah forcefully, striking him with a punch to the gut and sending him crashing into the ceiling, then plummeting to the carpet.

She's more powerful than the last time.

"I CAN'T HELP IT IF I'M DEAD! IT'S NOT MY FAULT!" she yelled.

Before Noah could lift his head, Diana snatched him up by his collar and tossed him across the room, smashing him against his door. "DO YOU THINK I WANTED

THINGS TO HAPPEN THIS WAY?"

Although she was outraged, Diana's violence wasn't causing Noah any harm. "No," he gasped. "I'm sorry, Diana. None of us wanted things to be this way. I know how you feel."

"ONE MINUTE, PEOPLE ARE MOURNING YOUR DEATH, THEN THE WORLD MOVES ON AND EVERYONE FORGETS ABOUT YOU LIKE YOU NEVER EVEN EXISTED. YOU DON'T KNOW HOW I FEEL! IT HURTS ME, KNOWING THAT I WILL NEVER HAVE A WEDDING DAY OR KIDS OF MY OWN!" she continued yelling, shoving him against the wall and destroying his room even more by lifting his drapes and bedsheets into the air.

"DAMMIT, I'LL NEVER KNOW WHAT MY KIDS WOULD'VE LOOKED LIKE OR WHAT THEY WOULD'VE DONE WITH THEIR LIVES!"

"You're right," Noah conceded. "Diana, I'll figure something out. I promise."

"THERE'S NOTHING TO FIGURE OUT! IT'S TOO LATE! CAN'T YOU SEE THAT?"

"DIANA, I'M SORRY! I'M SORRY THIS HAPPENED TO YOU!" Noah screamed with a look of despair.

Right away, Diana's wrath turned into misery. When she let go of Noah, the fire on her hands vanished. The wind stopped blowing, her hair finally relaxed, and Noah's materials dropped from the air and landed on his floor with a loud thump.

"Maybe I died for a reason! Maybe it was supposed to happen," she said morosely.

Noah immediately shook his head and readjusted his shirt. "No, Diana. Don't say things like that. You weren't supposed to die."

Though filled with grief, Diana was still unable to restrain herself from hitting Noah. She felt like nothing he said at this point could help her. Clobbering him was the only way she could release the tiny bit of energy she had left. "Yes, I was! They say everything happens for a reason!" she cried while punching him on his chest and shoulders.

"And guess what? I'm not holding you back from anything! You can do whatever you want with your life from now on! Besides, it's not like I uncontrollably thought about you one day and somehow magically caused you to come to me. It was the other way around, remember? You with all that 'You're the most beautiful woman I've ever seen' kind of talk. Oh, and how could I forget you also said, 'Diana I couldn't get you out of my mind.' 'I want you to be my girl.' Blah, blah, blah!" she said mockingly while continuing to slug him.

Suddenly, he laughed. "Wait! I didn't say it like that, and it's true you are the most beautiful woman I've ever seen."

Diana ignored him. "And then you come out of nowhere with the words 'I love you'!" she ranted, continuing to hit him.

Blocking Diana's shots, Noah smiled. "Because I do love you."

"Whatever!" Diana swung at Noah one last time, but he caught both of her forearms in mid-air and held them firmly. He then turned her around so that her back faced him. As he hugged her from behind, Diana had no choice but to settle down.

"Relax . . . Relax," Noah whispered while securely holding her and leaning back against his closet door.

"You're so lucky I'm drained right now," she said as she rested the back of her head on Noah's chest and caught her breath. "Ugh, it seems like you'll never be happy, no matter what I do. I know I can't give you the type of life you want to live—or the life either of us wants to live, for that matter. I don't know what else you want from me."

When Noah freed Diana from his grasp, she turned to him so that she could see his reaction on his face.

His expression was sincere. "Nothing! I don't want anything else from you. I'm sorry for taking out my frustration on you. I honestly didn't mean anything I said," Noah answered softly. "I just wish I could do something about our situation, because now I feel powerless."

"Maybe we have to realize that there's nothing else we can do. When it comes to love and life, we just got dealt a shitty hand," Diana grumbled.

Noah let out a slight chuckle. "We sure did." He hugged Diana before continuing. "The messed-up part is that you were taken away from your family too soon, and you deserve a second chance. I really thought I was going to give you the perfect birthday, but now I just wish I had a time machine to prevent that drunk driver from hitting you the night after your graduation."

"I know—but if I've learned anything from this, it's understanding that life isn't fair. What's crazy and really unfair is that we lived in the same city for our entire lives, but never met until ten months after my death. What are the chances of that?"

Diana wrapped her arms around the back of Noah's neck and sighed. "I know I didn't get a second chance at human life, but at least I got a second chance at love."

"We both did. And hey, I was stupid for falling for that scam, wasn't I?" he asked as he advanced closer toward Diana's face.

"Yeah, that was pretty stupid of you." Diana gave him a quick kiss on the lips and laughed. "But it's all right—you were just trying to make my ultimate wish come true on my birthday. I appreciate that! And I'm sorry for hitting you, silly."

Noah lifted his shoulder in a half shrug. "It's okay. Your punches tickle anyway."

Diana snickered and rolled her eyes. "Oh, shut—"

Noah placed his hands behind Diana's head and kissed her before she could finish her sentence.

During the heat of their passionate kiss, all of their anxieties were wiped away. This stress release was exactly what they needed. Still leaning against his closet, Noah smoothly slid his hands down from her hips to the back of her thighs and lifted her up off the ground as their lips remained locked. He then attempted to carry Diana to his bed and gently lie her down, but they unexpectedly fell onto the bed because he was unaware of his surroundings.

As their lips unlocked, Diana laughed while Noah lay on top of her. "I like it better when we do this instead of fighting," she mentioned joyfully.

"Me too."

Wrapping her legs around Noah, Diana caressed the back of his head as he seductively kissed her neck. Things between them were getting hot and steamy.

Noah's phone suddenly buzzed twice. "Uh, what now!" he muttered as he climbed off of her, feeling aggravated.

Clutching his phone and observing the notification, Noah saw that Diana's father (Barry Jr.) had sent him an email.

Diana saw the worried look on Noah's face as he read the message. "What's wrong?" she asked.

Noah handed her his phone. "It's your father. He wants to talk to me immediately. I wonder how long my phone has been buzzing—because he sent me this email hours ago."

"Oh my god, what happened now?" Diana wondered as

she began to read.

From: barryjrdivine@silversidemail.com
To: NoahKing@silversidemail.com
Subject: *We need to talk*

Hello Noah,
        I hope you are doing well. The reason I am contacting you is because my mother Joanna strongly believes that you've somehow been talking with my deceased daughter. Yes, I know this sounds crazy, but the loss of Diana has been tough on her, including me.

Due to her age and depression I think she has begun to associate you within a fantasy or a delusion of hers. You are a great therapist Noah, I'm sure of it and I want you to know that, but it's probably best if she doesn't attend any more of your sessions.

None of this is your fault by the way. It's just that these thoughts she's having of you are very unhealthy. I hope you understand where I'm coming from. I'm sure you will but my mother most likely won't.

Please contact me as soon as possible so that we can talk more about this.

After Diana read the email, she nervously raked her hands through her hair. "Noah, this is bad. They want to take her away from you for good. We need to talk to my Mom-Mom as soon as possible so that we can find a way to figure this out." She took Noah by the hand. "Hopefully, she's taking a nap right now and we'll be able to enter her dream."

When Diana placed her free hand on the wall and opened a portal to the second floor, they immediately saw the shimmering creek they'd sat by before in the spirit world. When they entered the portal and strolled through the sparkling grass, Diana spotted her Mom-Mom's dream portal floating right beside her. "I see it! There's her dream portal. Come on!"

They rushed through the portal. Entering Mrs. Divine's dream, Noah noticed that it was exactly how the old woman had described it. The sun was setting, giving the sky an astonishing orange glow, and Mrs. Divine's humongous house was right in front of the Silverside lake. From afar, they could see Mrs. Divine on her porch, peacefully rocking on her rocking chair.

When Diana and Noah approached the porch, Mrs. Divine grinned and waved at them. She greeted them as if she already knew they were coming to see her. The sight of Diana and Noah holding hands and walking together filled her with delight. "Aww, I finally get to see my favorite couple together at the same time!" she cried, getting up from her rocking chair to greet them. "Hey Noah, welcome to my dream world! And happy birthday, Diana! I sure wish your mother and father had the ability to come see you right now," Mrs. Divine added, wishing she could embrace her granddaughter.

"So do I, Mom-Mom—and thank you! How long have you been waiting here?" Diana wondered as she sat down on the empty rocking chair.

"I have no clue, sweetie. I've probably been sitting here for a long time, but you know I don't mind it."

"Hey, Mrs. Divine," Noah interjected cautiously. "I got an email from your son, and he wants to talk to me about you no longer attending the therapy sessions. He believes that you're becoming obsessed with me."

"Oh, don't you worry about him, baby. I can handle him. I'll put him right back in his place," Mrs. Divine answered confidently.

Diana tapped her fingers against her lips before saying, "Mom-Mom, did you tell my dad about Noah meeting me?"

Mrs. Divine innocently pinched her lips. "Listen, I got a little carried away when I saw your mom and dad trying to hook Noah up with Amber; so I may have told them that you and Noah are together," she explained.

Noah hung his head. "Mrs. Divine, I know it's great to tell the truth and all, but this may not have been the right situation to spill the beans about. If I were to tell your son the truth, not only would I look like a lunatic, but I could get kicked out of this internship program—and that would mean I could no longer be your therapist."

"Noah, I understand where you're coming from, sweetheart, I really do—but we can convince Diana's parents to believe us, I know we can. We shouldn't keep this secret from them any longer. Barry Jr. and Vivian honestly deserve to know the truth," Mrs. Divine replied soothingly.

Noah shook his head and began to pace back and forth on the porch.

Ugh, I don't know if I can do this. Revealing this big secret to them will cause all hell to break loose. This is not good!

Diana could tell that Noah was still concerned and unsure about what her Mom-Mom had said. She rose up from the rocking chair and interlocked her hands with his. "I know it sounds like a ridiculous thing to do, but maybe Mom-Mom Joanna is right. Telling them the truth may not be as bad as we think. Who knows—my mother and father may even take the news well."

"Diana, I'm not sure about this. Your parents are going

to snap! I can feel it in my gut."

"Just tell them some of the things I've told you. Like most of the things I've witnessed after my accident, and tell them about the time you watched me send a memory to my dad." Diana winked. "You've got this, Noah. I know you do. And look on the bright side: you're doing this to help my Mom-Mom stay in your sessions. I don't want them to send her off to someone else."

Noah sighed and lifted his head toward the sky with his eyes closed. "Oh, all right! I'll let you know if it goes south," he joked as he and Diana lovingly embraced each other.

Seeing the affection between Diana and Noah on display reminded Mrs. Divine of the love she and her husband had shared. "So . . . how was your night last night?" she asked, leering.

Diana and Noah looked at each other nervously. "Um, it was . . . ya know," Noah answered, stumbling on what to say, not even completing a sentence.

"We—we just talked the whole night, that's all," Diana said, smirking at Noah out of the corner of her eye.

24

THE TRUTH

Meanwhile, back at Noah's house, Mrs. King came rushing into his room in a panic.

After dashing inside, she saw him sleeping face-down on the floor. "This boy!" she muttered with a slight chuckle. "And oh my God! What in the world happened in here?" she wondered as she glanced at the drapes, sheets, and books that were strewn all over Noah's floor. "I suppose he must have been studying all night."

Out of the corner of her eye, she saw a wallet-sized picture of Diana hanging out of Noah's back pocket. It was the picture that Mrs. Divine had snuck into his pocket after their second session. It was a bit wrinkled due to his pants being washed and dried since then.

Pulling the picture from his pocket, Mrs. King felt perplexed. She couldn't figure out how Noah had gotten it, and she also noticed that the face in the picture looked familiar.

"Jesus! This was the girl I tried to revive at the hospital last year," Mrs. King whispered.

She tapped Noah on the back, attempting to wake him up. "Noah—Noah wake up, hon."

MEANWHILE, IN MRS. DIVINE'S DREAM

"Noah, thank you so much for doing this. Barry Jr. and Vivian are going to appreciate you just as much as I—"

"WHOA!" Noah shouted as his spiritual body quickly vanished.

Mrs. Divine was startled by what she'd just seen. "What happened?" she gasped.

Sitting next to her Mom-Mom, Diana let out a spontaneous giggle. "That's what happens when someone wakes up his physical body. I'm used to it by now," she explained as she looked wistfully in the direction where Noah had disappeared.

Mrs. Divine beamed at her. "You love him, don't you?"

Diana gave her Mom-Mom her brightest smile. "Yes, I really do! You were right: he's my Prince Charming. He's swept me right off my feet."

"I told you that day would come, didn't I?" Mrs. Divine said confidently.

"You sure did!"

"That's because God's work is never finished, baby girl. God's work is never finished," Mrs. Divine repeated quietly.

BACK AT THE KINGS' HOUSE

As Noah was sucked back into his body, he heard his mom's voice. "Hey Noah, wake up honey. I just received a call from Mr. Manning. Apparently, some of the elderly folks on the top floor of the Care Center are suffering from carbon monoxide poisoning. One of the members didn't shut off the oven and stove correctly."

Noah finished waking in a flash. *Oh no! Mr. Wise and Mrs. Divine live on the top floor,* he thought.

"How are Mr. Wise and Mrs. Divine doing?" he exclaimed aloud.

"It's not looking too good for them," Mrs. King answered gently. "Mr. Manning wanted to know if you could come to the hospital to see them before it's too late."

It took a while for Noah to fully process what his mother had just told him. Finally, he stood up. "I'll hurry and get cleaned up right away," he answered, rushing into the bathroom.

"I'll take you so that you can get in and walk around easily," Mrs. King answered, grabbing her hospital employee badge and keys from her purse. "Hey Robert, can you watch Nathan?" she called. "I'm about to take Noah to the hospital to see his patients."

"No problem, babe. Let me know how everything goes," Mr. King replied from where he and baby Nathan were sitting on the couch watching the news.

~~~

During the quiet and stressful car ride, Mrs. King pulled out the picture of Diana she'd found in Noah's back pocket. "Do you know this girl, Noah? Her picture was hanging out of your back pocket when you were sleeping."

Noah was caught off-guard. *What the hell? I don't remember ever having a picture of Diana on me.*

Not knowing how to react, he said the first thing that came to his mind. "Yeah, I kind of know her."

"You know her well enough to have a picture of her in your pocket? I don't remember you attending her funeral."

How in the world do you know she's dead? Noah thought.

Mrs. King continued before Noah could explain himself. "Look, the other night, I heard you call out the name Diana while you were sleeping in your room. Then, earlier this week, I heard you say it again. When I confronted you about it, you told me you were reciting lyrics from a song you heard on the radio. I knew that was a lie because you were calling out this name as if you were looking for someone . . ." Mrs. King kept her eyes on the road. "Is there anything you want to talk about?"

Aw shit. This is not good.

When Noah didn't answer, Mrs. King just sighed and said, "I'm only asking you this because I know that the girl in the picture is Diana."

Oh yeah—this is really not good! Noah was so frozen that only his mind could do the talking.

"I know I never really talk to you about what happens at work. That's because 90% of it is tragedies, and, last year, she was one of them. Last spring, sometime during the month of May, the paramedics brought her into the hospital after she was struck by a drunk driver. I did the best I could to revive her, but nothing worked, and that was the night she died. Telling her parents that their daughter was gone was the worst feeling ever. Her mother screamed 'Diana' over and over again for about an hour. . . So if you knew her, and her loss affected you in any way, you can let me know," Mrs. King proclaimed.

Hearing his mother's story made him want to confess, but he knew that would be a huge risk. Noah rubbed his temples. "Um, I wish there was a way I could explain this—but you won't understand," he declared.

Mrs. King began to decelerate the car. "Try me," she answered.

Noah stopped slouching in his seat and sat up. "Okay, Diana is, uh—Mrs. Divine's granddaughter. I never actually met her, though. I only know about her because Mrs. Divine talks about her all the time. I've been trying to find better ways to help her cope with Diana's death over the past few weeks," he admitted, deciding to only tell a half truth.

"That's it!" Mrs. King nodded and began to tap the steering wheel with her thumb. "But I still feel like there's more to this story. I'm your mother, Noah. I can tell when you aren't telling me everything. Why on Earth do you say her name randomly when you're alone? Especially if you've never met her?"

Noah was really struggling with not telling his mother the entire truth. *Man,* he thought, *I should just tell her everything right now. What do I have to lose?*

"All right, forget it!" he said, reaching a decision. "Mom—do you believe in the afterlife?"

Mrs. King didn't see that question coming, but she smiled and said, "You know what? Some doctors don't . . . but I most certainly do. There are just some things out there that science can't explain." She glanced at Noah quickly. "But why would you ask that? Wait, wait, wait, do you believe you're seeing her ghost? Or are you just dreaming about her?"

"Um, I'm seeing her in spirit form . . . and no, these definitely aren't dreams," Noah replied.

Mrs. King was flabbergasted by his answer, but she did

her best to listen and comprehend everything Noah said.

"Alrighty, then . . . So let me get this straight. You actually see Diana, the girl right here in this picture?" She held up the photo to Noah's face. "YOU ACTUALLY SEE HER SPIRIT?!"

Noah nodded. "I know it sounds absurd, but yes—I do."

His mother suddenly tightened her grip on the steering wheel, not having realized that this news would freak her out.

"Are you okay, Mom?" Noah asked, noticing the tension in his mother's face.

Mrs. King forced herself to relax by loosening her grip and taking deep breaths. "Oh, uh—yes, honey, I'm fine. Sorry about that. I just had to gather my thoughts. Okay, so when you see her spirit, what happens exactly? Do you two just have random conversations in your room?" Before Noah could answer, she added, "Oh my god! Diana's not trying to possess you or haunt our house, is she?"

"No, not at all!" Noah laughed. "Diana isn't trying to possess me, and she would never haunt our house. I don't think she's even capable of doing that."

"Okay! Thank God!" Mrs. King uttered in pure relief.

"Diana and I just communicate with each other." Noah slouched back in his seat again. "Mom, have you ever heard of astral projection?"

Mrs. King instantly displayed a look of excitement that revealed her geeky side. "Oh my gosh, are you kidding? Yes, I've heard of astral projection! I did a research paper about it in college a long time ago. Scientifically, they say it can't be proven, but then again, there are some things science can't explain. Besides, what do they know! Most scientists are so arrogant and think they're above everyone else in intelligence—bunch of know-it-alls," she rambled.

Suddenly, her eyebrows flared. "Hold on! Noah, can you astral project? Is that what you're about to tell me?" she asked with a look of curiosity and wonderment.

"Yeah. For some odd reason, I have the gift of astral projection. It just came out of nowhere—and you're taking this news way better than I expected," Noah answered, feeling a little less tense.

"To a nerd like myself, this is basically like finding out that your child has super powers." Mrs. King shook Noah's arm in excitement. "Wow! So you and Diana are doing more than just talking. You're actually traveling to other dimensions then! What is that like? You have to tell me all about it!"

"Yeah, we are . . . I'm sorry; I promise you I'll tell you more about it, but I'm still surprised by how well you're taking this. Are you being sarcastic, or are you actually okay with this?" Noah retorted.

"Oh, come on. Once again, I'm your mother. You know me: I'm all into the science theories, sci-fi stories, magic adventures, and spirit dimension stuff. And to add to that, why wouldn't I believe my own son?"

"Well, thanks, Mom. I've been holding this in for the longest time, and it really feels good to finally get it off my chest," Noah answered in relief.

Looking for a parking spot in the employee section as they pulled up to the hospital, Mrs. King slowly nodded. "So, are you two like—more than friends?" she questioned, finally finding a place to park.

Noah shook his head and laughed. "You just had to find a way to make things awkward, Mom," he said while exiting the car.

Mrs. King followed suit. "What? Hey, it's not like a mom finds out every day that her son is dating a ghost, ya know."

"She prefers to be called a spirit," Noah clarified.

Mrs. King smiled as they walked toward the hospital. "Oh, okay. So you two are together, then."

Noah didn't answer her this time.

After entering the hospital, Mrs. King collected Mr. Wise's and Mrs. Divine's information to figure out what rooms they were in. "Who do you want to see first?" she asked her son.

"We can go see Mr. Wise first," Noah answered.

"Okay. He's in room 302," Mrs. King answered as she led the way.

~~~

When Noah arrived outside the large hospital room minutes later, he peeked through the open doorway and saw what looked to be Mr. Wise's entire family surrounding him. Mr. Wise looked sickly, but he was cracking jokes and had a huge smile on his face. Everyone was laughing at his jokes and having a joyous time. You wouldn't have thought that Mr. Wise was dying at all.

There have to be about 50 people in here, Noah thought to himself as he studied the room.

Suddenly, a passing nurse stopped next to them. "If it isn't Dr. Natalie King!" she exclaimed. "What are you doing here? I thought you were on vacation?"

"Hey, Catherine. I'm just here helping my son Noah get around. He's here to see the man lying down in there; he's actually his therapist," Mrs. King explained, pointing to Mr. Wise.

"Oh, okay." Nurse Catherine turned to Noah. "Do you want to come in?"

"Sure!"

When Noah entered the room, the multiple

conversations and laughter died down. All eyes were now on him. "Hey guys, clear the way for the young brotha that just walked in," Mr. Wise ordered his family when he saw Noah standing like a deer in headlights in the crowd.

"That's my main man right there," he added in a happy, yet faint voice. "What's going on, champ?"

"Hey, Mr. Wise. It looks like you have all twelve of your grandchildren and twenty-seven of your great grandchildren here with you today," Noah replied as he approached the hospital bed and gently shook his Mr. Wise's hand.

"Yup, that's right—and my eight children are here too," Mr. Wise agreed.

Noah looked around the room at all of Mr. Wise's family members. "Hello, everyone. It's nice to finally meet you all."

"Hi!" Mr. Wise's family all answered.

Noah turned his attention back to the old man. "How are you feeling?" he asked, clutching onto his hand.

Mr. Wise coughed, then chuckled. "I'm feeling like shit, but it's okay. I'm happy because I know that today will be the day I finally check out of this world to see my wife Mary."

Noah patted his free hand on top of Mr. Wise's. "I hope I'm just as strong and determined as you when I'm your age. With everything you've been through, your love for your wife Mary stayed strong and never faded away."

"Young man, that's because true love is what drove me through night and day. Once you find the one, you'll know what I'm talking about," Mr. Wise told Noah before letting out one more cough and dozing off to sleep.

"Hope to see ya soon, Mr. Wise," Noah whispered right before leaving the room. He knew this would most likely be the last time he saw the old man.

"Are you okay?" Mrs. King asked when she met Noah in the hall.

Noah wiped a tear from his face. "Yeah, I think I'll be fine. Do you know where Mrs. Divine's room is?"

"Yes, she's in room 311."

Noah unleashed a harsh breath. "Okay," he said as nerves ran all over his body, not knowing if Mrs. Divine would be alive or not and knowing that she desperately wanted Barry Jr. and Vivian to know the truth about him and Diana.

BACK IN MRS. DIVINE'S DREAM

In the middle of Diana and Mrs. Divine's conversation, Diana started to see the older woman flicker in and out of sight, as if her soul did not know if it wanted to disappear or not. "Mom-Mom, what's going on? Are you okay?" she wondered with a troubled expression.

Abruptly, Mrs. Divine disappeared again, reappearing within a few seconds. She placed her hand on her upper chest in downright astonishment. "Um, Diana—for some reason, I'm in the hospital, and it seems like I'm going in and out of sleep!" she divulged.

"Oh my gosh, what happened?" Diana demanded.

Mrs. Divine shrugged. "I honestly have no clue. I went to sleep last night like I normally do, and I've been sitting here in my dream ever since. That means something must've happened while I was asleep."

Diana began to panic. "I wish there was a way I could go tell Noah to check on you right now."

Mrs. Divine's dream body began flickering again. "Noah's there! I just saw him enter the room," she mentioned before disappearing for good.

"MOM-MOM!" Diana shouted as her grandmother

vanished along with the rest of her dream world.

When it was all gone, Diana noticed that she was back in the spirit world, sitting all alone by the shimmering creek.

BACK AT THE HOSPITAL

Standing in Mrs. Divine's hospital room, Noah could see that Barry Jr. and Vivian looked distraught. "Thank you for coming, Noah," Barry Jr. exclaimed. "Listen, about the email . . . don't even worry about it. My focus has been completely redirected. I just want my mother to come back from this healthy and alive. God only knows what I'll do without her; even though she can be a thorn in my back sometimes." Barry Jr.'s tone was light, even though he was hurting internally.

"I hope she gets well too, Mr. Barry. Um, there's something I've been meaning to tell—"

Noah's mother walked into the room, interrupting him.

"Hello, Dr. Natalie. How are you?" Ms. Vivian asked as she hugged Mrs. King.

"Hi Vivian, and hello Barry. I'm sorry we have to meet again under these unfortunate circumstances," Mrs. King said sincerely.

"It's okay, Dr. Natalie. I'm starting to learn that this is all part of life's ups and downs. Thanks again for doing all that you could last year to save Diana," Barry Jr. answered.

"You're welcome. I really wish there was more I could have done." After taking some time to reflect, Mrs. King added, "So I see you've met my son Noah."

Barry Jr. and Vivian were stunned. "Wait a minute! Noah is your son?" Barry Jr. asked.

"Yes, he is," Mrs. King confirmed proudly.

"What a small world. Your son is the most polite,

humble, and mature young man we've ever met. He's a remarkable therapist, too," Vivian stated.

Out of nowhere, a voice spoke from the hospital bed. "Mmm. Hello, everyone," Mrs. Divine mumbled, waking up.

Noah could see that she was not well at all. She looked paler than usual, and her voice sounded frail.

"Hey, Mom! How are you feeling?" Barry Jr. asked, running to his mother's side.

"Not great, honey. Not great at all. What happened?"

"You're suffering from carbon monoxide poisoning. Someone forgot to turn the stove off properly at the Care Center last night. And the detector had a malfunction," Barry Jr. explained.

"Do you need anything?" Vivian wondered.

"Oh no, sweetheart. Thank you, though," Mrs. Divine answered. "And oh my, no wonder I feel so weak. I've never felt this way before. I barely have the strength to talk."

Mrs. King's professional instincts began to kick in, but she didn't want to seem overbearing. "I'll go notify one of the doctors on duty," she told everyone in the room.

"That's okay, dear. I'm fine, really. I don't need a doctor right now," Mrs. Divine said, stopping Mrs. King right in her tracks. "We all know there is nothing these doctors can do to save me, and I'm fine with that. I'm ready for my transition."

Barry Jr. began to tear up. He was not ready to accept the fact that his mother was dying. "Mom, don't talk like that. It's not too late! We still have time to save you!"

"Son, it's time! I know it! But everything will be okay in the end, believe me," Mrs. Divine whispered. She glanced over at Noah's mother, asking, "Who are you, young lady?"

"Momma Divine, this is Noah's mother, Dr. Natalie

King," Vivian explained.

Mrs. Divine used the little strength she had left to display her beautiful smile. "Well, aren't you just lovely. It's nice to finally meet you. I'm pretty sure my son and my daughter-in-law have already told you how great your son is," she said.

Mrs. King smiled. "Yes. I'm glad to hear my son made such a wonderful impact on you all."

Nodding in agreement, Mrs. Divine brought her attention to Noah. As they looked at each other, Noah could tell that something was on her mind.

Nerves jolted through his body. *What are you about to say?* he wondered. *I thought I was ready to reveal the truth to them, but I'm honestly not.*

"We have to tell them," Mrs. Divine said.

Everyone isn't going to take the news as well as my mom did, Noah thought.

Barry Jr. instantly looked concerned. "Tell us about what?" he wondered.

"We have to tell them about Diana," Mrs. Divine repeated, still staring at Noah.

Barry Jr. gently grabbed his mom by the hand. "Aw Mom, you just need some rest now. I'll ask Noah and his mother to step out for a while until your mind is right, and I'll see if the doctor can give you more medication."

"No!" Mrs. Divine shot back. "Let them stay!"

Breaking into a sweat, Noah placed his hands in his pockets and rocked back and forth on his heels. He knew it was time to defend Mrs. Divine. "Hey, so—um, Mrs. Divine has been telling you the truth," he finally said.

The room was dead silent, all eyes turning to Noah.

Oh my god, I need to just spit it out already. Here goes nothing.

"I know your daughter, Diana . . . and I love her, too," he stated firmly, feeling overwhelmingly relieved.

Vivian's eyes broadened as she gasped and placed her hand over her mouth. "Did you two meet while she was alive?" she asked. "Please tell me that's what you mean."

Nervous, Noah began to rock even harder on his heels. "No. Unfortunately, I didn't know her while she was alive. I truly wish I had. Diana and I met recently . . . I guess you can say I have the power to communicate with the dead, because we talk pretty much every day."

Frustrated and confused by what he was hearing, Barry Jr. marched toward Noah. "Please tell me you're just putting on an act for my mother, since she's most likely on her deathbed right now," he whispered to the younger man.

"Sorry, Mr. Barry, but this is no act," Noah whispered back.

A sudden rage came over Barry Jr., and he lost complete control of himself. He yanked Noah up by the collar of his shirt and forcibly held him against the wall.

I guess throwing me around runs in this family, Noah thought in surprise.

They were the same height and size, but Noah was much stronger than Barry Jr.; he could've easily pushed him off if he wanted to. Despite this, he allowed Diana's father to press him against the wall, thinking, *This is from built-up frustration. I have to find a way to calm him down.*

"This isn't fucking funny, kid! This is my deceased daughter you're talking about here! What kind of sick game are you playing!" the man cried.

"BARRY, STOP!" Vivian shouted frantically as she and Mrs. King attempted to shove him off Noah.

When the attempt failed, Mrs. King immediately shut the door. She did not want any employees or patients to find out about the altercation taking place. "All right, Barry and Vivian: I know this is extremely hard for you to process at the moment, but my son would never lie about anything as serious as this. I think we should hear him *and* your mother out."

After thinking about what Mrs. King had said, Barry Jr. finally started to relax and reluctantly released Noah from his grasp.

Mrs. Divine was heated with her son after witnessing how he reacted toward Noah. "Barry Vincent Divine Jr., if I could move right now, I would come over there and slap you for what you just did. None of this is a joke. And it isn't Noah's or Diana's fault that they fell in love at this particular time! You promised me you wouldn't get angry with him when he told you the truth, that you'd be on your best behavior. This was supposed be a pleasant conversation, remember!" she ranted while struggling to breathe properly. "You okay, baby?" she asked Noah, redirecting her attention.

Noah brushed himself off and adjusted his shirt. "Yes, I'm fine, Mrs. Divine. Thank you."

Mrs. Divine smiled. "Good! Then you can go ahead and tell them everything now, sweetie."

Noah nodded and timidly stared at Diana's parents. It was finally time for him to reveal the big secret. "The same day I met you at the Home Care Center, I met Diana," he explained. "I met her that night, actually."

Noah could sense their disbelief. "Look, I know this sounds unbelievable, and I know I may seem like a lunatic to you; but this special gift I have allows me to communicate with her and travel with her to several parts of the spirit dimension. After hanging out with her almost every day, our bond just grew stronger. And don't get me wrong, Diana would really like to communicate with you two as well—that's all she thinks about—but for some reason, she just can't."

Barry Jr. wasn't buying Noah's explanation. "You're telling me that we aren't able to communicate with our own daughter, but you are? What a bunch of BS! What is this gift of yours even called?"

"It's called astral projection, sir."

"Never heard of it."

"It's a real thing, and I'm not just saying that because he's my son," Mrs. King intervened. "I've researched it before. It reveals how our spirits are able to travel to different realms and dimensions."

Hearing what Mrs. King said, Vivian observed Noah, noticing his very serious demeanor. He wasn't fidgeting or darting his eyes. He was completely focused on getting his point across. "I believe he's telling the truth, Barry. Think about it—he has nothing to gain by telling us this, but he has a lot to lose. The only reason I could see someone taking that type of risk is if they're truly insane, or if they truly care. And dammit, I'm going to go out on a limb and say he cares, since he told us that he loves our daughter."

Diana's father began rubbing his neck, still infuriated. "I don't care what anyone says, I'm still not buying it. He has a lot to prove."

Mrs. Divine cleared her throat. "Barry Jr., you are the most stubborn man ever! Why aren't you hearing anyone out?"

"Because none of you get it! This is something you don't play with. Shit! Every single day, I wish I could rewind time and find a way to save Diana. It pains me, knowing that I wasn't there to protect my baby and prevent this from happening. All I want to do is hold her right now, but now all I can do is relive this nightmare over and over again! So this foolery needs to stop," Barry Jr. answered emotionally, starting to cry.

"No one is fooling around here but you!" Mrs. Divine

told him emphatically.

Noah had no choice but to interject there. "Diana told me about the night she died."

The room was filled with dead silence again.

"You gave her a $1,000 gift card as a graduation gift on the same night, right? And her last words to you were, 'I love you.'"

Noah could tell that Barry Jr. was finally starting to believe him because of the desolated look on his face.

"She also saw you and Ms. Vivian looking at a bunch of pictures of her while you two stayed in her bedroom after coming back from the hospital that night. You were telling your wife that everything would be okay. And recently you were at home in your living room, looking at a graduation picture of you and Diana hugging each other, and at that moment you had a vivid memory of what happened when that photo was taken."

Noah exhaled deeply. "Like I said before, I know this seems weird right now—finding out that your mother's therapist is in love with your deceased daughter. But trust me, there is a purpose to all of this. Diana and I just haven't quite figured it out yet."

While Barry Jr. and Vivian were still speechless, Mrs. Divine was overjoyed to see Noah finally tell them what he knew about Diana. She didn't care how her son or daughter-in-law took the news: all she wanted was for them to finally hear the truth from the brilliant young man she trusted the most. "Noah, come here, dear," she ordered.

Noah approached Mrs. Divine's bedside as fast as he could. "Yes, Mrs. Divine?"

She gripped his hands and locked eyes with him. "Thank you for telling them the truth. They needed to hear that. They may not understand all of this now, but they will understand it later."

"You're welcome. I'm just glad you're here to back me up. I can't thank you enough for that."

"Aw, of course. I would do anything for my grandbaby's Prince Charming. Now that you've done everything I needed you to do for me, I feel like it's time that I go now and finally be with my husband." Mrs. Divine raised her gaze to the ceiling. "And God, I really don't want to see my funeral or see people crying over me. I don't have time for all that. I just want to go straight to the stairway to heaven so that I can see Barry again."

Right after her final words, Mrs. Divine closed her eyes, and her heart monitor flat-lined. Noah's mother immediately rushed out the door to notify other doctors to come in to help revive her. Barry Jr. and Vivian held each other while balling their eyes out.

"No, Mom, don't go! Hang on, okay! I can't handle losing you, Dad, and Diana!" Barry Jr. wailed as he watched his mom lie there, lifeless. "I believe you now, Mom! Come back to me—please!"

Completely stunned, Noah felt Mrs. Divine's grip loosen in his hands. He'd never seen anyone die in front of him before, especially someone he actually knew. As tears flowed down his face, his mother ran back into the room with her team of doctors.

Watching the doctors operate on Mrs. Divine, time seemed to slow down for Noah. It seemed like they were attempting CPR on her for the longest time, but they soon realized that nothing would work. She was gone for good.

I have to tell Diana.

For a brief time, Noah stood completely still. When he finally began to move again, he got his mother's attention by saying, "Mom, we have to go."

By the look on Noah's face, Mrs. King could already tell that he wanted to get in contact with Diana as soon as possible.

After paying Barry Jr. and Vivian their proper respects, Noah and his mother headed out to the car. During the car ride, Noah was extremely silent.

"Hey, I don't want to be the bearer of more bad news here, but right before we left, I was notified that Mr. Wise passed away. I know this day has already been hard enough for you as is . . . Are you okay?" Mrs. King asked.

Noah looked out the passenger side window. "Yes, I'm fine. Mr. Wise was a great man, and he wanted nothing more than to see his wife, so I'm happy that he's getting the chance."

Although Noah knew that Mrs. Divine and Mr. Wise were headed to a better place, deep down, he felt a little empty. He was just starting to get used to seeing them every Saturday and hearing their stories, but now things would be different. As he continued looking out the passenger side window, he saw a family walking on the sidewalk together without a care in the world. It was obvious that their day was going great—but seeing this brought Noah back to what Diana had told him during their argument. The world doesn't stop when someone dies; time continues to move forward, and everyone else pretty much moves on with their lives, whether the dead like it or not.

~~~

Moments later, Noah and his mother finally arrived at the house. "You're about to go see Diana, aren't you?" Mrs. King wondered.

"Yeah. I have to see how she's holding up. I have no clue if she knows what happened today or not," Noah replied.

"I understand. I'll make sure your door stays shut and no one wakes you up. Go ahead and do what you need to do. I'll keep your dad and your little brother occupied," Mrs. King agreed.

Noah embraced his mother gratefully. "Thank you, Mom. For everything!" he said right before rushing into his room.

After shutting the door, Noah reached into his drawer and grabbed the sleeping pills he'd tucked away.

I swear, Mom, this is the last time I'll be taking one of these. This is just another emergency. Besides, you did say to go ahead and do what I need to do.

After taking a sleeping pill, Noah was out within an hour of lying down. In due time, he heard Diana's voice and felt her shaking his shoulder. "Noah! Good, you're finally up."

He saw that there was fear in her eyes. "Look, I think something is wrong with my Mom-Mom," she said. "Can you do me a favor and hop back into your body really quick to go check on her? Apparently, she's at the hospital."

"Diana, I'm so sorry that I have to be the one to tell you this, but your Mom-Mom passed away about an hour ago. I was there at the hospital when it happened," Noah told her while climbing to his feet.

Diana instantly fell to her knees and began to cry. "What? Tell me you're joking, please."

Noah crouched to the floor to comfort her. "I'm sorry," he said.

"I don't understand . . . How did this even happen?" she asked as she leaned her body into Noah.

"It was carbon monoxide poisoning. Apparently, one of the stoves on the top floor at the Care Center wasn't turned off properly, and the carbon monoxide detector wasn't working," Noah explained, continuing to comfort Diana.

"I don't know what to do. It feels like I just lost my best friend," Diana croaked.

"Before she died, she said that she wanted to go straight to the stairway to heaven to meet your Pop-Pop Barry," Noah said, hoping that this would make Diana feel better.

"Seriously, she said that?" Diana lifted her head from Noah's chest.

"Yeah."

For a while, Diana just stood still and pondered. "Let's go!" she finally spoke as she ran toward the wall. "I'm pretty sure I know where she's at now." She clutched Noah's left hand and opened up a portal to the second floor of the spirit dimension.

25

THE STAIRWAY TO HEAVEN

When they entered the portal and flew into the blue galaxy, Diana quickly took them to the silver staircase that led to the third floor of the spirit dimension. As they landed at the halfway point, they saw people in spirit form slowly walking up the stairs and entering the portal. "I guess Father Time already spoke with them. You don't think we missed her already, do you?" Noah wondered.

"I hope not," Diana answered as she and Noah searched through the crowd for her grandmother.

While swerving around multiple spirits, Noah caught a glimpse of Mr. Wise gleefully roaming up the stairs and clapping his hands. "Mr. Wise!" he exclaimed, speedily approaching the old man.

Mr. Wise's jaw dropped in amazement. "Noah! What are doing here? You didn't die, did ya? Or am I dreaming?"

"You aren't dreaming, sir, and I'm not dead either. I just have a gift that allows my spirit to travel to special places."

Mr. Wise exhaled with a whistle. "Whoa! Well, that's one hell of a gift!" Grabbing Noah's shoulder, he said, "Hey young brotha, I want to thank you again for everything you've done for me. Even when I cursed you out, you hung in there and remained positive, never giving up on me, and I completely respect that. Tell my family I love them and that I'm going to enjoy my time with my wife Mary now. They know her as Momma Mary," he explained, allowing Noah to embrace him.

During their embrace, the old man peeked over Noah's shoulder toward the golden portal. Right then, he saw his wife Mary standing inside of it waiting for him. "Oh, hallelujah! Speaking of Mary, there she is waving at me . . . Mary, dear, I can't believe it's you. Baby, I've missed you so much!"

When Noah turned around, he couldn't see what Mr. Wise was seeing. Staring directly at the illuminating portal, he saw a bright golden glimmering light and nothing else.

Overcome with joy, Mr. Wise swiftly rushed up the last few steps and jumped into the portal. After watching Mr. Wise vanish into the light, Noah turned around and saw Diana. She was hugging her grandmother as tightly as she could. They were the last people left on the stairway.

"Oh my god, Mom-Mom, I finally get to hold you again!" Diana rejoiced. "I've missed this so much."

"I know, sweetie. This is the best feeling in the world. I knew I would get to hold you again someday."

Noah allowed Diana and her grandmother to share their

special moment together for a good amount of time before welcoming himself into their presence.

"Hey, Mrs. Divine!" Noah interjected, trotting in their direction.

"Hi dear! You made it up here pretty fast. Did you fall asleep at the hospital?" she replied, giving him a warm embrace.

"Oh no, my mom and I came back home so that I could fall asleep there."

"Oh, I see. My, this place is absolutely breathtaking," she answered, observing the millions of stars flooding space. When she looked back down, she asked, "How were my son and Vivian before you left?"

"I can't lie, they looked pretty distraught—especially your son."

"Goodness, yes. I should've known. Noah, do me a favor and look after him while I'm gone. I know he'll need people around him like you and Vivian to keep him grounded. His life has been filled with so much turmoil. I don't want him to suffer from depression like I did."

"I'll be sure to look after him, Mrs. Divine. I promise."

"Thank you so much, Noah. I'm so glad I got the chance to meet you. Without you, I wouldn't have had anyone on Earth to talk to who understood what I was going through during my final days. Oh boy, I'm really going to miss you for the time being."

Noah smiled. "I'm going to miss you too, Mrs. Divine, especially our talks. I was really lucky to have met you as well, because if I hadn't, then we would not be in this predicament and I would never have met your granddaughter."

"You know what? You two may even have a greater love story than Barry and I." After releasing Noah, she gazed at him and Diana. "So, what are you going to do now?"

Noah and Diana hadn't thought about what was next for them until Mrs. Divine brought it up. They really didn't know what to say.

"Well, I'm sure you'll figure it out," Mrs. Divine added, right before patting their backs and strolling to the top of the stairway.

In that moment, Diana and Noah stared directly at each other. "Diana . . . I know you were waiting for your Mom-Mom to finally make it up here with you, and I know that you also want to go see your Pop-Pop Barry again. I'm not going to allow myself to hold you back from being in their heavenly presence. I think it's best if you go ahead with them," Noah said softly.

Diana struggled to respond without choking up. "That's true. I was waiting for my Mom-Mom, but things have changed since then, Noah. I don't know. I really don't want to leave you behind." Tears dripped like rain from her glistening hazel eyes.

Noah softly held her hands and swayed them back and forth. "It's okay, because I really don't want you to be alone. What would you do while I'm awake? Your Mom-Mom will be gone, we already know you can't enter your parents' dreams, and it looks like I'm not going to die anytime soon. Besides, I don't want you to see me grow all old while you stay young and beautiful. That would be embarrassing for me," he explained while lightly wiping the tears from Diana's face.

Diana swiftly gripped a handful of Noah's collar and pulled him closer to her. "You're never going to change, are you? Every decision you make is based on how you can help me. You never think about yourself, silly." She grinned.

"Because I love you, that's why." Noah told her,

planting a loving kiss on her lips.

I love you too, but I have to let you go now. You deserve a better life.

"Noah . . . . I think it's time that I think about you for a change. Let's say I decide to enter the third floor with my Mom-Mom. I wouldn't want you to torture yourself by not dating anyone, not getting married, having children, and creating a family. You deserve a life, too. So go ahead and go on real dates. I don't care if it's with Amber, Claudia, or whoever. Any girl will be lucky to have you. Just go ahead and be happy! I want you to create a brand new social life."

"I don't care about any of that. Diana, I don't need to have kids or get married to another woman. You and I have a very special connection that can't be broken. If I have to wait 100 years to finally see you again, then I will. You're the only one for me. I know you are!" Noah declared, finally saying his true feelings aloud.

Diana passionately kissed Noah and held him with all her might. She wanted time to freeze so that they could stay that way forever.

"BARRY!" Mrs. Divine screamed, interrupting her granddaughter's intimate moment with Noah as she approached the portal. "Oh my lord. Barry, is that you?"

When Diana swiveled her head, she saw her grandfather standing right inside the portal's entrance. She noticed that he didn't look the same as when she'd last seen him. He actually looked like his younger self. "Whoa! Pop-Pop Barry looks like he's in his mid-20s again."

Once more, Noah tried to view what was going on in the portal, but he couldn't see what Mrs. Divine and Diana were seeing. He was only capable of seeing the bright golden portal shine like the sun.

Mrs. Divine quickly dashed through the portal to hug and kiss her husband. Diana smiled joyfully as she witnessed them hold each other. "Aww, they're so cute! Mom-Mom has longed for this day," she uttered, gradually approaching the portal with Noah by her side.

As they stood in front of the glowing entryway, they did their best to say their final goodbyes. Diana wasn't prepared for it. She put her head down and contemplated what she would say.

"Hey, remember—this is not the end," Noah said, lifting her chin and meeting her mesmerizing eyes.

Diana bobbed her head, then looked toward the portal. She saw her Mom-Mom and Pop-Pop inside of it, holding and kissing each other like newlyweds. Even though Noah was much closer to the portal, he still saw nothing but a glowing light. "I don't know what I'm going to do without you . . . I'll miss you," Diana finally said, her voice breaking up.

"So will I," Noah agreed, doing his best to remain emotionally strong in front of her. "What you're going to do is check out this third floor with your grandparents and tell me all about it when I make it up here."

"Okay, silly!" Diana said, giggling and slowly walking away from him.

As she attempted to enter the portal, however, a force field instantly knocked her off of her feet.

"What in the world! Are you okay?" Noah asked as he caught Diana, preventing her from falling on her back.

"Yeah, I'm okay," she groaned.

Noah quickly turned to Father Time, who was standing right beside the portal. "What happened? How come she couldn't go in?"

Father Time took a second to think. "Hm. Well, it seems like she found her missing piece, but she still has some unfinished business on Earth," he explained.

Diana brushed herself off and pulled her hair back

behind her shoulders. "And what unfinished business might that be?" she questioned.

"And please, don't beat around the bush this time. We want you to get straight to the point," Noah put in.

Father Time released a slight chuckle. "Fine. It seems as though your parents and best friends still need your help. Thanks to Noah, your parents believe that they will have the opportunity to see you again; but they still feel guilty about your death and are suffering now that your Mom-Mom is gone. As far as your friends are concerned, they also feel guilty about your death and have lost faith and hope in the afterlife, but you still have the opportunity to change that. You can restore their faith," Father Time declared.

Diana shook her head. "I can't even contact them. How will that even work?"

"You have the power to contact them through him," Father Time explained, pointing to Noah and creating a portal that led back to Noah's room. "You and Noah were destined to find and help each other. When you two are finished with your duties, the universe will be calling for you to come back to enter your new home, Diana. I hope you're prepared."

Not knowing what to say, all Diana could do was nod. She was relieved to get to spend more time with Noah, but she also felt bummed about leaving her grandparents behind for the time being.

"Hey, we can fix this, okay? We'll find a way to heal your parents and your friends for good," Noah confirmed, taking Diana by the hand and entering the portal to his room.

26

THE LETTERS

After entering the room, Diana sat at the end of Noah's bed and huffed in aggravation. "What did he mean? How can I contact my family and friends through you?"

Noah placed his hands in his pockets and began to pace around the room. Multiple thoughts flurried through his mind, but he focused on just one. "Maybe you can tell me what you want to say, and I'll go relay the message."

"I guess that would be okay—but it would be a lot for you to remember. It would only be useful if I was capable of following you around and communicating with you while you were in your body," Diana said as she fell back onto the bed and closed her eyes.

She bit her lip, thinking deeply. "Hang on, let me think of something else."

Damn, I'm going to miss this girl and that lip bite of hers! Noah thought, distracted.

Suddenly, Diana sat up. "Hey, maybe I can go on your computer and log onto my *Gossip Place* account to message them and tell them everything that's happened."

Noah quickly shook his head. "No! Diana, that's not a good idea at all! If people see that your account has been recently active, all hell will break loose. Your friends and followers would assume your account was hacked. An investigation would take place, and then they would trace it back to my house because of the IP address on the computer. And I know I would do some time behind bars for that, especially if your Dad found out. God only knows how he feels about me at the moment. We have to talk about him later, too."

Diana palmed her face and took a deep breath. "Okay, nerd, maybe you're right," she teased after dropping her hand.

"I got it!" Noah shouted glancing at the notebook sticking out of his book bag. "You can write it all down! Write a letter to your parents, then write one to Amber and Samantha. That way, they know it's truly from you. You're capable of touching objects in my room, so this should work with no problem."

Diana liked his idea. "That's smart! We can go with that plan. Do you have a pen and sheets of paper?"

Hurriedly, Noah rummaged through his book bag, then handed Diana a pen, sheets of paper, and envelopes. Stepping away from her, he sat down on the side of his bed. "I'll leave you be for the moment. Just go ahead and pour your heart out."

Diana didn't respond, just giving him a familiar fond look. She sat down on his rolling chair and thought about what to write to Amber, Samantha, and her parents.

As Diana finally began writing, Noah gazed at the glum expression that entirely pervaded her face.

They both knew that their time together was coming to an end. They just didn't know when.

Why does life have to be such a cruel game? Noah thought. *I finally meet a woman I connect with on so many different levels, but we're literally separated by life and death. And now that we've established an unbreakable bond, she has to go. Out of my own selfishness, I would ask her to stay, but she doesn't deserve to suffer every day waiting for me to fall asleep just to see her. It's best if she goes with her Mom-Mom and Pop-Pop to the third floor. Seeing me every other night would just make matters worse. She would miss me more and more, and my sleeping schedule would be all messed up to the point where I might be awake for an entire week. I could also cause serious internal damage to my body by overusing those sleeping pills. Damn, this really sucks. I have to make sure that our last day together is perfect.*

All of sudden, he heard Diana start to cry. "Hey, is everything okay?" he asked cautiously, feeling the urge to go comfort her.

In a swift movement, Diana wiped the tears from her face. Her mind kept repeating the same question. *Why on Earth did my life have to be this way?*

She let out a harsh breath. "Yes, I'm fine. I just had a moment there, that's all."

She then continued writing, resisting the temptation to run into Noah's arms and cry on his shoulder.

An hour later, Diana finished writing the letters and placed them into the envelopes Noah had given her. "I hope this is enough," she said, sealing them. "Are you ready to send these off now?"

Noah grabbed the envelopes and slid them into his pockets. "All right . . . I'll come see you as soon as I get back, okay? So don't try to go into Heaven without saying goodbye first."

Diana's prepossessing smile rose on her face. "You know I would never do that to you, silly. You're the one who's good at disappearing on people without saying goodbye," she kidded. "Now go hop inside your body so that we can get this sad stuff out the way."

"On it!" Noah replied seconds before transitioning into his physical body.

In mid-transition, he wondered if Diana had only agreed to his request to spare his feelings. A part of him believed that she would be gone for good when he got back.

~~~

When Noah rose from his bed, he saw that the sealed envelopes were still in his hands. "This is it," he said to himself while pulling out his phone to send Amber a text:

(Noah)
Hey Amber

(Amber)
Hi Noah how are you?

I heard about what happened to Mrs. Divine.

Are you okay?

(Noah)
Yes I'm fine thank you.

I just hope Mr. Barry and
Ms. Vivian are doing well.

Do you think you and your
friend Samantha could meet me
somewhere?

It's important!

(Amber)
Sure but why me and Samantha?

And what is this about?

(Noah)
It's about Diana.

I know this seems weird, and it's
probably confusing you a little,
but I need you to trust me.

There is something I have to bring to
you two.

(Amber)
Okay!

And yes I must say I am
a little confused by this.

But I trust you.

When are you free?

(Noah)
I'm actually free now.

(Amber)
Okay cool come to my house
in a half an hour.

I'll have Samantha over
here in no time.

(Noah)
Okay thank you will do!

~~~

After the half hour flew by, Noah drove to Amber's mansion. As soon as he got there, he raced to her front door and rang the doorbell.

"Hey, Noah. Come on in!" Amber said, answering the door.

Entering the house, Noah spotted a light-skinned girl with curly black hair. She was sitting on the arm of Amber's brown leather couch. "Noah, this is Samantha! Samantha meet Noah," Amber said as she introduced them.

Noah beamed, gently shaking her hand. "Hello, Samantha. It's nice to finally meet you."

Samantha smiled back cheerfully, but the look in her eyes seemed permanently mournful. "It's nice to meet you too, Noah. I've heard a lot about you!" she replied.

"You brought something here for us, right?" Amber asked, getting straight to the point. "What does it have to do with Diana?"

Noah pulled a white envelope out of his pocket labeled Amber and Samantha.

Here goes nothing! he thought.

"There's a letter in here that Diana wrote for you two. She wants you to read it today." He handed Amber the envelope.

Samantha looked bewildered. "Where did you get this? When did you meet Diana? And why would you choose today?" she demanded, rapidly bombarding him with questions.

"Did Mrs. Divine give you this?" Amber asked in turn.

Noah shook his head. "No. It's a long story, and Samantha, I'm sorry, but I couldn't understand a word you just said."

"No, I'm sorry. I was talking really fast and overloaded you." Samantha took a breath, obviously trying to calm herself. "Do you at least know what the letter says?"

Noah shook his head again. "No, I haven't opened it or read it."

"Okay, so where did you get this mysterious letter from?" Samantha replied, continuing her interrogation.

"I really think I shouldn't answer that until you both read the letter first."

Samantha wasn't satisfied with this. "Oh. Well, have you ever met Diana?"

Noah smirked. "Again, I think I shouldn't answer that until you both read that letter."

"Noah, I swear to God, this better not be some cruel joke. I know her handwriting," Amber stated while opening the envelope.

"IT'S HER HANDWRITING!" Samantha shouted with teary eyes as she and Amber began to read the letter.

Amber & Samantha

My ladies!

I miss you two so much! Samantha, I know you're already crying. You were always the first one to cry, no matter what the situation was. Whether it was a romantic movie, our graduation, or one of those videos on social media where someone in the armed forces surprises their family for the holidays, we could always depend on you to cry first. All jokes aside (Samantha), I just want you to know that you CAN and SHOULD stop feeling guilty about my death. This was not your fault at all. The only one at fault for my death is that stupid drunk driver who is rotting in prison right now.

Samantha, I want you to do me a huge favor! Please step out of your house, come out of your shell, and start your filming and photography career immediately!

Go enjoy life, girl!

Now, Amber, I know our trio is dismantled now because you no longer have your go-to model for the clothing line, but that's okay. You'll eventually find another girlfriend/model to add to our former trio. And I honestly think you should model your clothes. That's right, you heard me . . . or, in other words: 'You read what I wrote.' You've been my best friend since we were kids, and we always promised each other to never end things on a bad note.

So I want you and Samantha to look on the bright side of things, because life as you know it is only the beginning of our spiritual journey. And you will see me again.

I know before reading this letter you both had lost all hope and faith in life after death, but trust me, that car accident was not the end of our story. Our story will continue forever and ever. I can't wait till we're all together again. We can live it up like old times! Today, I will finally be entering Heaven, so wish me luck! I know it's hard to say goodbye, and I didn't want to write anything too long and drawn out; so I'll just say this: We'll talk soon, my ladies!

P.S. The cute guy that handed you this letter is really cool. Trust me, I know! He's not a weirdo or a stalker. I know that's what you were assuming Samantha ;) He's honestly the most perfect man I've ever met.

Love,
Diana

After reading the letter, Amber and Samantha looked up at Noah. They were uncontrollably sobbing. "I don't understand—how in the world did she write this letter? Did she predict her death or something? And like Samantha asked, *when did you meet her*?" Amber demanded.

Noah didn't know which question to answer first.

"You can talk to spirits, can't you?" Samantha asked, sensing it instinctually.

Noah nodded. "Yeah, um . . . something like that. Today was the last day I could speak with her, though. She's going into heaven for good this time to be with her grandparents."

Amber was giving Noah a complete death stare. "Wait. Is she the so-called dead girlfriend you were telling me about?"

Noah scratched his head while feeling a bit nervous. "Yeah," he finally answered, beads of sweat forming on his forehead.

"You said this girlfriend died a couple years ago . . . but Diana died last year—ten months to be exact," Amber said with a curious smirk on her face.

"I know. I'm sorry for lying to you, but if I were completely honest with you about this whole Diana situation the last time we talked, I'm assuming you would have called the police and had me arrested for stalking or something," Noah responded.

"He makes a good point, ya know. I would have done the same thing," Samantha agreed.

Amber gave in. "Okay, fair enough."

"Noah, you said Diana is just now entering Heaven. She said the same thing in her letter . . . sooo where was she for the past ten months?" Samantha wondered.

"Oh god, how can I condense this?" Noah sighed. "Let's just say she was in the perfect *waiting room*." He started to chuckle. "Well perfect *waiting world*, I should say."

Amber and Samantha looked clueless at this. "Trust me, you'll understand all of this when you die," Noah added, starting to head toward the front door. "Sorry, but I have to hurry and go now to deliver this next letter to her parents."

"Hang on!" Samantha ordered, causing Noah to halt. She then ran to him and gave him a tight bear hug. "It was really nice meeting you, Noah! Thank you for doing this. I haven't felt this relieved and free in a long time."

Noah hugged her back. "You're welcome."

Amber joined in, making it a group hug. "I want to thank you too, Noah." She laughed. "Don't worry, we won't tell anyone about your secret gift or about this particular situation."

"Thank you for understanding, girls."

Their soothing embrace came to an end.

"Do you think Diana can see us right now? Because now that my faith is back, I have a feeling she's watching over me," Samantha asserted.

Noah crossed his arms. "Oh, I really don't think . . ." He trailed off. "You know what—yeah, she can. She's watching over the both of you right now."

"Good, because I want to thank her," Samantha said as she lifted her head and locked her gaze to the ceiling. "Diana, thank you for sending Noah just in the nick of time, because I was really at my low point. I was contemplating suicide, and I believe I would've acted on it if I hadn't seen your letter today. Every day has been hard for me because I dream about that car accident every night. It plays in my head over and over again, and I always felt like I could have prevented it. I would constantly tell myself that I should've picked you up earlier or chosen a different route, or that I shouldn't have tried to go to that party at all, especially since you were hesitant to go in the first place." She took a second to catch her breath. "I just felt this big weight of guilt on my chest, and that weight grew heavier and heavier each day. I gotta tell ya, Diana, life just doesn't seem real without you in it. Shit, life actually sucks without you in it, and I'm pretty sure Amber feels the same way; but don't worry, I'm not going to harm myself. Those thoughts are no longer in my brain now that I know you're looking over me. My new goal is to live for you, me, and Amber now. I'll make sure I live the best life possible, okay? And girl, make sure it's poppin' up there when it's my time to come too. It'll be just like old times," Samantha finished.

Irrepressibly sobbing, Amber chimed in. "Yes, thank you, Diana. We've been best friends since we were little kids, and not a day goes by where I don't think about you. The memories we've shared play in my head like a movie every time someone mentions your name. I must admit, I've been depressed, too. I know I do a good job of disguising it, but grief was truly eating me up inside. Without this letter, I don't know how long I would've been able to put up this front like everything is absolutely fine with me. Diana, I think you just saved me and Samantha's lives today. You came in the clutch, girl—as always. I love you and miss you so much. And I see why you attached yourself to Noah. He's a great guy, and I promise we'll look out for him while you're up there saving spots for us. I can't wait to see what our new journeys will be like. See you soon, Miss Diana Divine."

~~~

"Hey Noah, don't be afraid to keep in contact, okay," Amber said before Noah headed out.

"Sure, you got it Amber! I won't forget. I promise."

Moments later, after getting in his car, Noah sped straight down the road to the Divines' mansion, hoping that they would be there. When he approached the front door, he could see a car in the driveway. "Great, that means they must be home," he said to himself. "Ugh, this is going to be nerve-wracking."

After ringing the doorbell, his heart was pounding through his chest as he waited for someone to answer.

All of sudden, Barry Jr. opened the door. "Hey, it's you! Noah, I'm so sorry about before. I know I lashed out at you; I shouldn't have done that," he said quickly, hoping Noah would forgive him.

"It's okay, sir. I understand. I know you've been going through a lot over the past few years. No one should ever have to endure that much pain in one lifetime, so I understand. But, Mr. Barry, I'm actually here because there's something I have to give to you," Noah told him.

"And what's that?"

Noah pulled the envelope labeled 'Mom & Dad' out of his pocket and handed it to Diana's father. "That's Diana's handwriting!" Barry Jr. exclaimed as he opened the letter. "Vivian, come here!" he yelled.

When Vivian rushed over, he showed her the letter. "Look, Noah just gave this to me! It's our daughter's handwriting. This is from Diana!"

"All of the answers you need will be in that letter," Noah interjected smoothly. *I hope*, he added to himself.

All Noah could really think about after that was getting back home to see Diana again for the last time. "I um—I have to go now, but I'll see you two again soon, okay?" he said, standing there awkwardly.

Before Noah could even flinch, Vivian and Barry Jr. gave him a compressing hug as if he were their one and only son. "Okay, Noah. Thank you for everything! I mean it! Especially for making my daughter happy," Ms. Vivian divulged gleefully.

"I see that my mom was right the whole time. I wish I'd believed her much earlier before she passed on," Barry Jr. admitted before slowly exhaling, soaking in this entire experience. "I have so many questions for you, but you told me everything I need to know is in this letter; so I'll let you off the hook for now," he teased.

"Thank you." Noah smiled. "See ya soon."

Right after Noah left, Barry Jr. and Vivian began to read Diana's letter.

Mom & Dad

Hi Mom and Dad!

I'm going to be all over the place, so bear with me, please!

Sorry—I've been trying to reach you for the past ten months, but nothing worked until I recently found out that I could write a letter to you while in Noah's room. If you're reading this now, I am most likely in Heaven already. And don't worry, I'll be with Mom-Mom Joanna and Pop-Pop Barry the whole time.

Dad, I hope you don't harm Noah before reading this letter. I know he and Mom-Mom planned on revealing the truth about us to you before she passed. All I can do is hope that you haven't strangled the poor boy to death when he told you what you needed to know. Now, I know you and Mom weren't too fond of a guy I chose in my past; which is understandable, but you would be proud of this present guy. Noah is . . . well, was just right for me. He's a great guy, and I love him. But I guess you two would've already approved of him since you tried to set him up with Amber. And by the way, that really made me jealous—but it's all good!

Mom, I wonder if there's anyone in Heaven that can make Kitfo as good as you . . . Nah, probably not. I'm really missing those hugs from you and Dad right about now.

Remember how shocked people used to get when they would find out that you were my mother? People would always mistake you for my sister, but the truth is that not only were you my mother, you were also like the sister I never had because of how close we were. I could talk to you and Mom-Mom about anything, and I'm glad we never had a falling out.

I know you wished you could've helped me get my modeling career started. You've always played a major role when it came to encouraging me to follow my dreams. Even though I passed on before I could get started professionally, I want to thank you for being a great influence. I think I may have convinced Amber to model, so you might love helping her out with that!

Oh yeah, Mom, thank you for always being my partner in crime too. I want you to know that I hear your prayers every night and that I do my best to send you as many memories of us as possible. My God, I miss you with all my heart. I miss both of you.

Sorry, I'm crying right now.

And Noah just asked if I was alright ♡

Alrighty now, Diana—get yourself together and get to the point please! Told ya I would be all over the place.

Mom and Dad, I know you are still deeply depressed about my death, and I just learned that you two feel guilty about it somehow. I'm letting you both know right now that you don't need to feel that way. That tragic night was not caused by any of your actions, so please do me a favor and go to sleep tonight with a clear conscience. One day, you'll see me again. As for now, a part of me will always be in your hearts.

Whenever you're feeling down, just look at all of our home videos and photos to ease the pain, or look to the skies to feel my presence, because that's where my soul resides.

I miss you, Mom and Dad, and I'll see you two soon.

Love,
Diana

Finishing the letter, Diana's parents hugged each other and cried tears of joy. They wished that they could see their daughter at that moment, but it gave them comfort to know that they were definitely going to see her again someday. It was a bittersweet moment for them.

"We love you so much, Diana. We love you with all our hearts," Barry Jr. said with a peaceful sigh. Those were the only words he could let out.

27

OUR LAST NIGHT

When Noah finally arrived home, he stormed into his room, reached into his drawer, and chugged four sleeping pills. Within 10 minutes of spinning around and around in his rolling chair, he was asleep—or more like in a coma.

Now in his astral projection state, he exited his body and stood up off his rolling chair. "Diana!" he called. "Diana, where are you?"

There was no sign of Diana in his room.

I told her not to leave without saying goodbye . . . but something told me she was going to go anyway, he thought.

Noah suddenly heard familiar giggles coming from

across the hall. He knew it couldn't have been his parents because they were downstairs watching TV together. He opened his door and walked across the hall into his parents' room. Entering, he saw Diana playing with Nathan. She was making baby noises and funny faces at him while he was sitting up in his crib.

"Oh, there you are," Noah said with satisfaction.

"Hey!" Diana answered, turning to Noah with an elegant smile. "This little man just woke up, and I came in to check on him when I heard him yawn. We've been goofing around in here ever since." Sensing Noah's relief, she squinted at him. "You thought I left without saying goodbye, didn't you?"

Noah's gesture indicated that he did. "Yeah, pretty much." A wide grin spread across his face. "I'm glad that you're here, though. So when did you get here?"

"I've been here," Diana confirmed.

"Wait." Noah flared his eyebrows. "So when I hopped back into my body, you didn't go up to the spirit world?"

"Nope, I was still in your room. I watched you leave and everything. While I was here, a portal appeared by me, and I was able to watch over Amber and Samantha as they read my letter. Sorry about them sobbing all over your shirt, by the way. That was my fault. I was sending them all of the memories we shared together as they were reading. Shoot, I even cried like a baby when they felt my presence and began to talk to me. Thank God you were there to comfort for them.

"I also saw my parents hug you too before they read my letter. That was so cute! They were both thinking about me heavily in that moment. I had to turn away when they began to read my letter, though, because that was really just too sad to watch. And then finally I watched you storm into the house and run up the stairs." She giggled. "I called out to you, but you couldn't hear me because you were still in your body."

Suddenly, Nathan giggled a little louder than usual, which his parents heard on the baby monitor. As Mr. and Mrs. King started to make their way upstairs, Noah took Diana by the hand and began to speed-walk out of the room. "We have to go before my parents see a door shutting by itself," he explained.

After they reached his room and quietly closed the door just before his parents made it to the top of the steps, Noah saw Diana staring at his stereo with a confused look. "Hey, you fell asleep awfully fast," she said. "What did you do—because I definitely don't hear any '90s slow jams playing like last time."

"Oh, I just took four sleeping pills. You're supposed to take one, but I didn't feel like waiting a whole hour for it to kick in."

Diana gasped. "Noah, are you serious? You can kill yourself doing shit like that. We don't need your family grieving over your death, too," she pointed out with motherly sense. "Where are those sleeping pills?"

"In my top drawer," Noah answered. "And I know it's dangerous. My mom's told me a million times already. This was just an emergency."

When Diana opened the top drawer in Noah's dresser, she saw a picture of herself right next to the jar of sleeping pills. This steered their conversation in a new direction. "When did you get this picture?" she wondered, holding it in her hand.

Noah snickered. "My mom found it hanging out of my pants. I think your Mom-Mom must've slipped it into my back pocket when I wasn't looking during one of our sessions."

"Wow!" Diana found that to be hilarious. "I wouldn't

put it past her. That woman is something else!"

Grabbing the jar of sleeping pills, she tossed it out of Noah's cracked-open window.

Right after that, Diana huffed and folded her arms across her chest. She couldn't believe that her time with Noah was winding down. "So, this is really happening. Our final moments together," she said. "I wonder what's supposed to happen next."

Noah didn't want to think about it. He slowly caressed her hands. "I don't want to find out right away!" he exclaimed. "Spend one more night with me, please! Let's just use all the time we have together while we still can."

The heartfelt passion in Noah's voice made Diana's soul flutter. "Okay!" she answered, blushing. "I was hoping you'd say that."

"So where do you want to go? We can go to the spirit world with the beach again, or we could find a random spirit world to go to. That sounds like fun! Oh! Or maybe I could use a portal here on Earth to take us anywhere you want, like to China or Italy or Kenya," Noah babbled.

"I have a better idea!" Diana replied. "Let's just stay here all night and lie down together."

"Lie down? Are you sure?" Noah questioned, slightly confused by her answer.

"Yes. I've never been more sure of anything in my life," she assured him, jumping onto Noah's bed and patting his pillow.

"Well, okay then; you're the birthday girl," Noah said as he fell back onto his bed beside Diana.

As he lay on his back, Diana placed her head on his chest and wrapped an arm around his waist.

"I didn't get a chance to tell you this, but at the hospital, your Mom-Mom and I told your parents the truth about us. I told my mom too . . . Well, she kind of squeezed it out of me after finding your picture," Noah admitted, wrapping his arm around her.

"Really? How did they all take the news?" Diana asked, listening to Noah's heartbeat and the sound of his voice.

"Yeah, so, um, shit went south real quick! Your dad completely flipped out on me and held me up against the wall."

Diana lifted her head and met Noah's eyes with worry. "Oh my god! Something told me he would overreact." She felt guilty. "Sorry, I know you didn't really want to tell them because you knew this would happen."

"It's okay—your mom and my mom took it better than I expected them to; they even did their best to pull your Dad off of me. Eventually, he simmered down and listened to what I had to say. I have to admit, I probably would've reacted the same way if I were in his position," Noah rationalized. "I sat and thought about it; if I didn't know anything about this spirit dimension stuff and some random guy told me that he was in love with my deceased daughter and had been communicating with her, I'd probably want to punch him in the face."

"You make a great point, but he shouldn't have put his hands on you," Diana replied. "You've done so much for me and Mom-Mom Joanna. I love my dad, but he's lucky I wasn't there."

Noah nodded. "You should've seen your Mom-Mom when she snapped on your dad," he added. "She said, 'Barry Vincent Divine Jr., if I could move right now, I would come over there and slap you for what you just did.' She wanted to take his head off; but thank God everything was settled before she transcended."

Diana tried to hold in her laugh, but couldn't. "That sounds like my Mom-Mom all right . . . . Oh god! This was one crazy day."

~~~

By the time the evening arrived, Noah was slowly running his fingers through Diana's hair as he stared at the ceiling. "Diana?" he began.

"Yeah?"

"Out of all the things you could've done tonight, why did you choose to do this exactly?" Noah inquired as they continued to cuddle closely.

Diana sat up briefly to kiss him. She interlocked her left hand with his right hand and fixed her eyes on his. "Because I'll never have the chance to do something normal like this ever again. There are probably millions of couples around the world cuddling right now just like we are, but I guarantee you, they know they can do the same thing tomorrow, the next day, and the day after that." Pausing, she thought about what to say next. She knew her words would hold significance.

"Noah, you and I don't have tomorrow like everyone else does," she eventually said. "That's why we have to make this day count, and making it count means that I want you to keep holding onto me until the universe pulls me away." Finishing, planting an incredibly deep kiss on the love of her life.

As their lips continued to stay locked, Noah delicately but gently turned Diana to her back and caressed her thighs. And from there one thing led to another, and they made sensational love that evening for the last time, making it storm again in the city of Silverside.

When the evening darkened, they spent the night cuddling, talking about their childhood, high school, and college experiences and how they imagined their futures would've been if they weren't in this unfair predicament.

28

THE VISION

Diana gazed at the ceiling. "Let's say the accident never happened. Do you think we still would've met?" she asked Noah.

Continuing to hold her, Noah answered, "Absolutely, because I would've still gotten that internship at the Care Center."

"Oh yeah, that's right! And even though my Mom-Mom most likely wouldn't have signed up for the therapy sessions while I was alive, she would've definitely ran into you at the Care Center and asked what you were doing there."

Noah suddenly had a change of heart. "And I would've told her that I was there for my internship program, but now that I think about it, I wonder if that would've escalated to me meeting you. We probably wouldn't have met at all."

"Yes, we would have!" Diana asserted. "Remember, you made a good impression on her the first time you two met. After finding out that you were at the Care Center for your internship, my Mom-Mom would've swindled her way into signing up for your therapy sessions just so that she could introduce us to each other, since I always came to visit her. That's how clever she was."

Noah grinned, thinking about this fantasy encounter. "Wow, I can only imagine! I swear—when you walked through that door, I know I would've been stunned and wouldn't know what to say or do at first. But after a few minutes of getting myself together, I would've properly greeted you."

"How?" Diana wondered with pure excitement in her eyes. "Let's act like we're meeting in your office for the first time because my Mom-Mom introduced us. Ready?"

Noah felt confused. "What?"

"Come on, just play along," Diana commanded.

Noah drew in a long breath. "Okay, I'm ready."

Diana beamed. "Thank you! All right, go!"

Noah laughed. "I can't believe we're actually doing this. Okay, here it is! . . . . Hello there, Diana. It's nice to finally meet you! Your grandmother has told me so much about you."

"Hi, Noah. It's nice to meet you, too. And yeah, Mom-Mom Joanna has been going on and on about how fantastic you are. I love your name, by the way. It's lovely!"

"Not as lovely as Diana Divine!"

Diana laughed and interrupted their playful exaggeration. "My Mom-Mom would've intervened right after that and said that she had to go to the bathroom or something so that you and I could be alone together. And she would've made sure that I stayed in the office to talk to you more while she was gone. So what do you think would have happened then?"

Noah shrugged. "I don't know. Isn't this getting a little silly?"

Diana shook her head and kissed Noah on the cheek. "No, not at all. This is my last day here with you, and this story is just getting good; so let's continue to play along, please!"

Noah kissed her one more time before continuing. "You're right, this story is getting good! So, when your Mom-Mom left the room, I would've said: 'Hey Diana, I know that this is most likely unprofessional since I'm your Mom-Mom's therapist, but would you like to go on a date some time?'"

Diana tilted her head and smirked. "That sounds good," she answered, playing along. "I just have to think about it first. I'm really trying to focus on my career, and I don't know if I have time for dating."

"I see. Well, I completely respect that. So what do you do?"

"I'm professionally modeling now for a clothing line my friend and I co-own together."

"That's amazing! And I'm not surprised to hear that you

model either. You truly are a ravishing woman."

Diana smiled. "Ugh, every time you give me compliments, I get stuck and don't know what to say. I hate when I do that!" she finally replied, patting Noah on the chest. "Okay, hang on, let me get back into the daydream."

Taking a breath, she added, "Well, thank you. I appreciate the compliment!"

"You're welcome! So, um, can I have your number or follow you on *Gossip Place*?"

"Well, I'm not really on social media at all, and I don't just give out my number to strangers," Diana answered with a smirk.

"Hang on! Timeout!" Noah huffed, then snickered, "Wow, Diana, you would've made it that hard for a brotha?"

Diana shrugged. "Hey, I'm not like these fast girls. You would have to really work your charm to overcome my defensive shield."

Noah understood her point. "Okay, well, I would've gotten up from my chair, sat by you on the couch, and reached out a hand to shake, saying: 'Can we be friends starting now?'"

"Hm, that's clever! I would've shaken your hand and said: 'Yes, I would really like that!'"

"Okay then, Ms. Diana Divine, we are no longer strangers—so I guess I can have your number now?"

"Yes, now that you've earned it, I'll be glad to type my number into your phone."

"I know I failed on my first attempt, but I have to ask again, ha-ha! There is just something about your presence that's indescribable. So, here it is: Would you like to go to the beach with me? It's a public beach, so you don't have to worry about me trying to do anything suspicious. And it doesn't have to be called a date, either. Let's just say we're hanging out."

"Jeez! You're funny and persistent! How can I say no to you? . . . Sure, the beach sounds great! What will we do?"

"Oh, well, I was thinking we could enjoy our time on the boardwalk first—ya know, hop on the rides, go inside the corny haunted house—and after that, I will lose most of my money attempting to shoot through a mini rigged basketball hoop to win you a prize like a big teddy bear or something. When that's all done, we could enjoy a nice walk along the shore on the cool sand from the evening all the way till the nightfall."

Diana blushed. "Aww, Noah, I would've loved that. You're such a romantic. . . . You reminded her of him, ya know."

"Wait, is this playful daydream over?" Noah asked. "And I reminded who of who?"

"Yes, for now we're putting the daydream on hold," Diana told him. "And you reminded my Mom-Mom of my Pop-Pop Barry. You two are alike in a lot of ways. That's why she loved you so much! Especially for me."

Noah was surprised. "Whoa! That's amazing. I'm happy to hear that. She continuously talked about your Pop-Pop.

I can't wait to meet the guy."

"You're going to love him." Diana smiled. "All right, so obviously you and I would've clicked immediately. Heck, Mom-Mom Joanna even called it: we're soul mates."

At that moment, a tiny sparkling white portal emerged, levitating above them.

"What's going on?" Noah asked, fearing that the portal would take Diana away. "Are you doing this?" The portal began to expand and grow wider.

"No, I have no clue what that portal is doing here. It sort of looks like a memory portal, but I've never seen a memory portal do this before," Diana answered. "Let's just sit here and see what happens next."

Suddenly the portal expanded even more, engulfing Diana and Noah and violently transitioning them into an alternate reality—one where Diana's accident never happened.

ALTERNATE REALITY – The Proposal

Four years have passed since Mrs. Divine introduced Noah and Diana at the Care Center. It's now December 23rd, and Noah and Diana are enjoying their Christmas vacation in New York City. Diana's wearing a white beanie and a stylish red winter jacket. Noah's wearing a gray sweater with a black peacoat and jeans. They're ice skating at Rockefeller Center while the snow is gently falling in the midst of the magical night.

"I love it here. It looks picture perfect!" Diana says, idolizing the snowfall. In her mind, it looked as if graceful white stars were slowly falling from the sky to create a winter wonderland.

"It sure does. I feel like a couple in one of those cheesy Hallmark movies." Noah reaches in his pocket to check the time. *Okay, it's 7:45 and I'm right on schedule,* he thinks to himself.

In the process of ice skating, Noah suddenly stops them in the middle of the rink. He stares directly into Diana's eyes.

Bewildered, Diana asks, "Noah King, what are you up to now, silly?"

As the snow gently falls onto Noah's face, he gets down on one knee. Diana gasps in astonishment, covering her mouth with her mittens as tears begin to fill her eyes.

Noah then opens a small jewelry box that displays a glistening diamond ring inside. "Diana Divine, will you marry me?"

"Yes, Noah King! I'll marry you! I'll marry you a million times!" she cries, smiling brightly and crying tears of joy.

Noah stands up after placing the ring on Diana's finger. Savoring the moment, he hugs her with affection. All of a sudden, there are people clapping all around them, revealing that they'd seen what took place.

"That was breathtaking! I did not see that coming. How long were you planning this? I can't wait to tell Amber and Samantha," Diana babbles as she stares at the sparkling diamond ring on her finger.

Noah uses his scarf to wipe the melting snow off his

face. "Oh, I had this proposal planned for a long time. I always knew it would turn out great like this. Your Mom and Dad know, too. They're probably waiting by their phones to hear the good news."

"Noah, you never cease to amaze me . . . Oh my god!" She quickly starts to think about their wedding arrangements. "Can our wedding be in San Francisco, exactly where my Mom-Mom and Pop-Pop's wedding was? Ooh! And can our honeymoon be in Ethiopia, since it's my mom's home country? I never had the chance to go there." There's a huge smile on Diana's face. "I'm sorry, I forgot to ask you where you wanted to go. Are you okay with what I picked?"

Noah laughs and nods. "Of course I am! I'm okay with anything you choose. Everyone knows that the wedding day and honeymoon are when you treat your wife like a queen and do whatever she wants! I have no problem with that at all. It actually takes a lot of pressure off me. That way, I know I'm not making any mistakes or doing anything that makes my bride upset on those special days."

Diana kisses him on the lips. "Aw, you're so smart! Thankfully, I have a man who treats me like a queen every day of my life."

ALTERNATE REALITY – First Time For Everything

The following year, Diana is nine months pregnant with their first child. They're celebrating the baby shower at her parents' mansion.

"Okay, guys! Smile!" Samantha exclaims, kneeling in

front of Diana and Noah to capture a photo before they open their first gift.

"Did you get the picture?" Noah asks her pleasantly while hearing the continuous flicks.

"Yeah, I got just enough!" Samantha answers. "They came out great! Diana, you don't even look nine months pregnant. I don't know how you do it!"

Diana waves her off and smiles. "Oh Samantha, stop lying to me. It looks like I'm about to pop out of my gown any minute now."

"No it doesn't, girl, you're trippin'; and Samantha's right, you don't look nine months pregnant at all."

Amber is ready to get the baby shower officially started. "All right, now that we've got the first picture out the way, go ahead and open the first gift; which is my gift, by the way!" she informs everyone.

Opening the first gift together, Diana and Noah pull out a black and gold baby onesie that reads 'Cutest Godson Ever' on the front.

"Aw, thank you, Amber! And of course, you just had to design it and put yourself to work again. Do you even buy clothes anymore?" Diana jokingly asks.

Amber laughs. "I buy fabric, for the most part. Any clothes my godson receives from me will be designed by me. You know I'm addicted to creating! I can't help it."

Snickering, Samantha shakes her head. "When I'm the godmother of your next child, he or she will be my modeling baby. I'll have them plastered on billboards all over the country. So I'm going to need you and Noah to start on baby number two right away."

"What! Plastered on billboards all over the country? You just have to find a way to top me, don't ya," Amber tells Samantha.

"You two are something else! Whose gift are we opening next?" Noah asks.

Diana points to a big blue box near Noah's foot. "Babe, open that one."

Noah lifts the heavy box. "It says it's from Mom and Dad." He scans the living room. "Which mom and dad?"

"All of us," Barry Jr. and Vivian loudly answer at once.

Noah's mother nods in agreement. "Yes, I know your father's at work right now, but all of the parents pitched in to buy the gifts labeled Mom and Dad."

"Wow, you guys were on it!" Diana says.

"Yeah, they truly were!" Samantha puts in. "Their gifts are mostly what's taking up the living room right now. There are like eighty more Mom and Dad gifts where that came from."

"Eighty more!" Noah and Diana shout at the same time, turning to each other in surprise. "Well, Noah, it looks like we're going to be here all day."

That night, when Noah and Diana finally make it home to their condominium, Noah hurriedly plops a bunch of pillows on the couch for Diana to sit between.

"Today was long as hell. I'm all worn out!" he says, slowly helping Diana sit down.

Diana can relate. "Yes, it sure was. Thank God my parents let us keep most of the gifts at their house. It would have taken us hours to fit it all in here."

Noah doesn't answer Diana right away. He just sits beside her and gazes at her allure.

"Why are you so quiet all of a sudden, and why are you staring at me like that, silly?" she wonders.

Noah places his arm around her. "Because I have the most beautiful wife in the world. I can't help but stare at you."

Diana rests her head on Noah's shoulder. "Oh, whatever! You have to say that because we're married. You and I both know I look like a fat whale right now. I even feel like a fat whale."

"Well, you sure are one fat, sexy whale." He kisses her on the cheek after each word.

Diana laughs. "Boy, I can't deal with you!" Out of the blue, she pauses. "Uh-oh!"

"What? What is it?"

Diana quickly lifts her head and peers into Noah's eyes. "I think my water just broke."

"Holy shit! Are you sure?" Noah's heart began racing faster than the speed of light.

"Yup, I'm sure," Diana replies, starting to take deep breaths. "We have to go like right now."

"All right! Don't panic. Thank God the hospital is right down the road." Noah jumps off the couch and grabs his car keys. He runs toward the door, nearly forgetting his wife.

"NOAH!"

"Oh shit, yeah! Sorry, babe." He heads to the couch and uses all of his strength to pick Diana up. "All right, I gotcha. Just hang on tight, okay? We'll be in the car soon."

"OKAY!" she shouts as her contractions start.

After going down the elevator, running into the parking garage, and placing Diana safely in the car, Noah speeds off toward the hospital.

"Just breathe like they said in our Lamaze classes," Noah says, keeping one hand on the steering wheel and his other entwined with Diana's. "Inhale . . . now exhale. Inhale . . . now exhale," he repeats, actually doing the breathing exercise himself.

Diana starts giggling. "Noah, am I having the baby or is it you that's having the baby?"

"Right now, I feel like we both are." He quickly pulls into an emergency parking spot and runs to the passenger side door to pick up Diana. "HEY, I NEED HELP! MY WIFE IS HAVING A BABY!" Noah yells as he rushes into the emergency room holding Diana in his arms.

"Oh my god, honey! Her water broke already?" Mrs. King cries out of nowhere, noticing Noah standing in the hallway with a frantic look on his face. "She's a week early, but that's not a problem."

Noah is relieved. "Oh Mom, thank God you're here. And yes, her water broke."

"Hi Natalie! It looks like you're going to be a grandmother tonight," Diana says in between taking deep breaths.

Mrs. King claps with pure and utter joy. "I see, sweetheart. I can't wait! Someone bring me a wheelchair immediately and find me a free operating room. I'm about to have a grandson!"

A male nurse instantly runs to Mrs. King's side with a wheelchair. "You can place your wife down here, sir," the nurse says. "And congratulations, Dr. Natalie! Along with the lucky couple."

"Thank you, hon! Tell Nurse Catherine to call my family and tell them that the baby is coming," Mrs. King orders.

"Yes, ma'am!"

Seconds later, Mrs. King and her team of doctors rush Diana into the delivery room.

"Noah, don't let go of me!" Diana commands when they place her on the bed.

"Trust me, I won't! You're squeezing my hands tight enough as is," Noah tells her.

"How are you feeling? Do you need anything, ma'am?" one of the nurses asks Diana.

"DRUGS!!!" Diana screams. "GIVE ME DRUGS!"

"Yes, she'll need an epidural, quick!" Mrs. King orders. "She's about to go into labor. And give my son a surgical mask and scrubs, please!"

Diana begins sweating, screaming, and breathing more heavily.

"All right, Diana, we have you all set up to go now. You're doing great, sweetheart. On the count of three, I'm going to need you to push, okay?" Mrs. King says gently.

"OKAY!" Diana blurts.

"Noah, make sure you focus on your wife, honey!" his mother commands. "We need your help to guide her."

Noah is in complete shock and seems lost. "We're having a baby," he voices to himself. "Oh my god, I'm about to have a baby."

"NOAH, GET IT TOGETHER DAMMIT AND HELP ME PUSH." Diana squeezes his hand even harder.

"Ouch! Sorry, babe. Okay, Mom, I'm ready when you are."

"All right, 1 . . . 2 . . . 3, push!"

Diana uses all the strength she has left to push the baby out with all her might.

Mrs. King suddenly smiles. "I see the head. Just give me another good push on the count of three, sweetie."

After peeking over to see the baby's head, Noah starts to feel a little weak.

"Doctor Natalie, I think your son is about to faint," one of the nurses says.

"Oh no! Noah, please don't faint!" Mrs. King said, attempting to get her son's attention.

"NOT ON MY WATCH!" Diana pinches Noah's hand. "SINCE YOU CREATED THIS BABY WITH ME, YOU'RE GOING TO DELIVER THIS BABY WITH ME! WE'RE IN THIS TOGETHER!"

Noah immediately clenches his teeth. "SHIT!!! I'M HERE! I'M HERE!" he repeats. "Damn, that hurt."

"Here we go, last one. 1 . . . 2 . . . 3, push!"

After Diana's last push, she and Noah suddenly hear their baby crying for the first time as Mrs. King delivers a baby boy. "And here is my grandson, Noah Jr."

The team of nurses and doctors begin clapping and congratulating them.

"Here, Noah, cut the umbilical cord. I'll show you where to cut," Mrs. King says while cleaning the blood off of her newborn grandson.

After Noah cuts the umbilical cord, Mrs. King gently wraps her grandson in a baby hospital blanket and hands him to Noah. "Here's your son," she whispers as the baby stops crying and begins to fall asleep.

While holding his newborn child, Noah is speechless and stands completely still with a permanent smile. He's overwhelmed by the genuine innocence on his child's face. It wipes away all of the stress he was feeling during Diana's labor and turns it into everlasting internal peace.

"Go ahead and give him to Diana, hon," Mrs. King says soothingly. "The mother eventually has to hold her child too," she teases.

"Huh!" Noah utters, waking from his daze. "Oh yes, you're right. Are you ready to see your mom, little guy?" he slowly walks to Diana and hands her their son.

The second Diana has her baby in her arms is the moment she feels her life change. It feels like she has the world in her arms. She studies his eyes and chubby cheeks and soothingly touches his small hands. "Aw, Noah Jr., I finally get to see you and hold you. I love you so much, baby boy. I'm going to take extra care of you," Diana says while crying happy tears. "During the ultrasound, I could hear your heartbeat, but I could barely see you. But now you're here right in front of me."

Noah caresses his wife's hair and kisses her on her forehead. "He looks like you!"

"Really?" Diana shakes her head. "You think so? I actually think he looks like you."

"He looks like the both of you," Mrs. King intervenes.

"Yeah, I can see that!" Diana settles. "Oh my god, Noah, look at what we created! He's such a beautiful baby! I wish my Mom-Mom Joanna and Pop-Pop Barry were here to see this."

"I believe they're happily watching us right now as we speak. As a matter of fact, I know they are."

ALTERNATE REALITY – Home and Family Life

Years later, Noah and Diana are more than just a happy couple. They are now a happy family, living in a nice-sized home with four kids and an English bulldog.

On one bright and glamourous morning, the lawn is freshly cut, the birds are chirping, and Noah and Diana are in the kitchen together cooking breakfast for their children. As the bacon, eggs, and pancakes sizzle on the hot pans, each child comes running down the stairs one by one with their backpacks on, ready for school.

Fourteen-year-old Noah Jr. is the first one in the kitchen. "Hey Mom! Hey Dad! I'll be home at six today because I have football practice. It's the first official practice of the season," he reveals as he grabs an apple out of the fruit basket and takes a bite.

"Okay, honey. Did you remember to turn in your physical to your coach?" Diana asks.

"I turned it in yesterday morning," Noah Jr. answers as he sits at the table and scrolls through his cell phone.

"Jr., do you want any pancakes?" Noah asks his son.

"Um, I'll take three."

Noah slaps three pancakes onto his son's plate. "Thanks, Dad!" his son says.

"You're welcome, Jr. So what position are you playing this year?"

"Well, I tried out for running back, and I think I got it! I'm most likely going be the starting running back for the freshmen team," Noah Jr. joyfully replies. "I'm the fastest freshmen on the team, so I know I'll get a lot of playtime."

"That's amazing! I can't wait to check out your games this year! You probably get all that speed from me, even though I never played sports in high school," Noah tells his son.

Diana quickly slaps bacon and eggs onto Jr.'s plate. "He

probably gets that speed from my side of the family, since my Pop-Pop played football and ran track in high school," she tells her husband with a smile.

Noah places his arms around his wife's waist. "Let's just say he gets it from the both of us," he answers before kissing her.

"Fine." She kisses him back.

"EW!" yell their eleven-year-old twins, Dwayne and Diamond.

"EW what? You think when I kiss your mom, it's disgusting?" Noah asks his children.

"Yes! You two kiss each other all day. Can't you take a break for once?" Dwayne demands.

"Exactly! I would like to eat my breakfast without throwing up, please," Diamond put in.

"Without this love and affection your dad and I have for each other, you two wouldn't be here!" Diana pleasantly tells the twins as she gives them their breakfast.

"Hi Mommy! Hi Daddy! Hi Chester!" seven-year-old Joanna says happily, petting their English bulldog, who is asleep on his doggy bed.

"Look who it is! Joanna King, always the last one downstairs!" Noah says as he lifts his daughter into the air and kisses her on the cheek.

"Are you ready for your first day of 2nd grade, baby girl?" Diana asks her daughter after Noah places her down on the chair.

"Yes, Mommy! I hope all my friends are back this year," Joanna replies before biting a piece of bacon.

"Oh, I'm sure they'll be back," Diana assures her.

"After you all get back from school this evening, your mom and I are going to take you guys out to get some ice cream," Noah tells the children.

"Yes!" the twins both exclaim.

Noah Jr. zips up his backpack. "Sounds good to me!"

"Can I have chocolate ice cream?" Joanna asks.

"You can have whatever kind you want, baby," Diana tells her.

"Oh, Mom, don't forget that Aunt Samantha will be taking pictures of Dwayne and I tomorrow to model Aunt Amber's new children's clothing brand," Diamond reminds her mother.

"Yes, I know, Diamond! It's my clothing brand too, remember! I'm not just a model, ya know," Diana replies, kissing Diamond on the forehead. "You won't miss a thing, I promise."

Diamond smiles. "Okay, just making sure."

Dwayne takes a quick sip of his orange juice and places it on the table. "I don't mind doing this modeling thing, but why do they have to pair me and Diamond together during the photoshoots?"

For a brief moment, Noah Jr. stops looking at his phone and directs his attention toward his brother. "That's because you're quote 'cute twins,' and *cute twins* make Mom and Aunt Amber's company more money. It's the perfect marketing strategy. That's why the country adores your pictures so much and everyone wants you two to model for them."

Dwayne shrugs. "Oh. That makes sense."

Diana turns to her husband. "Jr. definitely gets most of his intelligence from you. I can say that much."

"I second that," Noah agrees.

"Mommy!" Joanna calls randomly.

"Yes, baby?"

"How long are you going to keep modeling?"

Noah Jr. sighs. "Please tell me this is your last year and that you'll stay behind the scenes operating your business after that."

Diana frowns. "Well, Joanna, I have no clue yet, honey. And Jr., why do you want me to be finished with modeling after this year?"

"Because all of the guys at school have crushes on you. Especially on the football team. Every time we talk about girls, your name always seems to pop up. Luckily, they don't disrespect you in any way while I'm right there, because I would probably be getting into fights all the time." Noah Jr. palms his forehead. "I know you love doing it, but it would be such a huge relief if you no longer modeled. I don't know what I'm going to do if I hear someone else say: 'Your mom's hot.'"

Noah laughs. "Son, that just comes with the territory. It's not like your mom is naked or even half naked in these pictures. Thank God she's fully dressed in all of them, or you truly would be getting into a bunch of fights at school. And by the way—your mom is hot!" he teases.

"Oh my god!" Noah Jr. sighs again. "It doesn't help that most of the girls in school like you too, Dad. After you picked me up from try-outs last week, the cheerleaders, the girls' soccer team, and the girls' field hockey team went crazy. They thought you modeled, too."

Diana taps her husband on the butt. "Well, your father is pretty hot too!" she jokes.

After laughing about everything, Diana takes her son's words into consideration. "In all seriousness, Jr., I'll think about stepping back and hiring new women to model in our clothes. If I did that, I could help Amber out with more of the designs."

"Thank you! And trust me—you can get right back to it after I graduate from high school," Noah Jr. implies.

"I want to model like you, Mommy," Joanna says out of the blue.

"You will, sweetheart! You can actually start whenever you want," Diana informs Joanna.

Noah gobbles down his eggs. "Man oh man, pretty soon everyone in this house is going to be big time models in the fashion industry. Everyone besides me, that is."

"Yeah, you can take me out of that equation too," Noah Jr. adds, placing his phone in his pocket and putting on his backpack.

"The bus is here!" Dwayne shouts as he peeks through the kitchen window after they all finish eating.

"Alrighty, then. Here are your packed lunches. Love you guys. And hey, walk to the bus, don't run! We don't need you all getting hurt right before school," Noah says as he hands each child a lunch on their way out the door.

"Jr., hold Joanna's hand for me, okay? Love you!" Diana commands.

"On it, Mom!" Noah Jr. replies, grabbing his little sister's hand.

As they watch their children get on the bus, Noah hugs his wife from behind. "We did a great job with them, didn't we?"

"We sure did! Do you want to make some more?" Diana teases as she turns to her husband and kisses him.

Noah shakes his head and laughs as the bus pulls away. "You know what I think: four is good enough for me."

Diana giggles. "I think so too, silly!"

29

BACK TO REALITY

Suddenly, the vision of their alternate reality vanished. They were now back in Noah's room, but there was an open portal on Noah's wall unveiling the silver stairway to the third floor.

"Wait—what happened?" Noah exclaimed. Tears were streaming down his face. "No, no, no, that was perfect! WHAT THE HELL HAPPENED?! I WANT THAT LIFE RIGHT THERE! YOU CAN'T JUST TAKE THAT SHIT AWAY! IT'S NOT FAIR! Hey universe, Father Time, do you hear me? You hear me, God? Whoever the hell hears me, give me that life right now! Just let me have it now, please!" he pled.

Diana turned and glanced up at Noah. "Noah . . . . I'm disappearing," she told him. Her spiritual body looked way more transparent than ever before. It seemed like Diana would evaporate at any moment. "That life was absolutely incredible, and I'm glad you and I both had a chance to see it. Now we know what our lives would've been like." She choked up. "But I can no longer be here in this world with you. My spiritual energy is dissipating; it's time for me go."

No, Diana, stay here with me, please. I don't want you go now. Dammit, I thought I would be prepared for this moment, but I'm not.

Noah knew he couldn't tell Diana what he was thinking because then she would enter Heaven with her soul filled with the ultimate guilt for leaving him behind.

"I really don't want to, but I have to go now." Diana repeatedly wiped the tears from her face. "You're going to walk with me to the portal, right?" she asked.

"Of course . . . but I don't think I'm going to be able to say goodbye," Noah admitted hoarsely as they both got off the bed and slowly walked toward the wall.

Diana gave him a quick kiss. "I know this hurts, but it's okay!" With a forced cheerful look, she whispered, "Hold my hand one last time."

She held out her right hand and intertwined it with Noah's left. "You don't have to say goodbye. Let's just say we'll see each other soon once we make it to the top of the steps."

Noah nodded and didn't say anything, since he knew he would end up getting choked up again if he spoke, and he didn't want Diana to see him like that in their final moments together.

"Remember what I said before, okay? You still have the opportunity to control your destiny. I want you to continue to live your life when I'm gone. Live it to fullest and experience having a wife and family of your own. Go travel the world and be great. Don't let me hold you back from that," Diana told him. They were slowly walking up the stairway one step at a time, trying to relish each second. Her spiritual body was whole again, now that they were out of his room and on the second floor of the spirit dimension.

Noah came to a complete stop. "No! I can't do it! You aren't holding me back from anything. Diana, remember what I told you."

He quickly pulled Diana close to him, with his arms fully wrapped around her waist. Diana passionately wrapped her arms around his neck and looked him in the eyes as their foreheads softly touched.

"I don't give a damn if I have to wait 90 to 100 years to see you again. If I have to wait that long, then I will. I know you want me to live my life to the fullest, and I'm letting you know right now that I will. It just won't be with another lover. You're the only woman for me. I know you are, and when I get back here to enter Heaven one day, you'll see me standing alone on these steps—waiting to see you again."

Abruptly, Noah laughed. "I'll probably have a bunch of wrinkles on my face, but I'll still be the same old me."

Will he really wait a century just for me? Diana wondered.

She smiled, although tears would not stop leaking down her cheeks. "Yeah, silly—but once you enter the portal, you'll look young again."

"Well, that's a blessing, isn't it?" Noah bantered.

"Yes, I guess it is." Diana paused briefly and thought about their alternate reality. "We would've had some beautiful babies, wouldn't we?"

Noah giggled and bobbed his head. "Yeah, we sure would have."

"I know it was just a vision of what could have been, but I miss those kids already." She cried on his shoulder. "The proposal was beautiful, the baby shower was beautiful, giving birth was beautiful, and our family was beautiful. My God, I miss it all."

Noah deeply inhaled and exhaled, still holding back his tears. "Me too . . . me too," he whispered.

After they finally made it to the top of the stairs, Noah passionately kissed her one last time, then hugged her as she buried her head in his chest. "I love you," she whispered. "I should've been told you that. It was long overdue."

"No, no, no, it was right on time," Noah answered sincerely. "Diana, I just want this moment to last forever."

He held her for as long as he could and took in her flowery lavender scent with each breath. In this heart-rending, yet miraculous moment, the stars above Noah and Diana twinkled brighter, illuminating the dark blue space that surrounded them. The silence of outer space combined with the sounds of their breathing resonated like a sweet melody in their ears.

Noah continued to cradle Diana. He did not want to let her go, and he literally felt like time had frozen.

"Hey, love birds!" Out of the blue, Father Time interrupted their intimate moment. "I'm sorry to intervene, but the universe's clock is ticking . . . So are you two ready?"

Diana reluctantly released Noah. "Ugh, I'm obviously not ready to leave him, but we both know I couldn't stay even if I wanted too."

When she turned around and looked at the portal, she saw her Mom-Mom and Pop-Pop waving and smiling at her. "There they are," she whispered while cheerfully waving back at them. And just like before, Noah still couldn't see anyone through the portal like Diana and Father Time could.

"Noah King, if your heart is still mine by the time you come back here, then I'll be right in that portal, ready to run back into your arms again," Diana said soothingly as she slowly backed into the portal. "See you soon, silly."

"Love you too, Diana—and see you soon," Noah quietly voiced to himself as he watched her disappear. "I'm going to miss that girl," he told Father Time as he pointed toward the portal. His tears were no longer held captive, and they poured down his cheeks like waterfalls.

Father Time didn't respond beyond nodding slightly and keeping a straight face.

After Noah wiped his face, he took a deep breath and looked at the portal again. "Aw, forget it!" he muttered as he attempted to dash into the golden doorway.

As soon as he was a few centimeters away from it, however, he ran into a strong force field. The force knocked him onto his back, causing him to fall down a few steps.

Father Time wanted to laugh really badly, but he kept his composure. "Um. Young man, sadly, I have to inform you that since you're still alive, you aren't able to enter the third floor yet, no matter how bad you want to go inside or how hard you try. It's just not your time yet."

"Thanks for the memo, Father Time. I just thought I'd give it a shot, that's all," Noah replied with a glum look, starting to slowly descend the stairs.

"Hold on, young man!" Father Time ordered.

Noah turned around with a joyful look on his face. He thought Father Time was going to find a way for him to enter the third floor to see Diana again.

I knew you were a cool guy!

Father Time suddenly opened up a portal that led to

Noah's room. "I can tell you've had a tough day. There's no need for you to walk that far just to get home. I'll cut ya some slack and let you take this quicker shortcut," he explained.

So he really can't help me, Noah thought.

Controlling his disappointment, he smirked and said, "Thank you—and I guess I'll be seeing you again sometime."

"Yes, you will—but that will be many, many, many years from now," Father time confirmed, watching Noah enter the portal.

That doesn't help at all! That just made my night even worse.

"You just had to be brutally honest, didn't you?" Noah muttered.

~ ~ ~

After reaching his room, Noah entered his body and tried to find a way to clear his mind. "What a shitty day. I've lost two clients that were like family to me, and I lost the love of my life all in one day," he said quietly to himself. "I don't know how I'm going to function."

He began by attempting to keep himself occupied. He needed to find a way to get back into the groove of his old but new reality, so he put on some exercise gear and jogged around most of the city until his legs went numb. Next, he showered until the warm water from the showerhead turned cold. Finally, he hopped on his bed, looked at the ceiling, and thought about Diana.

Diana, I really want to see you again, he thought as he fell into a deep sleep.

Only this time, he didn't astral project and Diana never came. The poor guy didn't even dream about anything that night. He just finally got the rest his body needed.

~~~

Waking up at the crack of dawn, he came to the realization that Diana was gone for good. "This is bullshit! Fuck this life!" he yelled. Out of anger, Noah threw his pillow at his computer, causing it to fall face down on the desk. "I didn't ask for this to happen, so why is it happening to me?"

Suddenly, he received an email from Mr. Wise's grandson.

From: lavellwise@silersidemail.com
To: NoahKing@silversidemail.com
Subject: *Lavell Wise (Grandson of Mr. Wise)*

Hey bro what's good!

You don't know who I am, but I saw you at the hospital with my grandfather yesterday. He talked about you a lot, and he really respected you as a man. I just wanted to share that with you. I know he could be a handful at times, but he truly meant the world to us.

I want to thank you for taking the time out to listen to his stories and being there for him on his final days.

My family and I are still trying to find some closure. Poppa Dave was the life of the family, but I'm sure we'll maintain.

Both of my grandparents are gone now. It doesn't even seem real at the moment. I guess overall I really just want to know how they're doing up there, even though I have no way of knowing.

From: NoahKing@silversidemail.com
To: lavellwise@silersidemail.com
Subject: *Lavell Wise (Grandson of Mr. Wise)*

Hey Lavell, your grandfather Mr. Wise truly loved you all. I could see the love on that man's face every time he talked about his family. I know the grieving process is a daily struggle, but I hope the little piece of information I'm about to tell you provides some closure.

Mr. Wise wanted me to let you all know that he loves you all and that he's with your Momma Mary now.

So my guess is that he's really enjoying himself in Heaven.

Every time I spoke with him, he would tell me that he was ready to be with your Momma Mary. On the day he passed, his eyes lit up when he saw your Momma Mary again. I've never seen him that excited before.

Now how do I know this? (You're probably asking yourself.)

Let's just say I had a vision about it!

From: lavellwise@silersidemail.com
To: NoahKing@silversidemail.com
Subject: *Lavell Wise (Grandson of Mr. Wise)*

Yo, I cried when I read that message. Don't tell anybody that, though.

This has definitely provided me with some closure, man. My

grandfather really loved my grandmother (Momma Mary) with every bone in his body, so what you just told me is certainly believable. I believe you.

You must be like a guru or something ha-ha.

I'll be sure to relay the message to my family. I know it will make them feel better than they do now.

Thanks again, bro.

After emailing Mr. Wise's grandson, Noah headed downstairs and walked outside to stand on his front porch.

Man, how selfish was I? There are probably over a billion spirits who would love a second chance at human life again, but I'm the one complaining. I know Mr. Wise and Mrs. Divine would not want to see me like this. And Diana sure as hell wouldn't want me to not care about my own life. I need to get it together for them. I need to live for them.

As he stared out into the morning sky with the golden sun gradually rising, he thought about all the things he already missed about Diana; like the way she gazed at him, the way she bit her lip, her cute laugh, and the energy she brought to him that made him feel like he could live forever.

Abruptly, his mother came out onto the porch with him and handed him a cup of coffee. "Hey hon, thinking about Diana?" she wondered while softly patting him on the back and staring out in the illuminating sky as the wind blew through her hair.

Noah nodded with a serious look. "Yeah. She's in Heaven with Mrs. Divine now, and unfortunately I can't travel there."

"It's okay, Romeo. You'll see Juliet again," his mother joked.

Noah snickered at his mother's remark.

"There's the smile I remember," Mrs. King said, reaching into the pocket of her robe. "So, I found these outside on the front lawn about an hour ago." She displayed the jar of sleeping pills in her hand.

Noah had guilt written all over his face. "Mom, I'm sorry about that, I just—"

"Just promise me you'll never use these again, and I'll pretend like this never happened," Mrs. King said pleasantly.

Noah smiled and turned his attention back to the morning sky, listening to the birds sing in the trees. "I promise," he said.

"You really miss her, huh?" Mrs. King wondered.

Noah nodded again and exhaled deeply. "Yeah, like crazy! Diana made our short time together feel like a lifetime."

"That's love for ya . . . Well, do you want to visit her gravesite or something? Or is there anything you need me to do to help?" Mrs. King asked, trying to make her son feel better.

Noah shook his head. "Nah, visiting her gravesite would just make it worse. Believe it or not, this actually helps me. The more I look up at the sky, the more I feel connected to her, like she's standing right next to me again. Last night, when I looked at the stars, I was hoping that she would somehow manage to come flying back to me," he answered.

Mrs. King wished that there was more she could do for her son, but she knew she didn't have the power to give him what he wanted. "I understand, hon. Hey, I'm gonna leave you be and head back in the house, okay? If you need me, just give me a call," she replied, walking into the house.

Noah looked up at the morning sky one last time and said, "I'll see you soon, Diana. I'll see you soon."

~~~

Throughout that year, Noah became good friends with Mr. Wise's grandson, Lavell. He also introduced Claudia to Amber and Samantha, which resulted in her becoming a new third member to their clique and a new model for Amber to use for her clothing line. Barry Jr. and Vivian joined Noah's family in attendance at his college graduation. And Noah kept the promise he made to Mrs. Divine and looked out for Diana's parents, constantly keeping in contact with them. Noah's mother always kept their secret about Diana between them, so his father and younger brother never knew about what had happened that year.

After graduating from Silverside University, Noah was hired at the Paradise Home Care Center as their permanent therapist. He could no longer astral project, no matter how hard he tried. The gift he once had was gone for good, and he eventually learned to live with that realization. From then on, he used his vacation days every year to travel to different countries. Throughout his time traveling, he would find ways to help humanity and nature, which granted him inner peace. He started off by donating large amounts of money to animal and children's charities across the globe, especially Christmas charities that helped poor and sick children. He then volunteered at local shelters and foster homes to help mentally and physically abused kids find good families. His new goal in life was to become a great human being and not just a great therapist.

In the end, no woman ever caught Noah's attention or

captivated his soul the way Diana had.

30

UNTIL WE MEET AGAIN

Seventy years later, Noah was sitting on the front porch of his parents' old home. He and his younger brother Nathan now owned the house together. They were sitting on their rocking chairs, staring out into the sunset and talking about life while Nathan's wife, children, grandchildren, and great grandchildren were putting the Thanksgiving food away.

"Well, brother, it looks like we have another Thanksgiving to look forward to," Nathan said as he rocked back and forth.

"My god!" Noah laughed. "I hope not! I'm ready to leave this world so I can see my girl again. I've lived here long enough. My time is up now. I can feel it."

"What girl?" Nathan chuckled. "Aw, here we go again with this crap. You never changed, you know that! Last year, when you told me you were in love with some ghost—"

"Spirit," Noah interjected.

"Whatever. When you told me you were in love with some spirit last year, I knew two things." Nathan held up two fingers.

Noah sat back and sneered. "Yeah? What's that, little brother?"

"I knew it was a good thing that you retired from the Care Center, because people don't need to hear your crazy stories—especially if your job is to counsel them through their craziness. And now I know why Mom asked me to look after you right before she and Dad passed away . . . The thing is—you always were a little psycho," he joked.

"Oh, shut up, Nathan. Believe it or not, you actually saw her before," Noah informed him.

Nathan looked confused. "Who, the spirit chick?"

"Yeah!" Noah quickly nodded. "When you were a baby, you smiled at her—twice!"

Out of nowhere, Nathan's sixteen-year-old great granddaughter Marie came outside to join them on the front porch. "Hello, Grandpa Nathan! Hello, Uncle Noah!" she said as she kissed them both on the cheek.

"Marie! Hey, sweetheart. What brings you out here with us old folks?" Nathan asked her.

"Well, me and the rest of the family were talking inside, and we were wondering . . . how come Uncle Noah never married or had kids with anyone?"

Nathan patted his leg and laughed hysterically. "Well, I

know why, sweetie, but you can ask him." He turned his attention to his brother. "And you know what, I never understood why you didn't go out with that Claudia girl. Man, she was a beautiful woman, and she really liked you too—everyone could tell. Shit! That entire trio liked you. You could have had Claudia, Amber, or Samantha. Woo! Man, they were finer than a mutha-fucka too boy! But you never made a move, so they eventually moved on and all got married and had kids. Way to blow your chances, brother!"

"I didn't blow anything!" Noah shot back. "They were just my friends, and they were never going to be anything more than that."

Marie turned to her uncle and intervened. "If they were just your friends, I understand. But, Uncle Noah, how come you never married or had children with anyone? Was it really hard for you to find love out there?"

At that exact moment, Noah decided to reveal the truth to his niece. "No, it wasn't hard for me to find love. See, the thing is—I had already found it. The reason I never married or had any kids with anyone is because the woman I love passed away a long time ago."

Marie's heart sank as she heard what her Uncle Noah revealed. She felt extremely bad for him. "Aw, she passed away while you two were dating?"

"AW MAN!" Nathan snickered. "Here comes the good part," he interjected.

Noah ignored his brother's slick comments. "No . . . she passed away before we ever had the chance to meet in the flesh, but in my younger days she would appear to me every time I astral projected."

Marie didn't seem convinced at all, but she did her best not to look doubtful.

"You know what, let's just say she appeared to me in

my dreams," Noah reiterated after seeing his niece's reaction.

"Oh, okay, cool. Now I get it!" she replied as her face returned to a pleasant look.

"In the short period of time we experienced together, she and I quickly fell in love. She was the most angelic and ravishing woman I'd ever seen, with a great personality to top it off. I never met anyone else like her; she was truly one of a kind."

"Aw, she must've been one amazing woman." Marie smiled. "So what was her name?"

"Her name was Diana. Diana Divine."

"Wow! She had a lovely name!" Marie replied.

"She sure did. I wish you could've seen the way she looked every time she smiled. Her smile could light up an entire galaxy." Noah looked up at the clouds. "But your grandpa never believed me when I told him that story last year, so I didn't bother telling anyone else about it. Besides, I don't need more people staring at me like some demented old man."

"Well, I believe you, Uncle Noah. And I hope I find true love like that one day," Marie said comfortingly.

Noah stood up from his rocking chair and sighed. "Oh, you will. You sure will! Everyone has a true love," he responded as he began to head into the house.

"Where are you heading off to, man?" Nathan questioned his brother.

"I'm an old man, and I'm about to take a nap in my room. I'll talk to you all later," Noah answered.

"Okay, Uncle Noah! See you soon," Marie said as she watched her uncle walk into the house.

Hearing the familiar words *see you soon* from his niece gave Noah chills and caused him to come to a complete stop for a brief moment. It gave him the urge to see Diana right away.

~~~

"Why were you teasing your brother like that, Grandpa? He's 91 years old. Couldn't you just play along like I did? He probably can't help the way his mind works at this age," Marie told her Grandpa Nathan.

"Oh, it's all good!" Nathan smiled. "He's my big brother, and even though I love him to death, I still like annoying him from time to time. It keeps us young. But he truly has lived a great life, and he's done miraculous deeds for people all over the world, even when he didn't have to. So many people love him like family because of the humanitarian he was. That man has no evil or negative bone in his body. My brother honestly should've been a Buddhist monk or a Pope; that's how in tune he is with nature and peace. He may be a little senile now, but his good deeds will never be forgotten."

~~~

When Noah entered his room, he slowly looked at the pictures of his father, his mother, and Nathan and remembered all of the great times they'd had together. Still reminiscing, he looked at his retirement plaque from the Paradise Home Care Center and the many charity awards he'd received over the years. He smiled, remembering what an honor it had been to receive those.

While thinking about the past, he remembered the wallet-sized photo of Diana he used to have. He started looking in his top drawer to see if he still had it. As he searched inside, he saw nothing there. Next, he attempted looking in his other drawers and desk and saw nothing.

"What did I do with that picture?" he wondered, rummaging through everything again.

After giving up on the search, he sat down at the side of his bed and began to take off his shoes. When he threw one of the shoes underneath his bed, he heard it land on something that sounded like paper. He got up to check out what was underneath his bed and spotted an old dusty envelope sitting right on the floor. "What in the world?" he said to himself, grabbing the envelope. Noah dusted the envelope off and saw that it was titled *Noah King*.

At that moment his eyes widened. "This is Diana's handwriting!" When he opened the envelope, he saw the wallet-sized photo of her he'd been looking for. It also included a letter.

Noah King

Hey, silly. I placed my picture in here, knowing that you would one day come looking for it and would hopefully come across this letter.

I just wanted to say thank you for showing me what the meaning of true love is.

Noah, when you met me, I was a depressed, scared, and lonely girl who had only had spurts of happiness. But you filled that void by becoming my Prince Charming. You were the missing piece that completed my puzzled life.

As I mentioned before, you honestly don't deserve to miss out on a wedding, kids, and grandkids because of me. But for some reason, I really feel like your crazy behind is actually going to sacrifice all of those things just to be with me again.

Whatever you choose to do and whatever happens, you will always be the love of my life.

I miss you already, Noah King.

See you soon.

Love,
Diana

After reading the letter, Noah folded it and kissed it right before lying down on his bed.

"Wow! This letter has been in my room all these years, and I've never noticed it." He giggled, placing the paper on his chest. "Well, at least I found it and have it with me now."

Moments later while lying on his side, he looked toward the window and into the sky. "I know I don't ask you for much, but, when I die, please take me straight to her," he mumbled right before falling asleep.

~~~

That night, Noah's wish would be granted. During the middle of Noah's sleep, his heart stopped beating and he peacefully passed away. When he opened his eyes right after that, he noticed a familiar blue tint on the ceiling.

"Am I dreaming?" he whispered to himself.

The ceiling magically unraveled, shining a big ray of light onto Noah and causing him to float toward it. The light took him to the silver stairway in the middle of the blue galaxy. He was the only spirit walking up the silver steps.

Making his way to the top of the stairs, he saw Father Time standing near the golden portal. "So, Noah King, we meet again!" Father Time said delightedly.

Noah smiled. "Yup. I hope I didn't take too long," he replied.

"No, you're right on time . . . and she's waiting for you," Father Time added, pointing toward the portal.

When Noah looked at the portal, it was no longer solid gold like he remembered from years before. It was now transparent, and from afar, he could see a silhouette of a woman sprinting in his direction as if she were about to run out of the portal.

A few seconds later, that silhouette cleared up and became more visible. It was Diana! She was running through the heavenly meadows toward Noah as fast as she could. It had been so long, Noah couldn't believe what he was seeing. There Diana was with her unblemished, glowing medium-brown skin, long black hair, and glimmering hazel eyes. The love of his life was back in his presence for good.

"DIANA!" Noah shouted as he quickly entered the golden portal.

At that instant, Noah's 91-year-old body suddenly transformed into the physical form of his 21-year-old self again. As he ran toward Diana with a huge grin, he saw tears of joy rolling down her face. Her long flowing hair blew in the mild wind, creating a masterpiece in motion.

The closer and closer they got to each other, the brighter their auras shone. Their spiritual connection was giving them a gravitational pull like magnets. Suddenly, from about two feet away, Diana leaped onto Noah and wrapped her legs around his waist. "Noah!" she cried.

As Noah caught her and held her tightly during their warm embrace, Diana planted a sensational kiss on him. "Your heart's still mine! I can't believe you waited. Well, I'm glad you waited!" she said, refusing to let go of him.

"I told you I would wait 100 years if I had to," Noah said as he spun them around.

When Noah placed Diana back on her feet, they continued hugging and repeatedly kissing each other.

"I missed you so much. I'm so glad I got my missing piece back," Diana stated while caressing the back of Noah's head.

That warm and electrifying spark between them was now rejuvenated to new heights.

"I missed you too! You want to hear something funny? I read that letter you left me right before I passed away," Noah admitted. "I should've found that thing years ago."

Diana laughed, but she couldn't care less. She was just excited to see him again. "Really? Silly, it was right underneath your bed." Her arms were still wrapped around his neck. "So, what did you do while I was gone?"

Noah shrugged and smiled. "Ah, nothing much. Just a bunch of humanitarian work. I did all I could to help people around the world so that I could somehow make the world a better place . . . That's about it," he responded humbly.

"Of course! The same old Noah, always putting other people before him," she said, giving him another kiss.

"So, what did you do up here while I wasn't around?" Noah asked as he glanced at the golden sky.

"Oh, it's a long story. There is so much for you to see and do here and so many people for you to meet. I mean, I barely even made a dent when it comes to exploring this place," Diana eagerly explained.

She could suddenly feel Noah letting her go as he tried to observe his surroundings. "Don't let me go of me yet! I promise I'll show you everything I've seen so far, and we can even explore the places I haven't seen yet. We can see it together. You're going to see my grandparents, my parents, your parents, the rest of our families and friends, and anyone else you want to visit in just a moment—but right now, please just continue to hold me, and don't ever leave my side again." Diana hugged him, placing the side of her face against his.

Noah chuckled, holding her tighter. "Anything for you! And don't worry, I'll never leave you again. We have the rest of eternity to be together," he whispered.

The sound of that made Diana's soul jitter.

"Thank God for that! I love you so much, Noah King!"

"I love you too, Diana Divine!"

The End

ABOUT THE AUTHOR

Leonard H. Williams III is also known as Lenny by his peers. He started to take writing seriously during his junior year in college, when his professor told him his creative writing was phenomenal and should be published. He's a very spiritual and peaceful person who believes that nature, the night sky, and dreams inspire a majority of his work. As a creator, he loves studying the works of Joshua Leonard, Martellus Bennett, J.K. Rowling, George Lucas, Steven Spielberg, Maya Angelou, Walt Disney, and Nicholas Sparks. He credits them for consistently instilling magic, love, and wonder in their material and hopes to make an impact with his writing like them one day.

SHE's DIVINE

Cover Design by Kerem Beyit
Business contact: kerembeyit@hotmail.com
kerembeyit.artstation.com

SPREAD THE MAGIC

-Lenny's Imagination